LETTERS FROM LEONARDO

Leonardo da Vinci has remained a constant source of interest and intrigue down the centuries, and there have been countless investigations of his skills in many diverse fields of art and science.

The one area of his life that has been overlooked is the last three years of his life in France – largely unrecorded – when he reflected on his successes and failures in life.

Iain Wodehouse-Easton, whose longstanding love affair with Italy inspired him to research extensively and recreate the missing years of Leonardo, in this novel brings a fresh insight into the mind of a man as fascinating today as ever.

The author has travelled many times from Leonardo's home town of Vinci, across Italy and up to his final home of Le Clos Lucé in Amboise to seek out the inner man, seldom revealed in his many writings.

LETTERS
FROM
LEONARDO

LETTERS FROM LEONARDO

A NOVEL BY
IAIN WODEHOUSE-EASTON

Published by FreeHand Publishing Limited
175 Munster Road, London, SW6 6DA
Registered Office Centurion House, 37 Jewry Street, London, EC3N 2ER
email: info@freehandpub.com
website: www.freehandpub.com

First published 2006

ISBN-10: 0-9551847-1-1
ISBN-13: 978-0-9551847-1-0

Design and production John Nicholls
Typeset in Plantin
Printed and bound in Great Britain by
William Clowes Ltd, Beccles, Suffolk

ACKNOWLEDGEMENTS

In gratitude for source material

Translations of original texts and archive material
by Marco Pareschi

Selected extracts from
The Literary Works of Leonardo da Vinci
by Jean Paul Richter
permission of Phaidon Press Ltd

FOR KATE, BRYONY AND LOUISE
and
ANN WODEHOUSE-EASTON

CONTENTS

THE LETTERS

The packages had looked insignificant at the bottom of a pile of old papers thrown haphazardly into a drawer and abandoned long ago. And I too had nearly overlooked them, as I was tired and reluctant to pay attention to anything else as midnight approached. Until the clue of the mirror-writing jumped from the sienna-inked pages. The indelible hand of Leonardo da Vinci.

The surface of the cloth binding them together with its oiled finish prompted me to investigate further. Someone had wanted to preserve the contents. Perhaps Francesco Melzi, his devoted pupil, who had trailed Leonardo to France at the end of his days, and inherited his folios; only for them to be sold on, when later generations lost interest.

The outer oilcloth had opened up to me as the ribbons fell away. It was not so much a folio as a miscellany of papers, some letters, some sketches, seemingly not marshalled in any specific order, but in three sections. A cache that someone had wanted to set aside, a keepsake, fond memories, perhaps of an unspoken love? Or the lazy neglect of a bundle of notes, a record of designs to be perfected, research to be pursued? Keynotes of a breakthrough in invention?

They had come into my possession by one of those quirks of fate - a purchase of cheap, battered old furniture at a derelict mansion. Lost in a bottom drawer under the lining of faded newspapers lay this package, unwittingly ignored for decades by many generations of the family.

The old lady who had owned the house was the last in line of once famous aristocrats, their most evident figure the

1

fourth Earl, who had spent many years in the eighteenth century on the Grand Tour of Italy. A keen collector, he had scavenged around Milan, Florence and Rome snapping up ancient statues, sculptures and vases from the past, as well as paintings and furniture from Renaissance Florence.

This artistic collection had once graced the mansion on the northern borders of Oxford, a house much less grand as ribbons of twentieth century house-building had encroached on its estate.

Now the collection was gone, disposed of glorious item by item down the generations to meet inheritance taxes and the occasional ill-gotten loss from gambling. When the old lady died, there was no one who cared about the house nor the remnants of its belongings. A hasty auction had cleaned them out, and the worm-ridden desk to me.

From my own scholarship one fact immediately entered my mind - Vasari, that sixteenth century biographer, had said of Leonardo: 'He never wrote of himself by himself. Everything we know of him is guesswork. In the multitude of his work only he remains hidden, purposely unexposed in the wealth of his very own inquisition on life.'

This package was a first sight from within to break through that blanket of mist.

1517

AMBOISE · LOIRE
FRANCE

I

Chateau d'Amboise, France. February, 1517

The dove in Leonardo's hand fluttered nervously as he gripped its legs between the fingers of his right hand. In the left a red chalk glided across the sketching pad, marking the bird's delicate outline and the minutiae of the feathered sinews as it struggled to power its wings free of his grasp.

How do we know this? Because it is written in the text of one sheet in this mysterious package. Together with a tightly drawn sketch of the bird's wing.

In this observation, on these pages, the principles of Flight are expressed in the ease with which the bird conquered the skies. It also records how readily it surpassed all man's attempts at that time to rise in the air above the battlefield of destruction upon which kings, princes, *conditorri,* popes and politicians were fighting so assiduously.

'To realise the freedom of manned Flight', he wrote on this sheet, 'now that would be a final and worthy ambition'. To be defined in the cluster of sketches and drawings, rediscovered in these Letters. Invention carried to its fullest expression. To be a lifetime's achievement. 'If time allows me'.

•

Fifty years later, perhaps too late for accuracy, Vasari had also noted in the margin of his portrait of Leonardo - 'A gentle giant'. Yet all we have from that latent witness, the prime chronicler of material evidence, is a dozen hollow pages. But now there is this package, oilcloth ribbon-wrapped wedges of papers encountered in the desk. More than fifty sheets of faded notes and coded letters.

The clutter of papers, jumbled in Latin and Italian, would take time to translate and sort, but the signature was immediately familiar - as it would have been to any other scholar of the period.

The characteristic writing running across the page from right to left - in mirror style - and the faded red ink, sienna in tone, matching sketches to be found in the royal collection in Windsor, or in the museums of Florence, Madrid, Milan, the Vatican and elsewhere. The indisputable hand of Leonardo da Vinci. But what substance in these texts? And how long in translation?

In camera obscura. Even that Leonardo thought through. The persistent observer, but never the object. Not in thousands of sheets, sketches or essays now in the public domain. One sketched self-portrait only late in those life-extending years. A deliberately stern mask.

So is the man to be found here?

II

Amboise. 19th February 1517

'Melzi, pupil friend, *saluté,* you must follow on soon and join me here in France. The King will surely welcome you and Salai, as he has done me in this foreign land. Think not of it as exile, for he proposes himself as a loyal and firm patron, with all our needs to be met, and the services of the Court at our disposal here at Amboise.

We are in better hands than those of Milan and Florence, who made me, only to ruin me. The young King sets on me too many projects already, but I am minded to keep one firmly in sight. The great mystery of Flight. Would that it gave the chance to escape this mortal coil and all its travails. If not for me, then perhaps for others.

I am in good company here, with souls collected from across the land, from city states, from afar. The Contessa di...'

The fragment is lost that would give her name, but the sense is of an ally, a fellow Italian, a lady-in-waiting, a favourite. What else could be her station that she figures so prominently in these records?

Can she be reliably connected with the body found under the battlements? Discovered not by royal guards from the Chateau d'Amboise itself, but by townspeople going about their daily business, in the first light of dawn, distressed at the sight of this bejewelled beauty broken and crushed. Perhaps.

How is that known too? From a note in one of his letters, but more fully in records held to this day in the town's archives. A town dominated by the spur upon which the chateau overlooks its citizens and the surrounding landscape. With views across the swirling Loire to the distant horizon. A citadel underpinned with one hundred feet high sheer walls, a fortress surviving the centuries with impunity, the ramp that leads up to the battlements a stiff climb.

The Contessa di Pavia was to prove the King's mistress. A beauty clearly renowned at Court and in place due to his patronage. With the role of tutor to the Dauphin, and an 'ambassador' to Renaissance Italy, to its artists and designers.

'A go-between,' an impolite comment at Court.

'The convenience of access to the King, excuses to visit him on many occasions.'

'And he to her apartments.'

'Without the Queen's blessing.'

'With her hatred barely suppressed.'

Soon after his arrival in Amboise, Leonardo records that the door of his study in the chateau had burst open when he was first unpacking and sorting his effects. The note is undated but this must have been within a week of King François I having delivered his promise of more secure patronage in France; well away from those in Italy, who had deserted the great man in frustration at incomplete commissions.

'Ser Leonardo?'

'Indeed'.

'I am the Contessa di Pavia. You must help me. Now you are here. I have insufficient friends at Court, and...'

'You have the one that matters, I am told. The King. Who else do you need?'

'There are those...'

'The Queen. You must expect that.'

'The King is not strong enough.'

'In two years he has subdued Lombardy and Savoy. Yet not even thirty.'

'He is not as strong as you think.'

'In your hands perhaps not', Leonardo had instinctively replied.

'You must be my ally. We are both from the same country. There are enemies at Court. Too many dangers.'

There had been sudden tortured screams from the castle depths at this moment. Cries that echoed around the corridors. Leonardo had been alarmed, but the Contessa surprisingly diffident.

'*Non ti riguarda*. Discount it. It will be the business of the Chamberlain, Artus. One of his Swiss mercenaries, no doubt. He dispenses justice for the slightest misdemeanour or mistake, treating them as animals, if he believes they have betrayed his trust. Artus will strangle the man's cries himself, if necessary.'

And another sheet of notes, from 1518, lifted to the fore,

ahead of its time. It is one of those that brings Leonardo into the open. Clearly written after events at the Great Ball had so nearly cost the Dauphin - and France - its very life. Dangers that had depressed Leonardo beyond belief, beyond faith in human nature.

Plus ça change, someone had scribbled in one corner.

'It is a dangerous world we live in', the first annotation. Later it was clear this was the hand of Machiavelli, with whom this sorry declaration was being shared. Niccolo Machiavelli, so often misunderstood, so constantly open to the vagaries of the politicians. Secretary of the Council of Florence, spinning lines adroitly between the competing factions, yet never trusted by any one side.

Machiavelli, a close friend, who had bought a vineyard of Leonardo's in San Casciano, south east of Florence, with its Chianti wines. Evidently this sad dissertation was with Machiavelli, his appendations all over this recording.

'One day the world may be safer,' Leonardo had answered. Though whether he believed it, or put it down for his own self-delusion is not clear. 'But only God knows when that shall be'.

Machiavelli's note: 'He is the one sound patron'.

Leonardo: 'In whom I am told we must trust'.

Francesco Melzi, his leading pupil, was in his mind too, for Leonardo's notes are quite specific.

Amboise. February 20th

> God has indeed done more for me than my own father or mother. Others had a more fortunate start, but as for me, I was taken from my mother when I was only two years old.

It was the best of intentions of my father, that I should come into the care of my grandparents and then at ten years be under his wing in Florence. But I missed her, as only an orphan can. Had I stayed in her embrace, should I have been a happy farmer, tilling the fields, uncomplicated in life other than the peasant's chase for sustenance, fodder?

Then beneath a tear-stained fold:

I saw her only a few times before I was forty. Though she was only two hours to the west of Florence, in Vinci.

On a second leaf:

Even though this short distance separated us, I held no record of her, was too young to sketch her. A blank page in my soul. She was married in convenience to a lime-burner to fill her day with fresh duties. On whom did her love shine?

My father married again and again. I had thirteen brothers and sisters. All of whom did not acknowledge me.

Melzi was to repeat on other occasions:

'It is no shame to be a bastard in these times.'

Leonardo:

But it meant I could not enter the Law, be a

notary, like my father, or go to university. In that respect I was cast with gravediggers, priests and criminals. A curious assembly indeed.

Machiavelli had noted:

'Yet invention has saved you. Brought you fame.'

And on the reverse of this inscription:

'Would that I had stayed in the fields, created one harvest of goodwill amongst my fellows, maybe invented a plough that lessened their labour, a machine to free the farmer from his yoke. Would that have been seen as an achievement? Would my mother have kept me close to her breast? Would my father have been proud of me then?'

These reflections slip off the end of the page and remain unanswered, as many were to the end of his life. There are no more clues on this sheet as to his feelings at the time for his father or mother. A suspicious or deliberate omission? Pain is much better carried hidden in the depths of the psyche. It is easier to act out the daily life than consider its imponderables.

III

Chateau d'Amboise, rooted to that spur of rock high above the town, overlooks the river Loire, and is amongst the most striking chateaux of the French countryside. It dominates the town, set beneath its cloud-clinging ramparts rising above the High Street.

In the beginning of the sixteenth century it was the preferred Court of the royal family and a centre of great activity. King François I had taken the throne at the age of twenty-one but soon established himself as a power in the land and adjacent city states, some of which he had militarily subdued before long. Lombardy was an early conquest, and it was in a benign period of rule there he had first seen the wonders of Leonardo's work and met the man.

The deal made between the King and Leonardo in early 1517 for his living in Amboise is recorded. That in exchange for 700 crowns a year, the great man would provide daily conversation, when called upon, and such design and invention in matters of military or household affairs as was demanded.

'You are of far greater interest in your thoughts than any other here', the King had observed.

A simple equation that led to designs for a summer palace nearby at Romorantin, with spectacular water cascades and garden features which would have been a wonder to behold, had they risen from the pages of his sketchbooks. Other royal commands supported masquerades, weddings and Court events intermixed with military devices to subordinate the nobles and mercenaries of rebellious city states.

'I choose to settle on the evolution of manned Flight', Leonardo had written in response to Francesco Melzi before his pupil arrived in Amboise. 'It can release man from all this fighting for ground. We can oversee events and sustain peace at last'.

Melzi was charged at that time with settling Leonardo's affairs in Florence and the various deposits of funds that were scattered around the bankers of Lombardy. Funds so often taken in commissions never completed. A patronage lost through too many projects being pursued at once and never fulfilled.

'There is not enough time', noted in Latin on a torn

sheet. Above that footnote, 'There never is enough time. Before long I shall not be able to contemplate even painting further.'

20th March 1517. Blois

> Ser Leonardo, you must paint a portrait of me. In secret for His Majesty's pleasure. I want it to be the finest effort of your well-worked limbs. An image that will please His Majesty. Of me, not *her*. Something that acts to stir his conscience... and with luck his balls.'

This frank inclusion, albeit within a secret message that must have come from the Queen, opens a door in the archives. At first this reference might relate to some imitation of the Mona Lisa, which the King was to buy, but this seems immediately too simple. Queen Claude was known to have received this purchase with equanimity, respecting her husband's judgement - and that of all since - that *La Gioconda* had some unique distinction, some rare appeal that was in the image, not the importance of the person herself.

It does not take long to unearth *her*. Hidden in other Court papers again - the Contessa di Pavia. Of whom there is no record on canvas, an absence with reason.

Yet, as these Letters unfold, one clear inference is that what is *not* shown on the page is as important as what is. On this first impression Leonardo is at Chateau Amboise, but all too soon is set apart in his own mansion at Le Clos Lucé, a guest on the edge of the family estate, at a distance from the daily politics of Court.

IV

Whilst most pages in the package seem to carry the imprint of Leonardo's hand, others do not. His signature can be seen often enough in notebooks in museums, collections, art and reference works, but are these sheets real or copies after all? Are those the work of one of his pupils, notes of a copyist, practising mirror-writing, attempting to borrow some of the magic? And those written in other hands?

The fragments at first seem a random miscellany, of uncertain worth. Some are badly torn, some have inks so faded that they are drained of text. One is stained with blood. Or is it wine, perhaps a tear. *If* they are genuine they have an instrinsic value even before the texts are established in translation. If they give new insights not already known, possibly a considerable worth.

But translation is only the start of this effort to overcome the resistance of the mirror-writing - a code simply designed to put off the lazy inquisitor, an appeal for privacy that Leonardo sought all his life with regard to his texts. A problem even for his closest associate and ally.

Francesco di Melzi, loyal pupil to the end - and beyond - was to gather all Leonardo's inheritance, thousands of individual sheets as willed and spend the rest of his life trying to catalogue them, binding together *codices* as he thought fit. He too must have paused in the decoding as he faced this enormous task, grieving for his lost master, as his life too became meaningless. But it is thanks to Melzi that so many of the notebooks, essays, papers, so much of the evidence, survived. More than was lost. Including this package?

But hitherto in the public domain nothing about the *inner* man revealed. No feelings, no private correspondence, no record from within. Machines, concepts, inventions, paintings from the greatest mind of all time. *But nothing about himself, by himself.*

Vasari gave us those brief dozen pages, but the inner man eluded him too. One marginal record of the visit by Cardinal Luigi of Aragon to the Court at Amboise in 1517, and the presentation of Leonardo. 'Our favourite engineer,' King François had said proudly on that occasion.

The great man escapes again.

V

It was to be in Amboise that Leonardo found time at last to contemplate life, and wrestle with his belief that he had failed. Improbably that was how he recorded his position.

'How much rather that I had concentrated on one sphere of interest, than swept across so many areas of inquisitiveness. So many sheets of proof and discovery, but has Man made proper use of such knowledge? I do not see it, nor gain any satisfaction from my compendium of information'.

'But some good will come of it all in time,' Melzi had responded vaguely.

'Not before my flesh has long rotted in the earth.'

But even that resting-place was disturbed in the later Revolution, and the mere remnants of his skeleton saved for reinternment in a small chapel, built into the battlement walls of the royal castle.

A month after his arrival, now at Le Clos Lucé, the nearby manor house gifted by the King, Leonardo came to pace the walled grounds of this quiet retreat. The long lawns, the sculptured box hedges, the flowered terraces, the detached view across to the town - all gave him a sheltered sense of well-being, as he reached sixty-five years of age, beyond normal expectancy, and began to wonder whether he had outstayed his welcome on earth.

2nd April 1517. Le Clos Lucé

Melzi, come soon. Bring not everything but
only those that register as important to the
end of my days. The notebooks, the accounts
and the drawings of Flight. Send the models
of craft on after.

There is so much imposed on me by the King
that I may suffer from his enthusiasm. We live
with his youth, rather than our age. There is a
wedding in the air, an alliance between France
and the Medici. As you might estimate, an
antidote to further war. I am to design the
celebrations, the fabrics and costumes for the
Grand Ball and the entertainments. It is all too
much. Come soon and bring that rascal Salai
with you. Maturina and I cannot cope.

His maidservant Maturina had accompanied him to
Amboise. They travelled by mule, with an escort, along the coast
of Liguria, through Savoy and across France to the Loire. A
journey of three months.

And here there is a note from Tuscany. Maybe proffered
so that Leonardo did not feel abandoned. The reaction of his
pupils to this latest command.

The inn. San Casciano, 30th April 1517

Salai listened to your plea and claimed you
miss us already, Maestro. Or possibly him.
We are gathered at the inn, swilling the

remaining fruits of the last vintage of your wines. The innkeeper insists we delay here in Florence until we have quaffed in full, until the coinage you left is used, so he is not in your debt for ever - if you are not to return.

Your humble pupil, Melzi.

And then a footnote.

On serious matters, I have yet to complete the withdrawals from your deposits with the Medici and Sforzas. These and other transactions prevent me from departing yet. We will make every effort to surrender our citizenship soon and travel to be with you in France.

VI

The beginning of the sixteenth century was a time of significant movement from religion to science, from fear of the unknown to the door of knowledge and by the release of the printed word, revolutionary challenges to god-fearing authority. But not to the freedom from petty squabbles, to local wars between city states. Not yet, whilst everyone was rooted to the ground.

At the centre of scientific enquiry was Leonardo. Setting aside fantasy and faulty belief, he posed many questions. Too many for religious authorities, new ideas borne with sound research, evident experimentation and clear logic. To counter explicit threats to his investigations, he kept much hidden in notebooks, recorded but not provided to hostile inquisitors.

He kept himself equally unrecorded, masked by the profusion of essays, theses and texts so as not to cause immediate alarm. Off the page. Now it is time to find that man, and back to the first report in this package, and the bird in his hand.

Chateau d'Amboise. February 1517

'Your dove, I believe. It tried to escape'.

The King's Chamberlain, Jerome Artus, stands at the door of Leonardo's study in the castle. A time before the King moved the great man into the manor house of Le Clos Lucé. A hawk, with blood dripping from its mouth, stands erect on the Chamberlain's gloved hand, the broken-backed bird in its claws.

'I set it free.'

'Ah, that magical condition - freedom. No one at Court is totally free, everyone has their station, and amongst those that are called to order I have the privileged place'.

The Chamberlain stood by habit at doorways, as if selecting those that could enter into an inner sanctum, at the security cordon of the chateau, or most importantly at the entrance to the royal apartments. Nothing passed the scan of his intelligence unnoticed, unassessed, everything pigeon-holed. A power that he knew often placed in his hands greater weight in court matters than that of his patron - the King himself.

Artus was a Swiss mercenary, bred for the position, who with insidious cunning drove the inner politics of the household without restriction, other than from Queen Claude, who in turn manipulated him for her own interest.

He took the blood-stained bird from the hawk's mouth and waved its lifeless body savagely above Leonardo's desk, the drops spattering the sheets of paper upon which the skeletal outlines of its bird's wing lay finely sketched.

Leonardo could only repeat himself: 'I set it free.'

'Then it did not understand the rules here.'

Leonardo: 'The King will be displeased.'

'I doubt it. With his blessing you may experiment with Flight. But not freedom. As the King's Chamberlain, his property is in my account. The dove did not have *my* permission to go free.'

'Freedom is the right of the innocent.'

'The dove may want to taste freedom, but Man is ill-suited to it. Why do you think we keep a strict account and everyone in harness? It occupies them fully. Avoids more serious trouble within the family.'

'One day the people must have true freedom.'

'Not in our lifetime. No invention of yours, Ser Leonardo, no flight of fancy will set them free of this world. You have your uses, but the role of the artist is to observe, to draw, paint, sculpt. To then be admired. But for those of us in power, Art is but an amusement, a *decoration,* not something to influence events. We do not pay for it to disturb our position. You ponder, but we act. That is why, Leonardo, all too soon it will be you that is forgotten. Not us.'

'Your position corrupts you.'

'The King needs me. An independent power at Court...'

'A mercenary.'

The Chamberlain spread his arms out, exaggerating the sweep of his heraldic cloak, the arms of the King's family woven across the back. 'I am an essential link in the chain of command. Power is a necessary force. Why do you think you are now in exile in France? Because those in Lombardy no longer have need of you. Your machines are spent, your works soon to be forgotten. Who will recall your theories? And what is this residue you have brought with you?'

He swept some loose sheets from Leonardo's table, with his viper-headed swagger stick. 'Some essays, unfinished sketches, unworkable designs, half-worked theories, meaningless texts. Who will value these scraps of paper, when they become withered leaves in some dust-ridden portfolio?' A gust of wind through the open window scattered other sheets to litter the four corners of the study. 'No, to influence events you have to take power, not merely doodle. It is kings, princes, politicians, masters of the realm, us *conditorri,* who will go down in memorable history. Not the individual. Amuse the King with your readings, but do not expect to gain further influence here.'

The Chamberlain finally threw the dead bird onto Leonardo's sketchpad, the blood draining across the lines of its feathered wings. Leonardo leaped up in anger, but unwittingly knocked his chalks and pads off the table. The Chamberlain ignored this accident and went to the door.

'You can analyse, dissect, draw, paint as much as you like, Ser Leonardo, but whilst you are on this earth, your feet must remain planted firmly on the ground. In the ring, on the field of play, with all the others. Where I can see you.' With that he swept out of the room with a final arrogant slash of his cloak across the old man's face.

Maturina appeared at the door, disturbed by the commotion. She had been Leonardo's maid in recent years, and despite the man's wanderings from Florence to Milan, to Urbino and to Rome, had remained steadfastly at hand. She too sacrificed her home in Vinci for the wider world, for the employment, for the desire to sustain this inspired master at full tilt.

'We are at peace here, Maturina, but not without battle to keep it so. The Court will provide but keep us caught up in its politics.'

'I know my position, my duties, and shall stick to them.'

'As you do so well. There are many challenges ahead, but I do not seek such pressures. This hand...'

'How much movement is there today in it, Master?'

That truth was becoming evident. Creeping paralysis was slowly locking the joints of Leonardo's right hand. It did not prevent him sketching with his left, but it slowed the painting, the designs, and laboured the writing when the weather was cold.

'It is getting worse.'

'May God slow its effect.'

'I shall need to rely on you, Maturina, even more.'

'It will not trouble me'. She gathered up the loose sheets of text in her generous arms and placed them at one end of the table. 'Shall I attempt to put them in some order?'

'Only I can do that. Until Melzi arrives.'

But it was the King who, later that day, commanded Leonardo's attention. The royal retinue was assembled on the bank at the conjunction of the rivers Schera and Sodro near Romorantin, a few kilometres south east of Amboise. Under discussion were drawings for the design of a royal hunting lodge of magical proportions, with the damming and diversion of the rivers' flow to create cascades in the gardens, together with Leonardo's plans to construct transportable houses nearby for the then transient Royal Court.

Bibliotheque d'Amboise. 1517

"Let the houses be movable and arranged in geometric interlocking parts around the centre. And this to be manageable with facility because such houses are at first made in pieces on the open spaces, and can then be fitted together with their timbers in the site where they are to be permanent. Let the men of the country partly inhabit the new houses when the Court is absent.

The main underground channel does not receive turbid waters, but that water runs in the ditches outside the town with four mills at the entrance and four at the outlet; and this to be done by damming the water above Romorantin. There should be fountains made in each piazza"

The King's instructions exist in the discarded plans.

"Divert the rivers if necessary. Let us have cascades that amaze our visitors. Outdo Milan, Florence and Rome."

Leonardo replied: 'The contours of the land, the flow of the rivers can be tamed to our purpose. With aqueducts, canals and waterwheels. It will be Nature that surprises us with its powers. It will take time, Your Majesty.' Yet it was not to be. The reasons can only be guessed, for some conflict between states, another battle perhaps had to be fought before this pleasure palace could be erected.

(Undated) Amboise

Melzi, another project has fallen into the wastebasket of excessive zeal. Romorantin would have consumed us all and still not been in justification. I am relieved of its weight.

I am not afraid of hard work, even in these advanced years, but I need you here as an intermediary, as an accountant of my time against all these desires of the King, Queen and Court. I face them alone and am overrun.

Bring my books so I can indulge myself in study rather than labour. Come soon. And

Salai sooner, if he is trying your nerves. I miss him dearly.

So, where in all this is the man? Not in the mass of essays, *codices,* or drawings already in the public domain. Many have guessed his feelings, seeing the inspiration behind that compendium of invention. They admired the enigmatic masterpiece, the few surviving paintings, but what they read, what they felt is not the man. In all his craftsmanship, ingenuity, the fascination with science, the workings of engineering, the cunning of the military mind, they do not hear from the man himself of himself. Each page of his notebooks is riveted with detail, nailing down new evidence, but they learn only of the machines, the designs, the aspiration. Not of himself. Astonished by his genius, they do not see beneath the surface of his life.

From the learned and famous there have been concocted hypotheses - an industry founded on air, on silence, on blank pages. One expert will have him as a painter, yet finds only fifteen pictures. Another has him a sculptor, only to criticise the Great Horse of Milan, that foundered, when the French smelted the bronze for cannon. Others see him as an engineer, his waterworks pre-empting canal and lock systems, though the great project of diverting the Arno to bring Florence trading on the sea proved geologically impossible.

Vasari gave us his dozen pages, yet the man eludes him too. Some overtones, some colour, but not the heart and mind. Written with the same lapse in time and truth as the gospellers of Jesus. History bent to need.

Delving into an essay of Leonardo's at random:

Why birds seldom fly in the direction of the current of the wind

It very seldom happens that the flight of the birds is made in the direction of the current of the wind, and this is due to the fact that this current envelops them and separates the feathers from the back and also chills the bared flesh. But the greatest drawback is that, after, the slantwise descent in movement cannot enter the wind and by its help be thrown upwards to its former elevation unless it turns backwards which would delay its journey.

An analysis, a depth of observation unsurpassed. The view looking out, not in.

But is there an iota about the man?

VII

The young Dauphin enters Leonardo's life soon after the latter's arrival in Amboise, and finds a regular place in the Letters, as if the old man found in the youth's eagerness a revival of enthusiasm, a lifting of spirit. A bond that inspired him to progress the future, at a time his own strength was waning. Or perhaps it was Salai he really missed whilst his wayward pupil and intimate friend dallied still in Vinci, and the Dauphin acted as a youthful proxy for the time being.

'I want to be the first to fly', is noted down on the side of one letter with the Dauphin's clumsy signature, as if the ambition is a simple one, merely to be fulfilled at some moment of convenience.

The King had later responded: 'Only, Leonardo, were

you to guarantee his safety. I cannot afford to lose him. The Queen is spent within.'

And glued to this another footnote, strangely linked. A report on an assignation between the Contessa and the King.

'We cannot meet so often, you are a danger, Madame.'

'Not to you, Sir, I trust.'

'Men would kill for your beauty.'

'I would only wish to please you.'

'These months you have. But the Queen does not like the thought of it. She intends to make mischief.'

'Make love to me, Sir. That is what matters.'

This is clearly not Leonardo's hand. But whose? An eavesdropped report, but on which side is the author, and why is it in this bundle? Lost, or a bargaining chip?

Queen Claude too is in evidence in a number of notations and her inheritance can be traced. A marriage of political suitability, bringing territories together, avoiding conflict in the field, a soft option.

'Ser Leonardo, is this corner of the Chateau not too modest for a man of your standing?' the Queen had enquired on her first visit to his study, before he had moved to Le Clos Lucé.

'Sufficient, Your Majesty. I have but two tasks to complete. The challenge of Flight and a personal folio, to put my affairs in order. As for Art, for Your Majesties...'

'The light is surely inadequate for painting, the stone walls too cold for your aged bones?'

At that moment a draught must have blown through and caused a log to be displaced from the open fire, and it had rolled across the room towards Leonardo. The Lady-in-Waiting had rushed to kick it out from under his feet, and then closed the door. An incident briefly recorded in the chateau archives.

Leonardo had commented to the Queen: 'I miss the heat of Tuscany.'

'If that is all you miss, Ser Leonardo, you are a lucky man. We are both stateless are we not? I have given up my lands, left behind everything I valued. My home, family, my privacy...'

'Yet, Your Majesty, for a great deal.'

'A great "arrangement". It seemed one's duty at the time, a course that would bring peace and stability in these dangerous times, some order between states. We all have enemies, but for me, what?'

'I am certain...' Leonardo had started to protest.

'I want you to paint the finest portrait your well-worked limbs can manage. A picture that will please His Majesty. Of me, not *her*.

'It is a commission that...'

'Is not beyond your talent. Do not fear my anger for too truthful a portrayal. I am no beauty. But you must bend the facts enough, that is all I require. A piece of art, not history.' But as ever, Leonardo was slow to respond even to this royal order. His mind was elsewhere, with Melzi and Salai, who were still in Vinci. If he had been at the inn where they were staying he would have heard their comments on his correspondence.

'Salai, listen... he misses us too much already':

"I fear the world has not learnt its lessons. There are rumours of fresh design that Milan has on retaking Lombardy from France. It is all the talk of the Court here in Amboise. Man never seems to learn. We are placed in the middle of this nonsense and the King is urging me on towards commanding Flight."

Salai, evidently in his cups: 'What does the old man want now?'

'His winged designs.' And then Melzi also well-refreshed with wine had added without proper thought: 'They'll never work, of course. But they will remind him of Tuscany's open airs. He's feeling truly lost already!'

Melzi, reading out loud: "I must use the last of my days to create a new freedom, to address human nature, to fly above conflict, to be out of reach, above the mess of this battlefield we call life. That, Melzi, is to be my inheritance, my last achievement, if there is time."

'He never gives up!'

'Nor seldom finishes either,' Melzi acknowledged. 'Hence no patrons at home.'

Salai: 'He is lost without us! We must move to Amboise as soon as we can complete packing his effects. We have to hold his hand, support his last ambition... in fact I shall set out and ride on ahead within the next ten days. Or the old fool will go under.'

VIII

The Chamberlain came into Leonardo's study abruptly, and surveyed the mounting piles of loose papers scattered around the room.

'So you commit everything to paper? A mistake. Do not be so concerned with the record. It is wiser to whisper than to scribe. The spoken word cannot be so easily proven. Your letters fix you in evidence.'

He picked randomly at the sketches on the table, but his attention alighted on one, a nude drawing of a young man, exposed to the front, full of detail.

'And what importance does this young man have?'

'It is my assistant, Salai.'

'You have put much effort into this extravagant illustration of youth, so attractive a body.'

'He assists me in my work in a supporting role, that is all. He offers himself up as a model. A natural opportunity...'

'For excessive study!'

'He came from off the streets, is keen to learn, and free with his time.'

The Chamberlain was unimpressed: 'And much else besides, no doubt. You should be careful here, Ser Leonardo, we do not take kindly to such things.'

After the departure of the Chamberlain, Leonardo added a footnote to his letter:

> Melzi, to hell with it. Expedite everything...
> and bring that rascal, Salai, with you. I miss
> him very much.
>
> Hurry to France.

IX

Leonardo frustrated himself and others. The original baggage brought from Florence to Amboise remained piled up in the corners of Le Clos Lucé, in the stables, hall, drawing room, study, and bedroom alike. Waiting for Melzi to take on the obligation.

Leonardo intended originally to spend the time at Amboise resolving this 'mess' - his own word for the pile of manuscripts and drawings. To him it was a bundle of failure, so little manifested in machines that often never worked. He lacked power to make his mechanics move and drive forward - even upwards. He was frustrated at this lack of power and will, which was slipping from his grasp under insidious paralysis in one hand and from age.

codex vitae 49

> Trees of information, their leaves falling,
> always adding to the detritus of life passed.

God is hidden, his purpose unclear, time short
and so much to be resolved. The body of man
reveals the entrails of life, twisted within the
gut, covered by thin layers of tissue; the skin
not the fabric but merely the outer garment,
within which we all lie exposed.

Where is the soul? Not yet found its place within
this body of creation. Where within the human
form does the elusive tincture of life reside?

How does it pass on its soul to the next
persona? If it does not, then where goes all the
inherited wisdom of the past?

This note brings a sense of doom into these Letters.
There is more frequent mention of a doctor and of Maturina
being closer in attention to his personal needs. Once the King
catches him as Leonardo trips on some stone steps.

'We cannot let you go yet, Messer da Vinci.' No, not
without the soul.

As the body weakens does the spirit rise in dependence?
Despite these first signs of defeat, Leonardo remained active in
mind and continued his investigations into Flight; at the same
time he accepted the obligations of creating *divertimenti* for the
King when events or celebrations demanded it.

In the Spring of 1517 he returned to his notebooks and
the investigations on anatomy, last pursued with vigour when
he had been living in Rome. This late burst of enquiry
instigated by a curiosity about his own condition, the very real
day-to-day change in the fluidity of his limbs, and the arthritic
constraints in the right hand manipulating images on canvas.

With his left, he continued using pen and ink, pencil or
chalk to sketch outlines, templates for machines and models, or
cartoons that would form unique images. One, from memory,

clearly of a youth with ringed curls on his head. Salai - even though the 'young' man had turned thirty?

codex vitae 66

> The beauty of a human body, the particular body that has kept itself vigorous, is reflected in the muscular structure of the young athlete.
>
> But the wisdom of age is no defence against the comparison with such evidence that the artist or sculptor feels obliged to portray in his work.

And added, as if Salai himself must have come to mind:

> Your body is smooth to the touch, white as marble, yet strong in form, lissom as a hound, moving with the stride of a horse. In its corners lie so many questions.

At this time King François issued strict instructions that the Court should not impose fanciful wishes upon the artist in residence, and attended Leonardo as often as possible when himself in Amboise. They would sit in the gardens, bathed in sunlight, reading from old texts, the prognostications of Aristotle, Pliny and others from ancient eras and compare their predictions with the advance of knowledge since.

'The pace of instruction is accelerating and we shall soon know the truths of life, though not in my time'.

The King saw his sage's failing energy before his eyes. 'Keep going; science shall extend our living.'

Leonardo: 'All is in Nature. We are all a circumstance of Nature.'

X

In the inner sanctum, the double-coded third folio within the package:

'The eye is the window of the soul.' Indeed, and these particular papers are the sheets between which the body lies. The touchstones of honesty that reveal more, the private worries, the inheritance of blame.

codex vitae 82

Mark these words with care, for they have stayed all my life. That the youth is the man, and the scales of skin which fall through the ages merely serve to replace impressions not the substance.

If a mother is persuaded to leave, when her child is but an infant then memory is too soft to lodge in his mind and recall is lost under the smothering flow of knowledge.

Growing is seen solely as the object, that experience will substitute for love, supposing the world can embrace it to the same extent as a mother. This is not so.

The lamb is permitted to grow yet merely for slaughter at a tender age, and within it is the whole child, the whole animal. For it looks out with an innocence and sees a wide landscape and its place upon it. But is consumed before it can learn to escape the paddock. The shepherd cares for his flock but only so that he can improve his lot, and move on to greater wealth.

Di Piero, *dispero*. A grandfather can hold a grandson in his weathered hands as a lamb in his pastoral care. An uncle can gather a nephew and teach him the beauty of the countryside. But a father should keep the child in his grasp until maturity.

The cruel waters of life flow too strong against a child of nature. The landscape of Tuscany paints a perfect picture but can be as dry as parchment upon which no text has yet been written.

The page ends at this point, the message still focused on the beginning of memory. The mother - his Caterina? His years in Anciano and Vinci lost in the sleeping mists of the rolling countryside. The dawn of his own experience reduced to the chores in the fields, the harvests rotating through the seasons, the plucking of the vines, the laboured sighs at the end of the hard-worked days. From outside, he remembers a childhood on the hillsides, gambolling with innocent lambs. Inside, the man formed early, wants to prove himself, wishing to make amends for the bastardy that kept him not from worth, but in law from the positions of importance.

Leonardo had taken his own road through the cities of Florence, Milan and Rome to end in this foreign field, to a manor house granted to him now by the King - the rest home of Le Clos-Lucé in Amboise. Where admirers and the curious continuously attempted to impose themselves on his time.

King François' image is impressed in a contemporary portrait, but not one painted by the fading wrists of Leonardo. That would no doubt have been seen by his patron as one task too many, once he had seen for himself the rigours of arthritis suspending the magic touch.

The King's sympathy was natural and extended into a private devotion to a genius recognised, now in the safety of his domain. He vowed to be with him to the end and at the end, the royal admiration solidly based, not fabricated from political or whimsical fancy.

In the portrait François has a small face perched upon the elaborate shoulders of a wide-sleeved gold cloth blouson, but it is the exaggeration of the unknown artist. The picture is of a man in his late twenties, confident, regal, as he had every right to be. With a short black beard, a cocked hat at a jaunty angle, and simmering eyes, he has a look of the young Henry VIII about him - someone he was to be in touch with later. Enthroned at a young age, François had succeeded in placing Lombardy under French rule, where his path crossed with that of Leonardo.

François and Leonardo. The young and the old. Royalty with respect. A King who used the affectionate "Father" to the great man in person.

Leonardo has included his gratitude in this package. To François, not Ser Piero.

Le Clos-Lucé. May 1517

> The father has been most warm in his generosity to me. Nothing is too demanding of his kindness. For it is not in wealth that I have need, but the comfort of his keep. Not in the goods of life, rather the spirit to persevere,

the encouragement to persist, not malinger.
So much remains unanswered.

The Court is a creation of his ambition to
have the finest artists, architects, painters and
artisans at the disposal of France, but all of
these are kept in their own places and do not
enjoy such a sanctuary as mine.

How is it in a young man, so suddenly brought
to rule, that so much warmth and charity can
prevail when rude ambition would be the
natural effect?

A private note, kept in the ledger perhaps for the day -
not too far ahead - when his account might be measured. But
why is it in this folio with the other Letters? Did Melzi work
with Salai to set aside a small treasury that held such insights
into the man?

The Court in those days was an itinerant body, constantly
on the move, and the inference here is that all other artists
moved with it as it ritually circumnavigated France, from
chateau to chateau, domain to domain, as it satisfied the
nobility, kept their allegiance in line, suppressed malicious
enterprise. Leonardo designed those movable houses for the
Court when at Romorantin, but it is not clear if they were built
and put into action. Like so much on the page, his creations
often lie buried between the bindings, hidden from view rather
than implemented. But the ideas were there. If this scheme was
not used, then instead there would have been a *caravanserai* of
wagons, swollen with all the trappings of the Court, its
furniture, tapestries, rush mats, curtains, bed boards, planks,
trestles, tablecloths, folding chairs, cutlery and tableware - all
that was necessary in advance of the royal appearance to
furnish otherwise empty residences and chateaux. When the

Court departed, all was boxed up again and taken on the next journey, leaving the chateaux silent - sometimes for decades.

For Leonardo, voyaging on the sea of life was past.

> His Majesty has made me promise to stay at Le Clos-Lucé.
>
> He sees the colour drain from my cheeks when a journey is proposed. I should not admit to infirmity, but it is upon me. I have outlived God's average.

Leonardo started so much, yet finished so little, and this gathering of Letters is no exception. Some hand has sifted them carefully - lovingly - from the mass of papers he left for Melzi to place in order. The commission that was largely to defeat him.

This most loyal pupil is slow to emerge from the shadows. Leonardo developed Melzi's skills not only to provide for his pupil's future as an artist but also in order to substitute the arthritic right hand in the few works he intended to complete. The brushstrokes vary the touch, but just as Leonardo himself had first contributed an angel to the work of Verrocchio, so now he passed on some of that talent to his devoted supporter.

Francesco in France. Maybe the coincidence did not seem ironic. But for him this exile would be a bridge to another future back in Florence. He does not reveal any anxious self-interest in his diaries but knew his master could not last much longer, and matched his energy with the benefit of younger years.

In his own record, written-up after he had left Amboise:

> The master would turn from one project to the next, amassing a pile of notes intended for the book of final words that we never managed in time.

He would sit in the study, before the roaring fire in winter and by the hour draw up schemes - not so much for the Court or King - but for his inner reflection on matters of nature or humanity.

He knew, not from mathematical assessment, but from experience the hollow fabric of man. The anatomy was on the page, the bodies dissected, yet the 'entrails of life' became of increasing concern towards the end. "Where next?" a favourite enigma.

I would wait for instruction on some new illustration, if his failed, in disgust. "In disgrace," to be his own judgement.

Maturina would bring hot water in a bowl within it a drop of olive oil, native from Tuscany, from his own tenancy in San Casciano, as a measure to soothe the limbs. The subtle aroma a reminder of our landscape lost in recent memory.

'You shall keep in trust with Messer Machiavelli, and his attention to the vineyard. I do not wish it to founder. The vine can outlast us all, as nature does Man.'

Melzi has added a note in a different ink at the margin:

Our conversation took hold in the future from that time on, but we were logging the present and the past, so it should not be lost to our hearts.

And later:

> We knew the cliff over which he would pass
> was on the horizon, and only the curvature of
> the earth kept it from sight. An (ironic) fact
> that he was to be constantly reminded of
> through the experiment with Flight.

> In the meantime we submerged ourselves in
> the forest of papers, so better to limit our view
> of finality.

There are however other clues as to the change in mood that was beginning to weigh heavily on Leonardo's mind.

The drawings, the illustrations of Man, these became more grotesque. Obsessively distorted in rage or pain, thin mean lines that coldly emphasised the conflict of old age. There is only the one self-portrait - made ahead of this time (drawn in 1512) - and there are strong visual similarities between these later riven old men and Leonardo himself, as if he was really drawing down his own expressions, his underlying feelings, and transferring them to the page in thin disguise.

The torment of old age. Success no nearer than when young. Reality drawing out the essential truths in life. A small cog in the wheel of fortune, the haphazard chaos that passes for development, greater intelligence, a better existence.

XI

At the beginning of the sixteenth century war was never far from France, and acted as a spur to the King's obsessive pursuit of Leonardo's invention. Portable siege machines, moving tanks, torpedoes, mines - already these weapons lay on the drawing boards of Leonardo's sketchpads. Hemmed in by pages of butterflies, petalled flowers, anatomical bodies, waterworks and winged creatures.

This treasure trove was not orderly and objects of Nature lay beside machines of war in folios as randomly as the moods of human nature swayed the interest of his patrons. There was conflict on the battlefield, more often than not conducted at arm's length by mercenaries, frequently drawn from the Swiss cantons. Marching from their mountain retreats, they offered leadership to the ragged armies of opportunists, to the politicians or great families who dominated city states in ever-rotating circles of power.

King François was not above this speculation. He had taken Lombardy soon after his rise to the throne, and with credit had left the burgeoning arts and sciences of the Renaissance to flourish. To his rear he held France in secure liaison by marriage and settlement, and was friends with Henry VIII of England, whom he was to meet years later on The Field of Cloth of Gold. For the present his exploration directed itself eastwards through Savoy to Liguria, Lombardy, Milan, Florence and, in tactical partnership to Rome. There was an uneasy peace, patrolled by threats and submissions, but the Court at Amboise kept its distance from the action if not the design.

'The King insists I pursue new weapons,' Leonardo records on a torn fragment, presumably to Melzi. 'Ensure my drawings of these machines are included in the baggage so at least I can pretend to study them, though I am tired of such investigation. I will develop Flight, but these other struggles frustrate me in old age. I long for peace and solitude.'

And a message from Machiavelli, discreet advice from an old friend:

Florence. 18th April 1517

Leave it to the politicians - and me - to decide the fate of Florence, Milan and Rome. There is enough intrigue to keep a thousand occupied each day, and we will not see your talent in the mists of this scheming.

I am minding the vineyard at San Casciano, and the harvest this year will fill amply the needs of the village. The vines are set well to burst with fruit later and we shall pick fully, so your interests are protected. I will bring wine to Amboise if business takes me there, with the chance to enjoy you again.

It is time however to put your share in my name, as you have offered so often. The vines need a close and interested eye upon them across the year.

Melzi has the Deeds and shall discuss the matter with you - if he ever gets on his way.

In the scatter of papers next to that note, in Leonardo's unique hand, the intrigue of Man linked with Nature:

The oyster opens completely when the moon is full; and when the crab sees it, it throws a piece of stone or seaweed into it and the oyster cannot close again, so that it serves the crab for a meal. So it is with him, who opens his mouth to tell a secret and thereby puts himself at the mercy of the indiscreet listener.

So Leonardo writes, observing treachery in animals as clearly as a human trait. But as he looks out to sea, scrutinising closely, recording specifically, he keeps the world from seeing him within, and whether this riddle resulted from a personal challenge is not known. The mask as ever does not slip.

Having suffered throughout life, now nearer to death he felt impelled to embark on these Letters, afraid that the record would never be straight, never true. And the truth? Maybe it never came to him either. "What are we but a biased judge of our own failure?"

King François evidently wanted continued invention, and Leonardo subscribed to his wishes. To a point. Imaginative masquerades, mechanical toys, elaborate costumes, one or two final paintings. These were threaded in the weave of his last days. Did he consider France exile, or had the nomad no longer any allegiance?

'We miss the heat of Tuscany,' the clue from within the chill walls of the chateau in that first winter. We, Maturina and Leonardo, it must be assumed, as this was before Melzi and Salai had arrived. Maturina, with him until the end, praying at his grave, receiving more than blessings from his Will. A dedicated handmaiden from Vinci, not out of the bustle of Florence or Milan. A peasant girl, just as his mother was.

Caterina - where are you, other than in the slimmest of genealogical volumes? A name upon the extended family tree, in small print, in the lightest of faint ochre on the parchment, in the forgotten margin.

'I barely saw my mother at all.' Yet she was living, now married by arrangement to a local craftsman, only twenty kilometres from Florence, still in the landscape of Vinci.

Was Maturina cast in the image of Caterina? Leonardo does not say, no sketch survives of either. Nor any indication yet that he planted them in memory on the page. Nor is he seen in the sweep of her bosom, nor at the breast. Maturina's presence alone a tribute to the need for caring, for loyal service, an anchor safely dug in to the rocky seabed of life.

And set against that security the chaos of life at Court. For now King François is angry at the arrival of an emissary from Rome. Why Leonardo had referred to it is a mystery other than for a sense of the ridiculous. A reminder that battles were never far away.

'Another emissary from Rome, Your Majesty,' the guard had announced.

'The second in a week.'

'His Holiness, Carlo Borgia, Cardinal of Urbino.'

'Now they try the church on me!'

The figure that appeared before the King was short in stature and age. This cardinal was just twelve years old, a nephew of the late Cesare Borgia, a political appointee. His cloak too big for his boots, dragging along the floor like a sweeper, making him appear as a servant rather than a master - indeed a master of nothing other than nepotism, a bought patronage from a corrupt and licentious Pope.

'Is this what Rome has come to?'

'Uncle Cesare was a cardinal at sixteen,' this figure had pip-squeaked.

'And unfrocked at twenty-two.'

Maybe this quaint insertion is a sentimental anecdote on Cesare, as Leonardo had been his chief engineer briefly when the mad man was campaigning to the north of Rome.

The mission of this impudent child is not recorded, but can be safely linked to the machinations and threats of further interstate strife. As so often this footnote is cast upon the same page as a completely different issue. The Dauphin is being taught to swim and is found with his governess - named as Louise - and the Queen beside the river with a small entourage.

The Dauphin is supported by inflated pigs' bladders under each arm and struggling to stay afloat in the stream with Louise's help.

Louise: 'His Majesty keeps losing his footing and falling under.'

Queen Claude: 'Do not let France fall from your grasp.' To Leonardo: 'You must give us a better invention than these to keep our "future" afloat. He is determined to risk his life before even the sight of a battlefield. You must engineer something soon.'

'It is a matter of design. We must move on from this simple device.'

'I don't expect it to defeat you.'

XII

A further contribution from Machiavelli:

Florence. (undated - May? 1517)

The Council of Florence has directed me as Secretary to conduct the negotiations for the settlement between Madeleine d'Auvergne, a daughter of France to Lorenzo Medici. Another brick in the building of peace between our states. More for the cause of good than the field of strife. Your machines of war yet again denied a purpose!

Leonardo, I shall be on your doorstep soon enough and pay you for your vines.

Is it by chance that this note is folded with a quite different reflection?

codex volante xxxi

A bird is an instrument working according to mathematical law, which instrument it is in the capacity of man to reproduce with all its movements but not with as much strength, though it is deficient only in power of maintaining equilibrium.

We may therefore say that such an instrument constructed by man is lacking in nothing except the life of the bird, and this life must needs be imitated by the engine of man.

The life which resides in the bird's members will without doubt better obey its needs than will that of man, which is separated from them and especially in the almost imperceptible movements which preserve equilibrium. We are able from this experience to deduce that the most obvious of these movements will be capable of being comprehended by man's understanding.

Leonardo's words - drawn down from his library of texts, and brought to the top of the pack. At Amboise, from the beginning he is obsessively studying the flight of birds, the grace of their wings, their effortless life afloat on the currents of warm air which the high battlements of the chateau drew nearer heaven.

He explains that easy drift across the sky in other notes, formed from anatomical principles. From the archives in Amboise there is further evidence of this pursuit of Flight. The motivation was underpinned by the King's instinct to remain superior in force against the states threatening his borders, and believing Leonardo could surmount the technical problems, he promoted trials.

The hills above Le Clos Lucé became the field of air upon which the prototype wooden craft were to be manoeuvred, in the first instance by hapless prisoners, strapped in to the heavy machines that took off from those heights but crashed immediately on the base of the cliffs below. It is uncertain how many died in these early attempts.

Le Clos Lucé. 15th May 1517

Melzi, ensure the latest models are in with the first of the baggage train. The King is most persistent in this endeavour and we cannot deprive many more souls of their lives in the error of our calculations.

Bring the three canvasses still to be finished. With those to hand perhaps we can distract His Majesty to wider interests. The Queen is most determined her portrait shall be the first priority and we meet at Blois in secret to further this work so as to surprise His Majesty in due course.

From this collection of notes, the thread of the Court is spinning, but it is the weave which Leonardo uses to conceal himself. Is he hiding behind the curtain of events, so no one can see the context in which he fell away towards death?

The life which resides in the bird's members...

Leonardo was searching for the power in Man that could lift him up amongst the birds and hawks that mastered the sky, but instead found energy draining from his own limbs. Most severely the creeping paralysis in his right painting hand - 'the creator of my art'. This anxiety burdened a number of Letters that can be dated to the middle of 1517. Not so much in the records themselves, rather in the lack of symmetry in some of the written lines and the images in the mirror now showing signs of distortion.

He struggled to determine from where the powering of flight might come; with pedals, cables, and a crank between these on a shaft to the rear of a winged design all drafted on paper? Gears and notched wheels to be turned furiously by the pilot to obtain lift beyond that provided by the upcurrents off the cliff face.

'We are not near a solution' is noted on the edge of a sheet dated April 1517. Beside this comment a diagram of such complexity that the craft looks impossible to build. 'The wood is yet too heavy and the canvas likewise.'

XIII

Chance brings the first mention of the Book. In the muddle of these texts it seems incidental, a common word in any text under translation today, but the printed word was of recent application at that time. It would have appeared natural if it was a bible, but there is no mention of such interest in any of his essays. He was not truly convinced of God's existence.

The first time it came to light was in the fire, and not as a printed edition at all.

Leonardo was asleep in his bedroom, at that time recently moved from the Chateau d'Amboise to his new home - Le Clos Lucé - the manor house 500 metres to the south on the edge of the town. Spring was late in 1517, and a large log fire was still kept in the room to protect the old bones, stoked up to last through the night as the temperature dropped.

That night there was a storm. Thunder and lightning attacked the house and great draughts blew through the cracks in the armoury of the leaded windows and down the chimneys. In Leonardo's darkened bedroom, loose papers, his day's work and drawings all blew across the room and onto the fireplace. He remained asleep.

Smoke only slowly built up, to emerge from under the door, but at that time there were no guards walking the corridors in the night. Rising vapours began to escape from the window and with them flame, as the burning papers tindered one of the long tapestries hanging from the cold walls. This illumination caught the eye of a late arrival on horseback to the residence.

This was Salai, who later records events in a message to Melzi, still in Vinci, winding up Leonardo's affairs. Salai, the bumptious young assistant, had become tired of waiting for the administration to be completed and had ridden ahead to surprise his Master.

45

'To alleviate that loneliness you must feel,' Salai had written presumptuously in his intended address.

But Salai proved to have a more urgent role in saving Leonardo that night - and the Book.

He had alerted the indolent nightwatchman at the gate by this night ride and, as he galloped through the archway, sighted the flaming smoke. Maturina was aroused and with others rushed straight to Leonardo's room and dragged out the great man as the oxygen of life began to fade.

'An angel!', had been Leonardo's first words on coming to, in the clear air of a side room.

'It is Salai, Master.'

'It cannot be, he is in Vinci.'

'No, it is me, dear Master. I came to surpise you, but you have turned the tables on me. We nearly lost you. The fire has taken hold of your possessions, the tapestries in your room, and they are beating the flames as best they can, even now.'

'The book, my book', Leonardo had immediately alerted Salai.

'What book, Sire?'

'The folder. A folio in hard covers. Beside the bed, underneath the side table. Rescue it. At once, enter if you can and save it. Bring it straight to me. Hurry.'

This duty done and the folder recovered, Salai tended his master in bed through the rest of the night, until Leonardo came back to his old self, shaken but once again alert. In the following days Maturina stood down to allow Salai to fulfil the duties she normally held. The slopping out the soil bucket, washing his body, oiling the cracks in his edifice. Laying on the hands as of a minister to a dearly loved one. Bringing him to life, to vitality.

Later, noted in the privacy of Salai's diary, the next words of his master:

'An angel, my angel. I cannot believe it is you, in the smoke of heaven.'

'It is me, Maestro, fixed on earth still.'

'Come closer. Let me touch you.'

The embrace had lasted long, and both were reluctant to part from this moment. Salai took off his outer garments and lay in his shift alongside Leonardo in the warmth and comfort of the bedclothes. Leonardo traced the line of his body, as if to sketch it.

'Beauty in all its hidden corners.'

But the touch was also of paralysis. 'The first time I felt', Salai noted later, 'the cold and stiffening rigidity of the fingers of his right hand upon me. Our textures clashed, and we both knew time was taking its toll'.

'I can touch art, but not satisfy it.' Leonardo's words before he slipped into a discontented slumber.

Salai: 'It hurt me to acknowledge that he would not live for ever. He had left Florence only months ahead of us, but it now seemed that years had intervened. The long journey, perhaps unwisely taken in approaching winter had brought a first frost to his limbs. His hair and beard seemed whiter than snow. I was shocked. It was then I changed from youth to maturity, as he did from old man to beleagured milestone *(sic transit)*.'

Leonardo, in the morning: 'I am becoming weaker, and cannot hide what is most obvious from you, dear Salai.' Then, gesticulating with his stronger left hand, he took hold of the book, now beside him.

'One day, at the end, I want you to have this folio. The truth. Your inheritance.'

'Master?'

'It is my Book of Reflections. It is me.'

XIV

'Enough of this gloom,' Leonardo had protested, once recovered, 'there is work to be done, and Melzi will be with us soon, with the models available for assessment and flight.'

Yet it was the Contessa who enters these private notes next. She slipped in to his bedroom, anxiously clutching her cloak tight to the body as if to make her look slimmer.

'The King indulges me with sumptuous dishes and wild fruits, when we are alone... after we have been together. Yet I try not to eat. Lose my figure and I lose him.'

'I doubt there is a risk of that.'

'We are due to meet again tomorrow. At Chambord. The hunting lodge that he is building for...' She turned to Leonardo in some agony, clutching her waist. 'Can you help stifle these pains?'

'That is a dangerous area,' Leonardo anticipated, but not that the Contessa would throw her cloak aside to reveal that she was naked under a loose linen shift. Grasping his arm and pulling it towards her, she opened the fabric to place his palm on her stomach, which she protested was swollen.

'I am not a doctor.'

'But a master of anatomy.'

'Has it occurred that you might be in the first stages of child-bearing?'

'The Queen!'

'She would take her revenge.'

'You must tell no one.'

'If this is the symptom, then it would tell of itself in time. Be careful.'

And was it by coincidence Queen Claude is known to have called upon the Chamberlain that same week? Or were these notes catalogued by some mischievous member of his spy network? For in the archives is the scent.

'She has flirted too often with the King. You must ensure, Artus, she gets that message.'

In the Chamberlain's own hand: 'I shall see to it.'

'She must go. But my hand must not be seen on it.'

'As you wish, Your Majesty.'

'The King must not know of it, either. He does not share our distaste for an excess of Italians at this Court.'

'They were once a threat to us Swiss, now it is France's turn. I shall work out what to do with her.'

In turn he summoned Louise, the Dauphin's governess, a suitable servant to carry secret messages within the royal apartments - under pain of punishment in the event of failure or indiscretion.

'Deliver this sealed note to the Contessa di Pavia after sundown. Say nothing, just take this warrant to her...

'But...'

'Nothing. Don't ever challenge my instructions, my authority.'

Louise froze to the spot, fearful of the envelope's contents. Its sentence one she could not guess, but she wanted instinctively to be separated from it. Then later, in the *post mortem,* the gossip that Artus started to touch the young girl, to stroke her hair, to brush his hands down her body.

'Remember, you owe me everything. Without me, you would be still in the gutter, in the pig stye, in the swill. You will be rewarded this time, when you have delivered. And *if* you keep your silence.'

Pinned to this sheet for some inexplicable reason, a record of Salai working on Leonardo to persevere in his inventions. Salai's vigour a counterblast to the tiring genius, who was found that day in a melancholy mood bent over his desk, sorting themes from theories, hypotheses from geometry. Salai, without invitation massaged his patron's shoulders.

'The artist bent to the wheel? Do not overtax yourself, Master. However much the paymaster presses.'

'There remains too much to do.'

'You are too easily tempted from your chosen subject, diverted by the expectations of others.'

'I shall never be finished. I still have to address such an array of matters. The King, the Queen, the Chamberlain, they all demand of my time.'

'Perhaps they are afraid of your invention, rather than admiring it. They wonder where your inner devotion lies. Maybe they just want to keep you occupied, not allow you to finish any one thing...'

'Before I am finished myself. For whom do I really do all this? My family has no interest in it.'

'Melzi and I are your family. Maturina too. We care to keep all our memories.'

'And you shall all have your rewards, as I have said. But my constructions, ideas, machines, paintings...'

'Residing with your patrons.'

'Who favour now Michelangelo, Raphael...'

'Your ideas shall outlast them. The cities and palaces have their monuments, but your ideas will still survive the longest in the record of your codices.'

'I doubt it.'

'Melzi shall agree with me, Master. He should be here any time, and will not accept this fall in faith.'

Then again in the confusion of these worksheets an intervention from a distracting influence.

The Dauphin, who came down from the Chateau d'Amboise to Le Clos Lucé at every opportunity, appears afresh in a brief report, dated that same May 1517, on the advancing life-saver project. Whether the drawing of this new device on its wearer is meant to be a close representation of the boy himself is not clear. There are no paintings of the Dauphin and the image is sketchy, ink running from the page as if the notes were made at the riverside.

The newly-designed lifebelt is drawn with a draughtsman's accuracy in that familiar red chalk and black ink. An inflated tube, with a breathing valve, formed from tightly sewn strips of leather, it is shown as fitting snugly around the waist and is restrained under the arms.

The governess, Louise: 'It is an ingenious idea, Ser Leonardo.'

The Dauphin: 'I can swim, I can swim.'

Leonardo: 'You can float, Sire. Float above the fish at least.'

Then the Dauphin's impatience: 'Is there anything you have not imagined, Messer Leonardo? Where are all those other inventions? In Tuscany yet? Will your man Melzi bring them here for me to play with?'

'He will bring some soon. Those models and designs for machines that are in the test of man. But much else is marooned on paper.'

'Above all, Ser Leonardo, I want to try your flying machines.' And pointing to the sky filled with swooping birds, 'like them, free.'

'If God and His Majesty permit'.

Then the first signs on the horizon of another force arriving to disturb the old man's dream of peace and quiet - the baggage train from Italy, that Melzi had organised to complete the transfer of Leonardo's possessions. Dust in the distance obscured the troop of horsemen and the baggage wagons on the rough tracks towards Amboise.

Yet to the sentries on the chateau battlements they were in view for some considerable time, moving across the landscape like ants at first, and then as more human forces as they came to the river crossing.

And before this invasion, is this the moment to remember Leonardo's earlier observation on the artist or creator?

Milan (undated - 1512?)

In order that the well-being of the body may

not sap that of the mind, the painter or draughtsman ought to remain solitary, and especially when intent on those studies and reflection of things which continually appear before his eyes and furnish material to be well kept in the memory.

Was he now in the Spring of 1517 - the Autumn of his life - to accept the contentment of having Melzi and Salai with him and turn to the royals of France as his real family? Had he finally left behind any hope of reconciliation with his own, who had abandoned him? Thirteen brothers and sisters busy with their lives in Florence, notaries, politicians, businessmen with considerable success and wealth. They had followed the straight and narrow path, whilst he had wandered from Florence, to Milan, to Rome and back again to Milan, an artist and engineer for sale, without roots.

That family is not in his notebooks, nor these Letters. Perhaps he knew they did not care, that none of them would expect to see him out, least to attend his funeral. Better to live out one's time with those that value your work, however feeble it became.

From another essay:

> What induces you, man, to depart from your home in town, to leave parents and friends, and go to the countryside over mountains and valleys, if it is not the beauty of the world of Nature, which if you consider well, you can only enjoy through the sense of sight.

Human nature was a cesspool, but true Nature a constant ally, if moody. Now that his sight was weakening and exercise more of an effort, he was preferring the warmth of the fireside at

Le Clos Lucé and his new family. These beckoned stronger than the challenges outside. Other than Flight and the arrangement of his papers there is no further record of major new projects. These two ambitions sufficed together with those entertainments that the King commissioned for Court celebrations.

When the vanguard of the baggage train arrived, Melzi was the first to leap from his sweating horse in the courtyard. A man now of twenty-five years, an artist in his own right, a dedicated pupil, he hugged his master and kept him in his grasp for several minutes, exhaustion stained on his dust-ridden beard and face.

They had ridden for over six weeks, avoiding the dangers of brigands in the mountains to move along the familiar route, the coast of Liguria, the southern shores of Provence, before turning north from Avignon to the Loire. Many stops had been needed to change the horses, to protect the mule wagons at night.

But now the goods were safely delivered, and the ever-present Dauphin pushed himself to the fore at once to disembark the large sections of flying machines that stood proud on one of the wagons.

XV

The Queen's portrait appears to be the last Leonardo undertook. Their meetings took place in the town of Blois, fifteen kilometres to the east of Amboise, then a safe distance from the prying eyes of the Court - and her husband. These records are in diaries, kept from the Court in her lifetime.

'You must render me beautiful...'

'Your Majesty!'

'No, I know it. A marriage made on earth is not defined by beauty. It has to be carved out of battle...'

'I would not agree..."

'Challenge not my judgement, Messer Leonardo, and I shall not question yours. I have seen what you can do with little in a face or body. Even The Florentine shows that. Aristocracy is not blessed with much in these stakes. They fight their way to the top. It's brawling muscle that counts in politics.'

'There is not a...'

'A degree of invention. That is all I ask. His Majesty must have a constant reminder of what might be, of where he can first look... for satisfaction.'

'His Majesty seems well pleased with...'

'*She* must not have everything her way. I intend to hang this portrait outside the royal bedchamber. So he cannot forget who is queen, so she cannot pass that door. I will guard the chamber!'

'You shall grace the chamber.'

'I shall own it by the sweat of my body.'

And for her rival in Amboise the warning was already delivered.

The Contessa had received the young governess, Louise, in her apartment, as she sat at her dressing-table. At first the shy girl hid the note within her dress.

'What brings you here?'

'I...'

'To gain some advice? Some lesson on how to manage at Court?'

Louise made no immediate movement, perhaps struck by the elaborate beauty of the king's mistress. The dark hair swirling from her shoulders. The proud breasts. A head seen sometimes covered with blonde hairpieces for effect. Just one device in the make-up of alternative characters and images to induce the King's attention.

The Contessa: 'There is a lot to learn. Who is one's

protector, on what side one can depend. Sometimes I feel no more than a stranger, an intruder, a guest.'

'A very important guest, surely?'

'Weight in some quarters, not in others. It is dangerous. For me, even perhaps for you. To stay in the swim, to be free is not always possible... to meet one's obligations.'

'I came to serve.'

'You may be freer, Louise, than I.'

'You are so beautiful.'

'You envy me?' The Contessa brushed the long dark hair, and surveyed herself in the mirror. 'Many do. But does that give them thought to remove me? Where can I stand with certainty? In whose hands?'

'That of His Majesty.'

'One man...'

'Surely?'

'I trust you are right.'

Then Louise, remembering the purpose of her visit, withdrew the Chamberlain's note from the pocket of her gown and timidly handed it to the Contessa.

'This is for you.' Before she could be questioned, she hurriedly left the apartment.

The note advises the Contessa to leave for Milan or Florence - and stay there. The words on this sheet, straight, uncluttered by doubt. Strangely it is folded now within another paper, a drawing of some plans for Chambord castle to the east of Amboise. Not yet on its final scale, the grandest of the Renaissance palaces, set within a vast enclosed forest park. It was a conception in King François' mind, a hunting lodge in the grand manner - perhaps an estate intended for the Contessa? For why is its plan attached to this particular note in Leonardo's folio? His sketch with it is a design for the central double-spiral staircase with an unique construction around a hollow core, demanding unequalled mathematics, the design mark of his genius. The trick being that the ascending party cannot see the descending but only hear the patter of their feet on the stone steps a mere metre away. A *trompe l'oeil* in three dimensions. A masterpiece of Renaissance art - and engineering. The Queen coming down, the King and Contessa going up, hidden, to bed?

Leonardo notes on Chambord: 'It will take a hundred years to complete'. Then in an unfamiliar script on the margin, someone had added: 'If she can last the course'.

XVI

Mentions of The Book do not appear again for some time but it was clearly of special importance to Leonardo; it holds clues to the heart of this elusive man, and through its mirror helps reflect light on these private writings.

All too soon, however the first dictation to his valued pupil:

'I wish you to draw up my Last Will and Testament, Melzi, to arrange my affairs in proper order against the day...'

'You ask me to do this when I have barely sat down in this place.'

'It is a matter that demands attention.'

'Not so immediately. There is plenty of time.'

'I fear not. We should be ready'

Melzi: 'I refuse, Maestro, to meet this request. There is to be time enough.'

'Do not be so sure.'

And there the matter seemed to have been set aside. For a while. Leonardo started the task of sorting all the papers, drawings and illustrated texts that Melzi had brought together with those he himself had stored at Le Clos Lucé. In private, including fragments from another folio in this package.

br12

I am within a family at last, safely in time to
retire to a final resting place and face death. I
prejudge the issue but there is need of
preparation. My instruction is that these
reflections are for the inner sanctum, and are
not to be unearthed for at least twenty years
after my demise, to keep scavengers from the
door of debate.

That God should have put me on this earth,
unheralded and made me wander the land in
search of truths, that weight now hangs heavily.

But the miserable life shall not pass without
leaving memory of ourselves in the minds of
mortals, and a record of our loves.

In rivers, the water that one touches is the last
of what has passed and the first of that which
comes: so with time present. Life if well spent
is long. But now long enough.

To he that sleepeth, what is sleep? It resembles
death. Why not let the record of one's work be
such that after death one may retain a
resemblance to perfect life, rather than having
during life made oneself resemble the hapless
dead by sleeping.

These diverse memoranda are written on a different
paper, a coarser weave, that Leonardo has drawn from a new
source. Maybe of French manufacture since it is distinct from

those codices driven by his energies in Florence or Milan.

br.12. Only later is it evident that this folio within the package belongs to a single strand of writing. Not letters as such, other than in the context of being of himself. No addresses. Simply *bibliotecca riflessi*. This library, these pages with such numeration in the top right corner all belong to this same Book of Reflections, the book he strangely was to entrust to Salai. To be kept from the popular gaze until the new wave of rivals at home - Michelangelo, Raphael and others - were also out of debate. Notes that not even Vasari was able to call upon.

The deduction from these inner writings is that he indeed kept them well out of sight, so that his public workmanship remained the only measure of his talent. Those texts on the universe, the four elements, the powers of Nature, mechanics, Flight, the arts, anatomy, mathematics, hydraulics, engineering, ballistics and others - this spread of talent was to be the body of work that he used as a smokescreen behind which he himself could hide.

Fifteen paintings survive, but out of how many? Even that is not known for sure. And whilst these put him most conspicuously on a pedestal, the admiration is in the subjects or technique rather than any discovery of the artist.

There must be earlier pages, enumerated before *br.12*, but already there is part of the body, the corpse missing. The heart, the soul? And who are these loves to which he refers?

Yet he was to write later, as he contemplated his Will: 'No being disappears into the void'.

But the man eludes all on this seductive stage, the house and walled gardens of Le Clos Lucé. The spreading lawns running eastwards from the mansion entrance, dipping to a hidden copse, whilst proud oaks dominate the sweep of flower beds. On the south side of the house, approached directly from french windows onto the terrace, Leonardo would see these gardens in classic Renaissance style. Boxed and low-priveted into squares to contain the plants, with eucalyptus, ash, chestnut and cypress pines to provide shape and shadow from hot summer suns. Below the garden wall, the land drops sharply away into a deep vale, that runs into the very edge of Amboise a few hundred metres away. On the town's pinnacle, well in sight is the Chateau d'Amboise, its grey stone walls contrasting with the soft rose brick and tufa facade of Le Clos Lucé.

Leonardo has included a pencil sketch of the exterior Gallery beneath the watchtower. Suspended along one wall, with a timbered roof and open walkway, it allowed creative festivities, commissioned by King François, to be watched in comfort. As the archives show, on one evening occasion these gardens being lit with four hundred candelabra for a feast - to make it seem "the night was driven away".

And with it preliminary outlines for new windows in the small chapel, where an adopted faith, a last minute conversion, is reflected in its frescoes, painted by his devotees, including Francesco da Melzi. The Annunciation. The End of the World. And, above, the Virgin of Light. Elements of faith that Leonardo possibly contemplated but could not bring himself to accept in his lifetime.

XVII

Chateau d'Amboise. (May?) 1517

A fragment from the castle archives, torn from the page:

"A most admirable lady."

The King was insisting on the painting being hung prominently at Court in the great antechamber. 'The

Florentine. I saw it in Milan and insisted on buying it from the Giocondas, despite their protest.'

'You have captured her beauty, Messer Leonardo, in a most individual way.'

'It was necessary to put her in the best possible light. There was less in life than is evident in her demeanour.'

Later, added in black ink attributed to the Chamberlain: 'I don't trust her. She keeps her eye on you, wherever you move.'

Leonardo: 'The eye is the window of the soul'.

Left unsaid, but in a separate note to Melzi: 'And what mischief, what intrigues at Court does she watch over?'

But the company of the Mona Lisa was not the only lady attached to Leonardo in Amboise. He was quietly studying, when the Contessa di Pavia came in unannounced through the terrace windows of Le Clos Lucé, open to the heat of the midday sun. Both these records are dated to the early summer of 1517, when May is listed as a particularly hot month.

'Teach me more that you have learnt from your studies of anatomy Ser Leonardo. I hear you have cut open more than thirty bodies of the poor dead. What did you find inside that makes us so interesting?'

'It was essential to study within, the better to portray the outside.'

'The workings of the body?'

'The entrails of life.'

'And did you find any spirits... or whatever lies at the heart of our souls?'

Then on contrived impulse she had repeated the invasion of his privacy, exposed the nakedness of her own concern. Pulling her gown aside, she thrust herself upon him.

'Examine my frailty once more. I have passed blood. I cannot be with child, but I must know what it is. For the King's sake.'

And then without his leave, lay down on the table top, as if ready for examination.

'I want a child by the King.'

'You think that will save your position? Is that wise?'

Leonardo felt obliged to examine her, superficially at first and then, as a doctor would, more purposefully, pressing the various parts of her abdomen.

'Further down.'

'I believe you imagine it.'

'Not so. There is also a general pain all over.'

'Perhaps you should have the King examine you? It could be a matter of the heart.'

'It is a matter of guts. There is something that does not fulfil the King. My lips may not satisfy him enough, not hold him tight. Put me to the test.'

'I cannot satisfy your curiosity. This test is not for me. I can paint you, varnish your looks, decorate your apartment, but not lay hands upon you.' Then as a knock came upon the study door, she rose swiftly, brought the ties of the gown together again, and fled out through the garden.

It was a call to action. The Dauphin wanted Leonardo to come to the new workshop specially provided for the great inventor in stables adjacent to the house. The models for flight were stored but still unpacked and impatience was riding the child's curiosity. 'When can I fly?'

'There is much to be done. These designs in miniature must be recreated to man's size and tested by pilots. Men of great strength, if we are ever to fly above the ground.'

'I shall ask my father to assign a full watch of carpenters for the structures and weavers for the cloth. We must make these machines work.'

'It has defeated man to-date. Do not be expectant. It will take time, maybe more than we have. Decades.'

'Do not die on me first, Ser Leonardo. I insist.'

codex volante xlii

Why is the fish in the water swifter than the bird in the air when it ought to be the contrary, since water is heavier and thicker than the air and the fish is heavier and has smaller wings than the bird? For this reason - the fish is not moved from its place by the swift currents of the water as is the bird by the fury of the winds amid the air.

This happens because the water is of itself thicker than the air and consequently heavier and it is therefore swifter in filling the vacuum which the fish leaves behind it in the place whence it departs. Also the water which it strikes ahead is not compressed as is the air in front of the bird. It is therefore swifter than the bird which has to meet compressed air ahead.

A footnote: "So, in life, we meet the pressures, the social airs and graces that fix us in place."

Time indeed for these Letters to further fix the man.

XVIII

The years in which Leonardo grew from a lost soul in the countryside of Vinci to the pupil in Florence, to the polymath beckoned by the Pope, the Sforzas, Medici and the *conditorri* in their ego-ridden ventures - these are tabulated by city records. The travels if not the man.

By his own admission he cast a thread of failure through many of these commissions. In his mind he never settled on the degree of his success. Now, with time for reflection, he sensed clearly those limitations to his skills that made him pause too long in much of his work, made him too slow, uncertain to finish. Was it pressure of time, the scope of his commissions that made him so unreliable, or was it that his theses fell on to the page with doubt, rather than certainty, embedded in them?

'I am a failure', is scribbled and heavily underlined beneath a set of drawings of complex machines on a loose sheet of paper in this package. Did these particular objects not meet their intended ambition, or was the man himself widening the comment to his entire work?

'You cannot bring this melancholy to France,' Melzi is known to have responded to such feelings of despair. 'There is much to be proud of, much that others can finish if you do not. You have set the path that they can follow, and good will come of it.'

'Each machine, whether of war or peaceful purpose, seems to make an advance, but only of a short duration, before something else replaces it, challenges its efficacy or countermands its gain. Will we ever end the cycle of misfortune?'

'Your work will stand the test of time,' Melzi insisted.

'The Chamberlain does not think so.'

'Then we shall work even harder to order it and preserve matters.'

Folios, essays, sketchbooks, theses, illustrations on the

workings of Man. Yet all this time he remained hidden behind the work. No notes on himself, nothing of his feelings. The ghost remaining out of sight, as if deliberately.

XIX

Amboise, May 1517

Events in the battlefields of Lombardy and Savoy were on the move. Though distant from Amboise, they kept King François' court constantly alert as he marshalled forces of state troops and the Swiss mercenaries to which much of the fighting was contracted. It is not clear from the Amboise archives how often he was in residence at this time, so mobile were political factions, the nobles' allegiance and military matters.

The King's deal with Leonardo remained however in place and was most generous and open in its arrangement. Seven hundred crowns a year deemed a full exchange for daily conversation whenever the King was in residence, together with the design of special entertainments. A deal of which he took full advantage, recognising in Leonardo the greatest intellect, the most stimulating and inventive mind. A perfect foil for the trials and tribulations at Court. A clear head, a sound mind set apart from the politics, the squabbling, the rivalries that ran vigorously beneath the surface. Family against family, cousins fighting cousins for territorial gain in a region of city states.

The King's mind, when he was allowed to free it, was on the future. The Renaissance was the advent of scientific analysis, trial by experiment, the proof of mathematics, the air clearing from religious mysticism. So much of its spirit to be found in

64

Leonardo. Yet on the ground the scuffles and skirmishes of Lombardy, Ferrara, Milan, Mantua, Urbino, Venice, Florence and papal Rome constantly diverted his attention.

These struggles kept the King away often and Leonardo's notes and sketches only refer to specific projects and certain celebrations for which work was commissioned. For much of the time, Chamberlain Artus ruled everyone other than the Queen and Dauphin. These he simply manipulated by intrigue and the Contessa di Pavia was under direct threat of this plotter, whilst he saw Leonardo as a competitor for the King's attention, and a source of uncontrollable power over his patron's wishes.

Thus an admonition from Melzi to Salai, who had misbehaved in some rash manner before the Chamberlain: 'Watch your step, you cannot be certain the man will not have you disenfranchised from your fortunate position within L's retinue.' Together with a footnote from Leonardo:

codex forza. iv

Weight is a power created by the motion that transports one element into another by means of force, and the length of its life corresponds to its efforts to regain its native place.

Force is the product of dearth and profusion. It is the child of material motion and the grandchild of spiritual motion, and the mother and origin of weight.

Weight is confined to the elements of water and earth, but force is unlimited: for by it infinite worlds could be set in motion were it possible to make instruments by which this force might be generated.

This essay on gravity would not be in with these Letters if it were not for the annotation in a foreign hand: 'My force is only limited by the King, and then only when we are in his sights.'

But when the attack came it was from an unexpected quarter and when the Court was least prepared. The incident is described in full in a summons to try the four prisoners attached to a personal note from the King himself.

"Messer Leonardo da Vinci, in whom I always had my trust, I now place my gratitude for protecting France at an hour of great need." The future of France that is the Dauphin.

The celebrations were in process for the announcement of a betrothal of Madeleine d'Auvergne and Lorenzo Medici. A contract to avoid war, a settlement in peace, rather than on the battlefield. Another convenience to maintain power, a delicate balance between Florence and Lombardy's present overlord. An agreement that kept out others, protected trade and wealth.

Except others took offence.

The assassins were not noticed at the border, and must have slipped easily through the many isolated areas on this notional barrier, somewhere between Savoy and Provence.

Easily disguised as traders rather than a military, mercenary group of no more perhaps than a dozen in total.

Four arrived at Amboise as the evening celebrations were starting, as guests in fancy dress made their way to the chateau. Whether they had luck, had watched from the surrounding hills or from some inn for the right moment, that was not extracted from them before they died. But the Masked Ball gave them every chance to present themselves at the great gateway in costume as they mingled with the assembling guests. Daggers and short swords well hidden within their elaborate disguise, they were readily able to swill past the guards in the tide of excited humanity.

The Court collected in the Grand Ballroom, a mass of brightly costumed revellers, dancing under the magnificent candelabra of a thousand candles raised and suspended in the centre on a rope woven of ancient flax secured to a side pillar.

Leonardo was in attendance, to one side of the revolving mass, beside the pillar, safe under the colonnades amongst the observers. The guardians, the Chamberlain, the Ladies-in-Waiting, the old retainers were all off duty, except the Captain-of-the Guard, besworded and proud, and even he a little relaxed with a cup of greeting.

The table plan and drawn faces exist in a faded painting, placing the royal family set back from the dance at a high table on one side, spread with extravagant dishes and generous gifts of food from the provinces. The intended couple sit on either wing, separated for a little longer, but expected to become in favour of each other in time. Given time. As in the grand scheme of such things.

In the records it was the Dauphin who insisted his governess, Louise, take to the dance floor with him. He was unaffected by shyness, keen to show the steps he had so recently learnt, willing to be with the one person nearest his age.

An act that started the mayhem.

The foreign mercenaries infiltrated the Ballroom, and stood unnoticed at the edge of the swinging courtiers dancing excitedly. Then they struck.

The first seized the Dauphin and gripped him from behind, a dagger at his throat. The others formed a circle around their captive and shouted at the orchestra to cease playing. As the danger rippled through the crowd, the bandmaster held his baton high and the playing stopped.

This silenced the dancers, who came abruptly to a standstill, to find themselves in a standoff with a group of armed men rooted to the centre of the great room, as they themselves backed away to the sides. The light from the great candelabra fell in focus on the assassins and their prisoner, the braziers on the side walls glowing but not so brightly as to distract attention.

'Your Majesty. We demand France withdraws from Milan.'

'And who are we? What are these illegal instruments demanding such a contract?'

'In the name of Milan... and Rome...'

'Another papal plot!'

Queen Claude was on her feet beside King François, who sat steadfast in the face of this danger. His hand restrained her, as she made a move to reach her son. The guests fell back further to the sides of the room, a great mass of audience lining the pit in which this fateful contest was to be fought. The King exchanged glances with his Captain-of-the-Guard who was hemmed in by the crowd. Leonardo stood momentarily transfixed at this infidelity and leant against the pillar supporting the central dome and instinctively pulled at the rope as if to shake the candelabra from its mountings but his attempt was enfeebled by the numbness in his right hand.

The assembly stood transfixed, rooted to the spot as the King pondered his next move, his answer. No one else felt able to act, with the Dauphin's life at risk.

'You would make him a hostage to fortune, would you?' King François challenged the commander of the group.

'We insist on a pledge to withdraw, and we shall take this boy as our ward in this bargain.'

The silence of this mass continued, everyone paused in their life, uncertain what next to do, who should act.

It was Leonardo who earned the King's praise. The one man in the room to examine the problem, to quickly analyse the options, to provide the answer.

In the shadows, with an unseen but overwhelming sense of anger he found reserves of energy, the source of power to unmount the Captain-of-the-Guard's sword from its impeded scabbard and raise it in one great cutting sweep of demonic strength and bring it down to cut the rope retaining the candelabra on its mountings.

For a moment Leonardo could see no movement and few others knew of his action. Then a speck of plaster fell from the great ornament's mounting in the roof.

Too small to be noticed by the assassins.

But then more plaster and dust began to appear as the heavy weight of the massive wooden object began to shift on its mountings. To this point no one had shown knowledge of any movement, but even as a corner of his eye picked up the signals, the King did not change his stare from the commander's eye.

'You think that we would let you go from here? With our inheritance?'

'You must.'

'I must nothing.'

The pause in proceedings is recorded as in seconds, but it must have seemed a lifetime to Leonardo, anxious as to what he had set in train, waiting to shout to the Dauphin to run at a given moment.

But it was Louise, his governess, who spotted the candelabra break from its moorings as the rope finally severed, who first gave the game away, by glancing upwards.

The commander and his soldiers of fortune believed this to be a device, a tactic to distract their attention, and remained steadfast in the centre of the room. The last to realise that their fate was about to be decided, that they would be broken on the wheel.

The great wooden candelabra broke free, and with a final shudder as its weight overtook the fastenings, started to descend upon the intruders beneath. And the Dauphin.

Louise screamed at that point and the Dauphin looked up, and sensing the paralysis in the commander's mind, twisted himself free of the man and his weapon and threw himself at his governess at the very moment the great wheel of candles fell upon the assassins and crushed them to the floor in a cloud of dust and wax.

A fraction outside the area of damage, with its broken captors, the Dauphin stood, frozen in the space he had created. When the last of a thousand glass beads of the shattered candelabra had finally come to rest, there was complete silence from the asembled company.

'Vive le Roi! Vive la France!' It was the Dauphin's voice that broke the air.

'Vive la France.' The company spoke in unison.

Reassured, the Dauphin rushed over to Louise and fell into her embrace.

'Bandmaster. Play us out.' The King had recovered his authority. But no one danced.

The intruders were dragged from the wreckage, moaning under the weight of their shattered limbs, white-faced. The entire assembly watched, before servants rushed forward with brooms to clear the dance floor.

'Damned Italians!' The Queen had spoken. Then seeing Leonardo, 'Excepting your presence, Sire.'

XX

A new sheet in Leonardo's hand dated May 1517:

br.18

Then it was that I thought again of my own mortality. The Dauphin's life had been almost taken. Too young, whilst mine was so nearly gone. Human nature is of the most selfish kind, yet the time given to me by God, if he exists, has run its course.

With so little resolved. Ever projects lie in the cartoons I scribble, the rough edges of invention, essays of the possible. Schemes that often lack the power to drive them. It is time to wrap these goods in ledgers that others can examine and develop. With their own tools.

The evening shadows cast themselves across the pages. My notebooks full, my heart slow. My limbs weakening.

This mordant text identifies itself as from the *bibliotecca riflessi* – the Book of Reflections. Pinched with it is a note from the hand of Melzi:

The codices are in need of binding, so that we have folios of logical order. You must not deny me the effort, Maestro, as no one other than yourself can marshall the evidence into correct sequence. The mathematics of your designs are not self-evident.

Behind the chaos of his papers lay the life's work, its lack of order contrasting with the pure lines on the page. Orderly texts, running from right to left across the page, in the mirror of his thoughts, encoded within his mind to deter the casual observer, the indolent copyist.

Further events at Court interrupted progress on this task, and Leonardo lacked the energy to be disciplined at this stage, wanting to rest from his labours rather than increase them. He was already sixty-five years old - more than a stay of execution. A lifetime achieved through strength of will, furious effort and attacks on so many fields of endeavour. He had other things on his mind. His money still deposited in Florence with the Medici. The King's generosity meant he would not lack, but Leonardo knew he would never travel back himself, that he had separated for ever from his birthplace, from the landscape that had nourished his original thinking. Melzi would be sent back to retrieve the funds.

Here another preparatory note, perhaps for the Book of Reflections, but sent as a missive to Machiavelli, with whom he was already in correspondence regarding the shares in his vineyard at San Casciano, in the light of his permanent exile.

Le Clos Lucé. 4th June 1517

In the silver of the mirror, my hair has turned pure white. The last glimmer of colour wasted away, washed from my beard. The follicles are brittle now, hairs break off and are not replaced. In the strands of my words on the page the thread, like that rope, is breaking too. The store is emptying.

Then in a different ink, written later:

Events at the Ball have turned the mirror over too. Italians at this court are suspect. What proof of intrigue is not clear. There is no evidence that the intruders, those assassins, had allies in Amboise. There was no sign of contact. They burst upon the scene unannounced, but the excuse is given. The Contessa is fearful that the Chamberlain will take advantage of this situation.

There are other fragments to suggest the Contessa di Pavia kept as close to Leonardo as she could, to attach his secure position to herself. However the attempt to persuade him to paint her portrait - for the King - failed.

'I need your help more than ever,' she said, bursting into his study one day, as he struggled to sort his papers. 'I am not sure I can survive at Court, yet I must not show anxiety either, lest it is interpreted as guilt, or something to do with the insurgents. Besides where else is there for me to go now?'

Leonardo: 'The Queen will believe you are amongst the plotters. Or make a case of it.'

'You have the ear of the King...'

'In matters of design, painting, entertainments, flight. But it is better you talk with Machiavelli, when he comes. He has access to all avenues.'

'They are saying I am involved. That I helped them into the chateau.'

'I trust they are wrong.'

'Of course. I had nothing to do with them. How could you think so.'

'The greatest danger is a conflict of the heart. Your motives.'

The Contessa burst into unrestrained tears. 'Do not side with them, I beg you, Ser Leonardo. You know I had nothing to do with it. Surely, you believe me?'

'The facts will not matter. They have all the means they need to...'

'Force a confession?'

'To the Queen the facts will not mean anything.'

'You must help me. Talk with His Majesty, I insist.' The Contessa had not shown Leonardo the warning note she received from the Chamberlain. It had not carried a signature, but she knew it could only be from that office. A threat no less real because it was unsigned. A first shot across the bows. Maybe she was ashamed of it, or felt it would oblige Leonardo too much, make him complicit in her actions.

It is evident Melzi and Salai formed the old man's private screen against all comers other than the royals themselves. The Contessa was reluctant to test this barrier too often. She falls outside the second batch of Letters within this folio, which are grouped for a reason. They are between Salai and Leonardo. Intimate exchanges, and just as love letters are stored in a bottom drawer, accumulating their wealth across a great span of time, so these must cover a considerable period. Possibly over the last years in Florence and into Amboise.

Vinci. June 13 (15 --?)

Salai, you cannot expect me to go on paying your dues. The debts can be cleared this time, but it must be the last.

And on another brief note: (undated)

> I trust the rumours are untrue. You should
> keep surer company when you visit the back
> streets of Milan.

In contrast:

> I am sure we can come to some arrangement.
> I told you I would always support your
> endeavours in this regard. In turn you must
> care for me when I am wounded.

In what regard? Salai had a reputation as a mischief-maker. This is at least known from other records. He had not been accused, as Leonardo had as a young man, of sodomy. A contrived charge, assembled by other rivals when Leonardo and two others had fought a battle on the streets of Florence when he was eighteen. The case dismissed, but a legacy that remains caught in the binding of history.

The evidence of Leonardo's increasing fallibility is in the chateau archives. There was a case of food poisoning and once again his life had been spared by the vigilance of his servants. Maturina had been absent for some reason, and the food prepared outside.

The lack of notes suggests Melzi and Salai were not present either. Leonardo was found slumped in a passageway, clutching his throat, the breath struggling to escape his windpipe. The doctor was called just in time. As he noted the yellow sickly spume dribbling out from the old man's mouth, he must have made a quick diagnosis. Milk was forced down Leonardo's throat and then salt water, which brought up all that was left in his stomach.

It had been a close run thing, as Leonardo acknowledged later. Salai had been recalled and immediately took up station at his bedside, then within it, as Leonardo privately records.

br.22

We lay the whole day beside each other, unable to determine the author of this deed. It smelled of a deliberate act, not a casual misfortune. Then, to remedy my anxiety, Salai read from his workbooks, so I could amend the errors of his study. An easier task than finishing my own essays which are becoming too much. We talked to the end of light and I knew it was time I should decide on the Will. I must give him security in the years ahead when I am gone. An inheritance he can return home with and start anew. Without me.

A footnote:

I shall miss him. His healing hands have brought me much comfort.

Salai had come to take up a special place in Leonardo's heart, for even in the years before their removal to France he was always in close attendance. A young acolyte who saved his master's life - and his spirit in Amboise. Devotion manifest.

In the documents attached to the Will:

By the laying on of hands, we are united, you and I. There shall indeed be a reward in heaven, and you shall be blessed whilst you are upon this earth.

A prediction of some substance.

XXI

The arrival of summer brought a shift from war to invention - and the progress of Flight. With the interstate conflicts distant from Amboise and in the hands of mercenaries, the King increased his attention on Leonardo and added to his workload, just when the great man felt his age weigh heavily.

Though King François was Leonardo's constant patron, the royal commands do not feature heavily in these Letters. Because their agreement was centred on conversation, all that needed to be reviewed, argued and debated would have been left in the air, unrecorded by the archivists.

Rare confirmation:

17th June 1517

His Majesty always wanted it thus. That we should be free of others, free of the Court diarists. All else needed to have the benefit of his signature, but our conversations were at liberty to roam across the realms of his kingdom and my invention.

This plan allowed me to examine his inner thoughts and express mine.

'I have a kingdom, but its borders change from year to year. I have gained territory but not peace. The city states rebel. The nobles demand more for themselves, for their allegiance. I sit at the top of the pyramid, but at the base there are loose foundations.'

Leonardo: 'The world is changing. There is movement from religion to science, from darkness to light, from the history of fear to the belief of proof. Knowledge will free us from anxiety, from the threat of neighbours.'

'But I sense never from war.'

'That it might is a course to be pursued.'

'Through the frontier of Flight?'

'Possibly, Your Majesty. It is a threshold over which we may soon cross. It would allow us to oversee any enemy, to stop his advances, to outflank his manoeuvres with foresight.'

'What progress in your designs?'

'The new craft is almost ready. We do not have timbers of the lightness I would wish, but we may achieve some lift, when we fly from the cliff-top.'

'With whom as a pilot?'

'That is a dilemma. To determine whose safety we can risk.'

'There is a solution. We have two prisoners. Suspects amongst the chateau servants, who may have assisted the Italian intruders. They have not broken yet, but my Chamberlain is certain of their guilt. You shall have one of them to test the craft.'

'He may not survive the experience.'

'Then we must continue to induce the other to tell us what we need to know. It is an apposite solution. You shall have one for the test. If he survives it may indicate his honesty. Proof of his innocence. A real test indeed.'

The test is well recorded. Leonardo's craft was brought by his carpenters before the royal party assembled on the high bluff to the east of the chateau. A sheer drop of over two hundred feet to the river Loire in the valley below provided unrestricted space in which the craft could meet its examination. And the pilot's destiny.

The Captain-of-the-Guard and a platoon of soldiers

brought up the prisoner. Ominously he was offered the services of a priest. Then with much fuss he was strapped into the new design of Leonardo's birdwing.

It is on the page, sketched out by him clearly, dimensions noted. The structure is complete within a framework in which the man straps the device to his chest, bent forward, stooping at a slight upward angle and after running to gain initial lift would switch his feet onto two pedals and the rope pulley system. The pilot is then required to pedal furiously in order to bring about a flapping of the cloth wings in imitation of a bird, and to do so fast enough to achieve and maintain lift. Assisted by Leonardo's knowledge of the natural upcurrents upon which other birds could be seen to float.

"The prisoner was immediately reluctant to be brought forward in this contraption nearer the edge of the cliff. He struggled with the weight of the object. His eyes were staring at the chasm, his face as white as bleached linen."

The Captain finally prompted him with his sword, a reminder of his fate if he did not proceed. Reluctantly the man started to run down the slope, and at the exhortation of the soldiers, ran faster towards the edge and passing over, began to pedal with all his strength - out into space.

For a moment he seemed to obtain lift; for a moment or two he joined the birds circling above the cliff face, but then the weight of the structure overtook his efforts. He swerved to one side, as if in a controlled manoeuvre, glided a short distance, but then quickly spiralled into a vertical dive and dropped like a stone down and down until he plunged into trees at the base of the cliff.

"He never reached the liquid release of the river. Pardoned, he only found heaven."

And then stuck to the back of this record a quite separate matter - maybe this file being one of failures. An exchange with the Queen, who was clearly in a state of some anger.

Blois. 8th July 1517.

'The portrait is not good enough, Messer Leonardo. Put my very best face on it. Address the problem. As a painter of the greatest talent, the challenge shall be met by you. Recreate, exaggerate, if you must. If anyone at Court should mock, they insult both of us. We shall find them room in the dungeon, don't you think?'

Leonardo apparently had not answered.

The Queen had sent a second note: 'As the expert, Messer Leonardo, on the human condition and the body - as an anatomist, take the scalpel to me. The portrait must reflect these skills, I insist. His Majesty is to be pleased. Not with her, but me. I shall see to her in my own way. But you must make me look as good as her. So history records me thus. If not perfect, which I am surely not, then as an enigmatic beauty. You must manage that, and by the time of the masquerade.'

XXII

These Letters lead into the trap Leonardo engineered deliberately. The texts are preoccupied with events at Court, with the pursuit of Flight, with conflict on the fields of battle, with every distraction recorded other than the man himself. So no one can find a way through to the privacy inside the shell.

Yet now, a very different clue. A lock of hair. Pressed between two sheets of paper, folded twice and secured with wax. The first item in the third folio. The seal suggests a private note of great significance, together with this lost heirloom. The lock is dark brown and still soft to the touch. The hair of a young person at Amboise or of someone taken when they had been young and immediately stored?

The candidates? A young girl? Possibly, but where to start a search, unless through his models, their subtle forms only sketched on the pages of the past? An unknown, or the famous in his portraits - Ginevra de'Benci, La Gioconda, or to arguably the most beautiful of all - Cecilia Gallerani? Which one of these suggests a colour match good enough to give confidence?

His mother? The one memento, the one lifeline to Caterina, a parting gift? A token of love, to be touched in moments of despair, a reminder that he was still loved, even if from afar?

Or Salai? An entrant into the equation of love. An affectionate token, or a snip of the scissors in some idle moment, a trifle, casually passed over the evening table in an impudent gesture? Yet treasured in secret.

(undated)

On St. Mary Magdalene's day - 22 July - 1490
Giacomo Capriotti, named also Salai, came to

live with me, when ten years or so of age. Thief, liar, obstinate, glutton. The next day I had clothes made for him, a pair of pants, and a jacket, for which I put aside money to pay for these things. This money disappeared and no account could be made of it though he looked guiltily at me.

The very same Salai who was with him twenty nine years later at the end. A strong candidate indeed. Not as young as the old man made out. Everything is relative.

Or the lock a gesture from Niccolo Machiavelli? There was no intimacy between them beyond the vineyard ownership and the call of duty, so unlikely, other than this prince of darkness steps into the limelight at unexpected moments.

Chateau d'Amboise, 20th July 1517

Machiavelli arrived to negotiate on behalf of the Medici the dowry of Madeleine d'Auvergne, the share of the nuptial bounty for their already amply filled coffers. The price of peace, a battle won by armistice.

In the notes, Niccolo: 'Much is agreed. Between Florence and France. The finances. I bring the "Letters of Proposal" '.

Leonardo: 'And the welfare of the couple?'

'They will get on together. We - and politics - shall see to that.'

'To make it last?'

Machiavelli: 'Exactly.'

'How to ensure man loves another, loves peace enough? If we could settle that once and for all, one's other achievements would pale into insignificance.'

'Cure human nature?'

'Or fulfil God's wish? I am noting what I can for the

record before it is too late. Melzi is to help me assemble this poor inheritance, these battered remnants, and put my affairs in order. I will entrust my letters, my papers, the remaining contracts and plans to him.'

Melzi must have entered the room. The mature student, who had become the faithful disciple, the administrative head of the household.

Machiavelli: 'You are to inherit all this!' He had gestured to the sweep of loose papers spread across the tables and floor.

Melzi's words are noted, it would seem, as if Leonardo had briefly left the room.

Melzi: 'I have not worked all this time to carry the weight of my master's genius. I will assist with gathering the folios, but there is much more yet to come from the maestro, of that I am certain. I refuse to pre-empt destiny, time itself. I shall continue to serve, whilst I am allowed to polish my skills at his side.'

Machiavelli altered course, on Leonardo's return: 'The arrangements for the betrothal?'

'Since the danger at the Ball, His Majesty insists on a private gathering to be arranged on a date unknown but to a few. You, Niccolo shall be a witness for Florence, I for independence. The royal family and the couple to be protected by the Swiss guard. These alone will be present.'

'And the celebrations upon this success?'

'A masquerade will be held at another time, when we have safety on our side. I shall be obliged to prepare some new *triomphe de jolie* for the event. Another burden.'

XXIII

Amboise, August 1517

The failure of the first test flight suited the Chamberlain well. The rising influence of Leonardo over the King was arrested, the redirection of priorities reversed. The cost of one human being to be accounted for, even if he was a prisoner, but listed on the conscience of the inventor, not the comptroller.

Leonardo made a preliminary sketch of this dark giant of a man. Perhaps intended to be a token gift for the Queen with whom Artus continued to effect control over the royal subjects in the King's absence. Times when they could settle scores, despatch dissidents, twist the tortured arms of recalcitrant servants or petty thieves.

The drawing shows a high forehead, thick dark beard, long unkempt black hair, fingernails bitten to the quick. On his shoulders the cloak he wore as his badge of office with the royal crest, the salamander of François I emblazoned on its back in rich red and gold braid. A symbol of authority that stood out on the sinister black cloth. It suited him well that the achievement of Flight did not yet seem in prospect. A situation however that would stand only until a lighter structure appeared from the drawing-board of the great man. Yet that suffered an accident, as is too innocently recorded in the chateau archives.

Chateau d'Amboise no.112, August 1517

"The night before the next proving flight, the lighter craft had been secured in a paddock near the hillside from which it was to make an attempt. Ready for an early morning departure. This was to be launched from the East Cliff. The craft was shown on the plan as having ties from the wings to the ground to prevent gusts of wind lifting it off in the night. There was a shepherd posted as sentry for the machine and his flock. In the morning he was gone, and the craft in broken pieces at the corner of the field."

Witness R.

Why? Can it be assumed the breakage resulted from grazing sheep, their guardian fast asleep? That the ropes to keep them from lusher grass had fallen by themselves at the thrust of these hungry animals? The enquiry resolved nothing, an accident assumed.

But Melzi with Salai had pursued the matter further, and his brief report is in the folio:

'The hoof marks of four horses were to be seen in the mud at the gate into the field, where the sentry had been posted. His crook lay by the road, but there were no footmarks, as if he had been lifted from the ground and carried away. Then, on closer inspection, we found the same signs of horse around the area of postings securing the craft.'

Leonardo does not record what anger he laid at any person's door, but this page has a large letter C assigned to it, and his suspicions must have fallen on the Chamberlain and his men.

'There must be no mistake in future. It makes me more determined than ever.'

And in his random manner of folding in one sheet with another, leaving the connection to be reckoned, is an extract from the Book of Reflections, as he concentrated on the issue of motive power to drive these flying machines.

br 24

A current of water is the concourse of the reflections which rebound from the bank of a river towards the centre, in which concourse the two streams of water thrown back from the opposite banks of the river encounter each other.

So it is in life. The course to steer is never followed as set at the beginning. The search for the truth, for fearless knowledge is twisted by the rebounds of science, the curves of algebra, the conundrums of mathematics. And accidents of fate.

Salai has written over this:

Darkness in mood does not suit you, Maestro. Consider this: That you have more direction in understanding than the rest of us together.

On the reverse, in Leonardo's familiar mirror-script:

br.25

The tide in the water is as the flow of my designs. Constantly on the move, but seeming to return to the drawing-board of failure. The wings will not fly, the spring-car unable to travel uphill before exhausting the rider. The parachute uncertainly at present dropping death not saving life. The auto-gyro glued to the ground whilst four men pedal the gears to the limit of their energy.

For so many machines we lack power, and
they remain marooned on paper as do I. One
sketch, one look into the mirror enough to
warn me of age, the lines of time running out.

However King François made great efforts to maintain
Leonardo's spirit. Having brought him to Amboise specifically
to enjoy his conversation, his thoughts and inspired theories, he
easily detected any lapse in the old man's vigour. He would
enter Le Clos Lucé through the tunnel from the Chateau
d'Amboise that runs down inside the hill directly to Leonardo's
drawing-room. The King kept this route for his private use, for
those intimate exchanges that enlivened the burden of royal
responsibilities. François shouldered the weight of his duties
and campaigns with ease, but within the privacy of Leonardo's
study allowed himself to expose the other cheek - the
tribulations of keeping the Court together, the nobles faithful,
the spies in the open, the jealousies at bay.

The royal diary shows that these exchanges were
increasingly at Leonardo's bedside. A custom to be followed as
the sage became prone to passing sickness or succumbed to
ailments. Indeed the entries show the King took a particular
pleasure in administering medicines, dismissing the hovering
physicians, whose flickering doubts only made Leonardo
anxious of his condition. The creeping paralysis in Leonardo's
right hand became a noticeable manifestation of his
deteriorating state, but it was not his writing and sketching
hand. These skills he could use, even if the manner of painting
with his right became restricted when holding the palette and
brushes. Suitable excuses to resist at least the Contessa's
persistent wishes.

The King would read aloud to Leonardo from the
novelty of printed books, in plain satisfaction of adding
something to the man's vast knowledge, as if he wanted to fill
his mind to the brim, to spark new inventions, new avenues of

investigation. Leonardo would plead exhaustion, but the King would not accept such a state, nor that Leonardo was finished, or that the avalanche of ideas could ever fail.

Those same declining powers that were falling from a great height, but at a pace that left little scope for fresh initiatives. In the time available on earth.

XXIV

Chateau d'Amboise, August 1517

The masquerade was intended to be a delayed celebration of the betrothal. After the attempted abduction of the Dauphin had cast a storm cloud over any celebrations, the Court had been obliged to retire, as if in mourning, from outward displays of extravagant entertainment.

At the private gathering arranged at the specific instructions of the King, there were indeed in attendance only a few apart from the couple and the royal family. The Chamberlain, Leonardo, Machiavelli and the Swiss guard. The register shows their signatures alone.

The Court archives reveal also who was to be excluded. Not least amongst these was the Contessa di Pavia. An accompanying footnote, written by one of the diarists, suggests that she had left the town of Amboise, but it does not say for how long or to where she had retired, and whether with the King's discreet help. She chose to keep out of sight and out of mind. For the present.

It would be natural to assume she would have considered returning to her native Pavia, but unfulfilled ambition, unsatisfied love for the King or the belief that the insurgents had only endangered her position at the margin, may have kept her hopes alive. Presumably she had not yet managed to speak with Machiavelli as he focused on the couple's interests and the contract between them - and their states. He makes no mention of her.

Queen Claude had her own ambitions and in the lodge at Blois plagued Leonardo for attention. He reports the visit to her for an inspection of the portrait that he continued to work on lamely, discreetly.

'Art modifies the truth,' she noted on seeing the enhancements the old man had wrung from his weakening brushstrokes. 'You have done well, Messer Leonardo. It looks not like me, but better.'

'I tried to capture... my fingers are becoming poor at definition.'

'Worry no further. The Court can take the view the King fell in love with me. There will not be a record of *her*, will there, maestro!'

'No indeed, Your Majesty.'

The Queen had settled in the chair, facing Leonardo angrily at first, but now did so stoically.

'It is not easy to lie, have lived a lie, each day, through the night, with his passion spent on her. How do you believe that feels?'

'I am sure His Majesty will be pleased with this portrait.'

'Enough to *fuck* me tonight?'

The Queen had swept out, leaving the artist to complete his estimation of her from memory. But not before insisting Leonardo present his costume designs for the masqueraders, who were to lead the entertainment.

These costumes are seen in beautiful sketches within the archives. Elaborate headdresses, flourished fronts to the detailed garments, breastworks of minute intricacy, feathered caps, extravagant cuffs, tailored waistcoats. It must have been at the time of rehearsal that the Contessa also sighted these fantastical outfits. Perhaps she returned to watch from the shadows, or saw seamstresses in the town preparing the gowns, and decided to steal one for herself that incorporated a mask. It was a risky choice - that of an elegant butterfly.

The masquerade itself brought the Court back to pleasure. The orchestra greeted the partygoers as they invaded the chateau ballroom once more and music swirled the dancers in excited circles. Others indulged in the grandest buffet that had ever been spread before them. The young couple, now relaxed with each other, led the dancing and inspired everyone to sustain the celebrations towards midnight.

At the appointed hour gongs announced the finale. A parade of young courtiers in a diversity of styles, some representative of a city state or region, others reflecting one of the arts or an aspect of nature, strode in with outfits that magnified the skills of Leonardo in design, and the seamstresses in their needlework.

Then on a final float, a prototype machine dedicated to Flight, with beside it young women costumed as birds of paradise and butterflies. The whole assembly stood aside to let this elaborate construction be slowly drawn forward in presentation to the royal family at the top table.

The King and Queen watched in rapture as this latest creation of Leonardo's triumphed.

It came to a stop in front of them and each masked servant and girl afloat produced a shower of butterflies from a container under their garments and flooded the air of the chamber with these winged messengers. Until a final flourish from one - the Contessa - unmasking herself, attempted to hand the King himself a single purple emperor butterfly proffered in her hand.

She looked momentarily pleased with herself, as if this gesture would appease everyone, not least the Queen. But when the stunned King - and his horrified Queen - stayed silent at this unwarranted licence, the Contessa panicked. Instead of the hoped-for smile of greeting, she knew she was to be unacknowledged.

The Contessa stood her ground for a moment longer, than in the face of silence from the court, fled the room.

The Queen: 'A dangerous piece of mischief, Messer Leonardo... for the benefit of Florence?'

'Not of my making, Your Majesty. I condemn the use of my creations for this.'

King François broke everyone's silence. 'To the dance. To

dance. Bandmaster.' The Queen immediately left the scene with her Ladies-in-Waiting. The Chamberlain followed.

Leonardo recorded that night in his notebook: 'My creation has been abused. I fear we shall all lose our heads at this rate.'

XXV

Doubts.

Why are there separate packages within this bundle of Letters? What has seemed a random collection of gossip, court dealings, delivery instructions, distress signals, and appeals to Melzi, Salai and Machiavelli - all these are less relevant than those Letters that express doubts.

Where lies the man behind the Book of Reflections in all this mess? What residue is left of it, a folio which infirmity or death had intercepted? Those sheets that carry the tell-tale signature - *br* - did not show anything like a full sequence.

Leonardo's doubts. Are these revealed only on certain pages of his life? Is that why so many are missing, or did Melzi prune the inheritance to keep their secrets, whilst King François, his Queen, the Court did not doubt him, whatever past patrons felt. Quite the opposite, they are intrigued by his ingenuity, invention in entertainments, the elaborate plans for Romorantin and Chambord. Nothing seemed to be limiting his talents other than time - and the fingers of paralysis.

Melzi ploughed through the organisation of this lifetime's essays, theses, sketches and the notebooks, determined to retain the genius in view, the master of many fields, a man of certainty in design, in anatomy, in paint, in engineering, in hydraulics, in everything. To then hide any paper of Leonardo's self-doubt, and in so doing, conceal the man himself?

Yet here, on the page:

> It is not only my mortality that I doubt. More
> I look upon those empty pages upon which a
> theorem, only half-fixed, waits for a
> resolution, challenging my capacity for
> further insight.

93

How many investigations am I to leave unfulfilled? Poor Melzi must catalogue these texts and sort the wheat from the chaff.

His health, too, was exercising his mind:

Le Clos Lucé. 25th August 1517

Melzi has attended to my needs and called in a doctor, who says he cannot loosen the paralysis that daily creeps its way towards rigidity. My fingers are stiff with worry and self-doubt. The palette loosened in my hand. His sole prescription more exercise of the digits. It is easier for him to propose than I to fulfil.

Whether I can finish the Queen's portrait in time, with a strong sufficiency of talent is under question. She insists but I have to warn her. She sees my malady but is reluctant to let me have a stay on its execution. His Majesty, unaware of this gift in the making, is irritated - at least for the present - with lack of progress on other projects. Romorantin, that summer palace of fountains and cascades has been postponed in favour of Chambord. Yet this hunting lodge that is so large in scale to rival any chateau, is beyond us all.

I cannot complete many of these ambitions. Time is not on my side and I must attend to my own Will and Testament, before that escapes me.

Melzi guides this process, as if his fingerprints are upon the outer cloth, tying the ribbons. The written scripts are becoming uneven. He alone is that close to the feelings of Leonardo to bar investigation of the inner truths. The watchkeeper at the gate.

Yet Salai is present too in these notes. At the bedside of his master, mellowing with the years, patently forgiven the indiscretions of youth. He would lie on the bed, beside Leonardo, in the habitual afternoon rest, and learn to read, so that he could, in due course, keep his master's mind ever alert to the changing records of time, the dramatic advances that were flowing from the printed page, the release of knowledge to the whole continent.

'The fear of God is passing'.

'A God about whom we know next to nothing,' Leonardo replied. 'And whom I doubt until science can prove Him.'

Melzi: 'Too late one becomes curious about His existence, more certain He has to exist.'

'But in what form? Can He help me now? I doubt it.'

Here a loose fragment, attached to the folio for no apparent reason, unless Leonardo's sight was beginning to weaken.

codex vitae.vii

Shadow is the obstruction of light. Shadows appear to me to be of supreme importance in perspective, because without them opaque and solid bodies will be ill defined; that which is contained within its outlines and the outlines themselves will be ill understood unless it is shown against a background of a different tone.

Therefore I state as a proposition concerning

> shadows that every opaque body is surrounded and
> its whole surface enveloped in shadow and light.

Wise old man, surrounded by opacity throughout his existence. A mass of observation of other objects, external forces, but the inky surface of these texts shaded by the forest of words, the skilfully placed sketches, the mirror of script.

Shadows cast deliberately.

> The distance between the eye and the body
> under examination determines how much the
> part that is illuminated increases and that in
> shadow diminishes.

Clever ghost.

There is one other figure in the shadows, Maturina, but she also is elusive. She has contributed no words to the file, for an obvious reason. She could not read or write.

Yet she was to be with Leonardo to the end, when he reached the age of sixty-seven. More than a lifetime in those days. So, how old was she, this faithful handmaiden? If she was there at his side as he left Florence that would make her not much younger than him. A companion, servant, ally or housemaid? Or a substitute for Caterina? A mother figure by proxy.

Perhaps she had been commissioned by Caterina to keep an eye on the erratic genius that was her son. A link with Vinci, a thread by which to hang a sense of belonging. Possibly a source of occasional reports.

br 29

> I owe much to Maturina, and she shall be
> remembered in my Will. To her unbound loyalty

I respond with thanks. Now she has been brought to a foreign place at my behest, she must be rewarded.

The woman at my side, the seamstress, water-carrier, the cook. The layer-on of hands. The sympathetic ear, the unquestioning servant of my needs.

There must have been more in this vein, but the page is torn, the gratitude unfinished. Maturina would not expect more than the Will instructed. She would not recognise these notes, nor could interpret them anyway. She lived amongst the sketches, the texts, the diagrams of dissected life, but could only shuffle them into loose piles on his desk. Not inquisitive, not knowing.

There is no portrait of Maturina in his notebooks, no rounded figure of a servant that would lead us to presume her form. She is in the shadows, working under the cover of darkness, helping to lift him wearily to bed, in the candlelight tending to his sores, to the stiff bones. Massaging essential oils into the swollen fingers before he attempted to complete the last portraits. Mothering Maturina, a woman's lot, second in life, a rock to which the rope of life was firmly attached. Melzi and others had their roles to play, but Maturina kept his soul, nourished its body, ordered the house and made it a home.

With Salai at his other side?

XXVI

The Dauphin was the one who became the driving force behind the flying trials. By dint of frustration at not being allowed to engage in any pilot activities, he vested himself with powers of persistence to have carpenters, craftsmen and weavers of cloth assigned in quantity to the project. The King indulged him, but at a cost to Leonardo's willpower and health, and other priorities.

'I have isolated Flight as my last great project, but had intended I should be allowed to advance it at my own pace,' Leonardo complained to Melzi, as they struggled with the other matter in hand - the ordering of his life's works.

'And my Will and Last Testament.'

'Later, Leonardo, later.'

codex volante. xix

The principles of Flight with which man is to glide above the earth are grounded in the movement of wings in the manner of birds.

Man must find the impetus, which is the power transmitted from the mover to the movable thing, and maintained by the wave of the air which this mover produces.

But we do not yet have this power; only the capacity of a man to pedal the gears fast enough yet barely sufficient to move him and his craft above the ground.

To fly from the cliff is to demonstrate Flight but
not in constant motion. The weight of the craft
must be less than that hitherto constructed in
relation to the lift.

Precisely. But of no satisfaction to the Dauphin, who
attended the old man's study on frequent occasions at Le
Clos Lucé.

'Messer Leonardo, we must succeed, and soon.'

'It is something in God's gift, if anyone's. He has not
revealed the final equation to us, and we must be patient if we
are to enter his universe of the sky.'

'But your trust is in science, not God.'

'Indeed. But it eludes us yet, and we must be equally patient.'

But it was politics once again that interfered with
Leonardo's progress, in the form of Niccolo Machiavelli, that
other interloper in these texts. To the city states the manipulator
of politics, but to Leonardo a friend. Their separate talents and
unusual dedication to their chosen professions set them apart.
They were deeply involved in day-to-day events, yet a greater
part of them is not on the pages of their correspondence.

Secretary to the Council of Florence, Machiavelli was at
the pinnacle of his career, yet as vulnerable as the common
man to the exchanges of princely power, the politics of greed.

He came to see Leonardo in the privacy of Le Clos Lucé
that autumn, once his public business had been completed at
the Chateau d'Amboise, the dowries sorted, the goods and
chattels divided, the documents signed, to enjoy the relative
calm in the shaded gardens.

'The Ball. It is a dangerous world we live in!'

'One day it may be safer. But only God knows when that
shall be.'

'He is the one sound patron.'

Leonardo: 'In whom all trust, but me.'

Leonardo was in bed, suffering from a cold or some form

of influenza. Maturina had insisted he stay warm as she fired up the logs. Melzi took notes. This ailment, of considerable concern to all in view of his age, had also brought on a stiffness in other limbs beyond the lapse in his hand. He was in reflective mood.

'God - if He is watching over me - may have done more than my own father. Or my mother could. You, Niccolo had a fortunate start, but I lost her to the countryside when very young. It was the best of intentions of my father, but I missed her, as only an orphan can. If I had stayed in her embrace, in village life, would I have been a contented farmer, tilling the fields, uncomplicated in life, a peasant's chase for sustenance, for fodder?'

And later: 'I was to see her only five times again before I was forty. Yet she was only two hours ride away. No letters, she could not write, could not bridge that short distance between us. I never knew where her love shone. Then my father married thrice more and I had thirteen brothers and sisters. Yet all were to deny me access to their position. He denied me much in the way of privilege, as if he wanted me to struggle in life, to prove my own abilities in some vain form of pride.

Machiavelli: 'He meant well. I am sure that he had your best interests at heart, and did such things as opened a door to your talents.'

'I doubt it. If I had stayed in Vinci and had spent my energies on the condition of the farmers, he would not have seen that as any achievement. Nor perhaps would my mother have had cause to be proud of me.

Maturina must have come in and attended to Leonardo. A cough, a splutter of indignation or a call for water?

Leonardo:'I am beginning to wither on the vine.'

Machiavelli: 'Soldier on. Resist those at Court who seek to destroy your ambition of Flight. Make them wither first. Whoever they are.'

Machiavelli sensed more than anyone that there were hidden threats to Leonardo and his favoured position. No man was entirely safe.

Machiavelli's journeys to and from Amboise took time and were not embarked upon lightly. He had many obligations in his work as Secretary to the Council in Florence, and no doubt they kept him from further visits. Life was shortened by the brutal truths of sickness, power-plays, treason, in-fighting, and battles on the field of play that ended in death more often than not. The gift of patronage was a loose bond, certain for a while, but subject to the winds of change. It required constant attention and served them both with irregularity and anxiety.

Leonardo: 'No peace for the wicked.'

Machiavelli: 'Nor for the valiant. Not least for the artist.'

Not even for the ill, for the Contessa emerged later from the shadows to pay a surprise visit to Leonardo in the hope that he could influence matters in her favour. To encourage the King to install her once more in his affections.

'Explain I had nothing to do with the intruders. They may have been from Lombardy, seeking revenge for His Majesty's control of their lands, but I had nothing to do with it.'

'I know that, but who will be persuaded? You should stay quiet for a while longer, then take up your duties, when events have moved on. Step forward again then, but not before the distractions of the Court are concentrated elsewhere. In time they shall be.'

'I cannot wait. I do not trust the Chamberlain. His Majesty will abandon me.'

'His patronage is subject to the same chance as all of us. Chambord is in prospect, your best opportunity to serve there, out of reach of others here at Court.'

But it is unclear whether the Contessa took his immediate advice. Whilst she felt in Leonardo she had her most favourable ally, his preoccupations were his Will, Flight and survival itself, as weakening health made him concentrate on the close 'family' around him.

Amongst those, Salai was increasingly at his right hand. In a preamble to the Will, written maybe when Leonardo first fell worryingly ill, steps to ensure Salai received *the* gift. The Book of Reflections.

> Faithful Salai: You are to retain this work as your inheritance. What you have given me I return in favour with this private testimony to be kept within your ownership for at least twenty years from my passing.

> It records my true feelings. Connections, loves, that could not be declared at the time. Those that have thrown wild accusations in the courts, will find they misjudged me entirely. The artist and model. The artist and the one true love amongst the fairer sex. To hell with all my critics, for they only ever understood the half of it.

> In time you may use it to your necessity, when the world has moved on and focused on new heroes, if it so suits your purpose to dispose of any value it might have.

Vasari, writing on Leonardo those fifty years later, does not draw upon it as a source, and Salai, for his own reasons, never used the option entrusted to him by the dying man.

> We have travelled far together. From obscurity to the great halls of patrons, from ignorance to appreciation. But you have brought hidden wealth to me, not them. These folios will be in your domain soon.

The note is indicative of the increasing frequency of Leonardo's illness. Now sixty five, but described when younger as beautiful in feature, admired for his inordinate strength, bending iron rods with ease; yet bringing these same strong hands to a delicate tuning of the lyre. Beauty reflected in his drawings and paintings. And found in Salai? Perhaps the double-coded texts in these Letters will give further insights? But not before the exuberant Dauphin has burst into Leonardo's bedroom.

'Ser Leonardo, are you yet alive?'

'God, if he exists is playing with my life.'

Ser, the notary, the title his father held, as did his great grandfather and predecessors settled in Florence. Notaries, lawyers by expectation, family tradition. Denied to Leonardo by birth, illegitimacy, if not shame. Too late to be acknowledged now.

br. 33

I did not yearn for acknowledgement at that time. I was young and in the fields, there was no anticipation of success or recognition then. My horizon clouded by the storms of nature ravaging the olive groves, vineyards and fields which supplied our sustenance. By the rains that both nourished and destroyed our crops.

I expected inclusion. Caterina was taken and married to ward off the danger of attachment. Thus my mother I lost to the convenience of position.

Grandparents serve you well, but age you before time; let you roam unhindered, grateful for the dispersal of energy that eludes them;

leave you to the study of nature and the open skies of exploration, but create the introspection of an untapped mind.

The real challenges Leonardo faced occurred when he went to live in Florence at seventeen; he was accounted for in the census as being at his father's residence. He was registered there, but almost certainly lived at Verrocchio's studio, not amongst the new family that his father had accumulated.

The first sign of artistic endeavour had been sighted earlier, when Leonardo was seven, with the decoration of a carved shield - the first images in grotesque relief that he was to use throughout life. Not in the familiar polished portraits of the famous, but in the anger of notebook sketches, the distorted features of old men, whether in battle scenes or stormy seas, contrasting with fine lines of anatomy; these grim realities he imposed on the beauty of the body. Men constantly portrayed old before their years. Men without wives or daughters to mellow them? Mirrors of his own existence, the old man within, hidden behind the skin of health? The Dauphin for one knew him only as an old man. Respect accorded, but still pushing to the limit the ambition to fly. At the risk of France.

The Dauphin's persistence noted:

'Is it not time for the next lift into the air, as you have promised?'

Leonardo, no doubt too weak at that moment to fight: 'We shall try again soon, when the carpenters have strutted a lighter craft, but this boundary may remain beyond our talents.'

XXVII

An outline sketch of a young woman drops from the folio.

The lines are drawn very finely, and suggest an image created some time before his exile to France, for their gentleness is in stark contrast to later works, when the faltering hands came into play.

C.C. - or is it C.G? - as the only notation.

The girl - or young woman - is seated, but sits with her back erect, a factor conditioned by something clutched close to the body, the faint outline of a pet on her lap that is seemingly trying to escape.

There is an enigmatic smile, but more naturally expressed than that of the Mona Lisa - an innocent look, almost virginal, with a sense of intimacy that passes only between lovers, rather than artist to model.

Perhaps this is a study for those attempts to unearth the workings of the human soul - the invisible elements that evaded his anatomical dissections of men and women. Those muscular diagrams displayed the entrails of the human form, assiduously drawn in the minutest detail, becoming grotesques at the end. But this sketch concentrates on youth in its fresh simplicity and innocence. Who was she, and what part had she played in his life? A model, simply hired for effect or practice, or someone he had come to know more intimately?

What is revealed is a passion for the feminine form, gracefully expressed in a brevity of lines, yet revealing much. This is not some peasant, but a girl with an air of nobility, a presence that confirmed status; an uplift in rank or position, reached through beauty alone?

So many clues drop from these pages, but it is the archives at Amboise that shelter other truths, and Melzi who first strung together the platform of threats, which had begun to impose themselves on the group at Le Clos Lucé.

'The poisoning. Accidents can happen, but with frequency, Maestro?' he had thrown at Leonardo one day. 'It seems beyond belief that anyone at Court should seek to put your life at risk. Who could have instigated that?'

'Someone who might believe that I was in league with the Contessa di Pavia. That she had a connection with the insurgents. The Queen almost said as much."

'In the heat of the moment.'

'Whereas the Chamberlain would consider in the cold light of dawn, and draw his own conclusions.'

'As he is paid to do.'

'Indeed. He will make whatever connections suit his purpose.'

'Which is?'

'To reduce the influence of us Italians at Court. To undermine that special relationship you have with His Majesty.'

'He need have no fear of that.'

'We know that. But the envious mind, the jealous heart, will reign uppermost in his logic.'

Francesco Melzi. The volunteer, who had given up his wealthy family background in Milan to follow the wayward artist, abandoning Law in pursuit of creative licence. At an early age he had thrown off the cloak of security and cast his lot with Leonardo, learning the craft of painting with determination, until over the years he could pass muster - and reframe his patron in the chapel windows at Le Clos Lucé. Comptroller. The role Melzi now happily adopted was that of manager of Leonardo's affairs in Amboise. There was no one else competent. Salai, now a portrait painter too, if of lesser skill, who had moved on from his wayward youth, nevertheless did not take to orderliness. Baptista de Villanis who had been hired to accompany the caravan from Milan on its journey of exile - attendant, but not organiser. It was Melzi, who burdened himself with the muddle of folios, the roll of paintings, the pieces of engineering, the battens of the flying craft, the canvas wings and the scattering of illustrations that remained piled up in the gallery of the stable block.

Leonardo did make one sketch of Melzi, perhaps scamped in an idle moment, or in reflection of his role. Presented as a round-faced, bold full figure, clothed imperiously in a fine cloak in the Florentine fashion. Plump waist, strong limbs, staunch legs, footed in shining buckled shoes. A representation of Melzi as he might have remained, had he prospered in Milan, rather than thrown in his lot with the artist.

On another sheet - a later annotation, no doubt - 'You must see me as I am now, Maestro, not as what could have been. I do not regret my move. Paint me in the humility of my present position.' A request Leonardo must have ignored.

Melzi was in a quandary. If he took upon himself to intercede and visit the Contessa, who had retired temporarily to a nearby town in an act of discretion, any sightings would strengthen suspicion of complicity. He wanted to act as an intermediary, but could see no way to do this without making the situation worse. The Chamberlain, as far as he knew, viewed him as merely a member of staff, the burgeoning artist rather than an intriguer, and Melzi felt it was important to maintain this position. There was enough scheming at Court already.

But the King's occasional absence was the opportunity that the Chamberlain - and the Queen - used to manipulate affairs to their chosen agenda. Since the Ball, the prisoners had been repeatedly tortured, but had not yet confessed to an insider connection. 'Which doesn't mean there isn't one,' their jailer noted.

XXVIII

Melzi constructed a daily routine, built around the need to bring order to all Leonardo's artefacts. He had little guidance from his master, who found activity increasingly difficult - a reality that led the King to make more frequent visits to Le Clos Lucé. That had been the bargain and he meant to keep it - conversation whenever State or Court duties permitted - and enlightenment on the march of science. The subjects were endless, and remained fresh in the mind of the old man, if not in the body.

Melzi would shuffle through the folios, essays, notebooks to find some order. Travels well recorded, works expanded as each patron in turn sought to exploit his gifts. Pleas from popes, city elders, monks, princesses and warlords alike that had arrived in endless succession. A flow that had only slowed when Michelangelo and Raphael took precedence with the patrons for whom Leonardo failed to finish works. The monks who demanded their money back. The Borgias that dispensed with his war services. The diversion of the Arno abandoned. The drainage of the Roman marshes unfulfilled. The bronze of the great horse for Ludovico Sforza broken up by French artillerymen for cannon before it left the mould. The clay model used for archery practice.

br.35

Fame brought me more of everything. Work, obligation; more work, but insufficent riches. A treadmill of experience that left me no peace, no order in my life. No life of my own.

Fame is desirable in youth, fed in middle age, but serves poorly when older. Then it does not pay a living, nor hold attention from the younger generation. Patrons will have their own heroes, their architects and soon my plans will be buried in the indifference of archives.

To Melzi:'We shall never finish putting this house in order.'

'Maestro, a lexicon of your work would have been of great assistance.'

'There never was time.'

'We should have started long ago.'

'Now it is too late, I fear. You shall have to deal with all this once I am gone.'

'Do not presume that will be soon.'

'We know it shall be.' Leonardo apparently had dropped a sheet of papers from his right hand. The rebellious fingers too stiff to grasp documents as firmly as they had once. Too fixed to handle the flex of paint brushes. 'We must not fool ourselves. Time is not on my side. I have outlived the average, achieved a second life.'

Leonardo walked the gardens of Le Clos Lucé each day, avoiding the task in hand, reluctant some days to face the work. Once that would never have been the problem. Now it was the inevitable.

"No being disappears into the void". These mortal words were to be repeated, as he instructed Melzi later to prepare his Will and Last Testament.

But they haunt these Letters, these reflections. The words are indeed perceptive, not least of himself. Leonardo had long lived in a void of misfortune. The childhood separation from his mother and father, her lifelong detachment from his circumstance, these factors were not unusual then. Nor the bastardy itself. But he was lost in the space between them.

His situation had acted as a barrier to formal learning, and made Leonardo determined to mine his own talents and steer an individual course of his own making, on his own terms. Then he chose to stay in the void he created, within the public eye, but masked by his genius. Sufficient that the works speaks for themselves.

King François was to say to Benevenuto Cellini, the great sculptor: "I believe no other man had been born who knew as much about sculpture, painting and architecture, but still more he was a very great philosopher."

Leonardo, adjudicating on others, on so many subjects, yet not himself: "The Medici made me and ruined me."

This a reminder that he was in Amboise in part because of the death of Guiliano de Medici in March 1516, and by the loss of this patron any hope of finding further fruitful employment in Florence and Rome. He had been ignored by Lorenzo the Magnificent at the start of his career and passed on to Ludovico Sforza - Il Moro - in Milan. This led to the most productive phase of this life, yet later the Medici were to underuse his services in favour of the newer, younger artists. Only King François was left in admiration. Late in the day, very late.

But others at Court sought to impose themselves:

codex vitae.xix

Words which do not satisfy the ear of the listener weary him or vex him, and you will often see symptoms of this in the frequent yawns of such listeners; therefore when you speak before men whose good will you desire, and see such an excess of fatigue, abridge your speech, or change the subject; for if you do otherwise you will earn dislike and hostility instead of the hoped for favour.

> And if you want to see in what a man takes
> pleasure, without hearing him speak, change
> the subject of your discourse in speaking to
> him and, when he presently becomes intent
> and does not yawn nor wrinkle his brow and
> the like, you may be certain that the matter
> which you are speaking is agreeable to him.

Quite.

Vasari reports that Leonardo used to buy caged birds in order to release them, for he had pity for their plight. From these Letters it is easy to conclude that the man himself felt caged. Trapped by success as much as failure. For each invention or work of art that brought admiration, so there was a critic. No one ignored him.

At Amboise the Chamberlain resented Leonardo's assumption of a position of confidence with the young King. The Queen kept a certain distance, having to concede the afternoons to the two men's conversations. She bridged it with the demands of the secret portrait, but the moments of truth were few and far between. A slight resentment rather than jealousy. Many courtiers were disappointed too that some interest had been diverted from their attempts to gain influence. Leonardo, the innocent in all this, not needing to fight, nor wanting to become embattled any more in the mire of politics, was made aware of the hostile factions against him.

codex forza. vii

> Weight is a factor of motion that changes the
> means by which force is exerted and it
> prolongs the settlement of stability.

111

Exactly. But the further series of accidents that befell him, the fires, the impending damage to his flying machines - were these coincidences or the forces of resentment and jealousy piling up against him? Who had risked the introduction of poison? Who was hiding in the shadows, wanted him dead?

Perhaps Leonardo had some premonition that his papers would be destroyed rather than nourished. Forgotten rather than form the basis of scientific advance.

br.36

Nothing will become of them. Youth shall find its own popularity and with blind aspiration seek to establish its own credentials. No one will print these works of mine.

My fault, no less, for not ordering them in time. But no weight do I seek at this point to lever such ambition. My handiwork stands on the pages for all to see. If not use.

On a separate note: Melzi, you must do your best.

The entertainments Leonardo organised for the King, the final portrait, the effort on Flight, these were sufficient to keep himself alert. But he still felt too close to the politics and in-fighting, and Life was then a cruel and haphazard existence, with dangerous contests determined on the field of battle using crude weapons.

codex forza. xix

Creatures shall be seen on the earth who will always be fighting one with another, with the greatest losses and frequent deaths on either side. There will be no bounds to their malice; by their strong limbs a great portion of the trees in the vast forests of the world shall be laid low, and when they are filled with food the gratification of their desire shall be to deal out death, affliction, labour, terror and banishment to every living thing.

Philosopher? Prescient soothsayer. Foreseeing the reasons his work could vanish into the mist.

XXIX

Vasari tells us how Melzi had come into Leonardo's life and home. 'Messer Francesco da Melzi, a gentleman of Milan, who in the time of Leonardo's first acquaintance was a very beautiful young man, and much loved by him.'

Francesco's parents owned a large estate at Vaprio, near Milan. In 1507 Melzi would have been fifteen, but what was an early physical attraction blossomed into a private relationship of trust. Master and disciple. A pupil painter, soon accomplished in his own right, Melzi later became Leonardo's right hand, travelling everywhere with him, and finally to Amboise.

"There he helped finish the last works of art as the old man's brush hand became paralysed. He devoted his life to the genius."

Amboise. 15th November 15--

Bring with you those effects you know are most of importance to me. I do not have to list them as you made the account in the first place.

I entrust with you the funds held at Santa Maria Nuova. Bring them safely under guard yet leave five hundred écus soleil in deposit for emergencies.

Lastly bring yourself and the workings of companionship that bind us together in perpetuity.

This letter is out of order and the torn date must be 1516 not 1517, but it has emerged at random from translation, a small glimpse on paper of their relationship and trust in life.

In the chapel of Le Clos Lucé the frescoes painted by the school of Leonardo, including Melzi, later adorned the walls of the chapel, a permanent tribute in commemoration. The Annunciation, the Virgin of Light, the End of the World. Alpha and Omega. The beginning and the end. Birth and death. And for Leonardo the ages in-between, the attachment of youth to his studio, to his staff. Their energy as much as beauty uplifted and inspired him

'Melzi, I insist on dictating my Will and Last Testament.'

'Yes, Master, but not at present. We have much still to do.'

It was a matter the pupil did not want to undertake before it became necessary. Put off today what you can do tomorrow. Maybe he had learnt from the old man, the great unfinisher, the maddening genius who so frustrated his patrons. Or more likely, Melzi no more wanted to face the inevitability of death than Leonardo himself. A life incomplete, scattered in notebooks and loose papers. "Not much to account for."

But it was not Melzi - a safe pair of hands - who was to be the next cypher for danger. An unsigned note had been circulating in the King's absence with a challenging accusation.

It reads: "Messer Leonardo, being acquainted with the manner of young men, and in favour of their company, made the practice of enjoying to the fullest their vulgar ways, which are not to be condoned, nor accepted at Court."

This piece of mischief may have been seen by the great man to be just that, a scandalous assertion - whether deemed true or not - that would suffice to lay fire to the smoke of political infighting at Amboise.

Whether Salai had been the cause of this attack is not clear; his impudence was waning and his recklessness long behind. But his close attention to Leonardo in his retiring rooms, particularly when he had moments of fatigue or illness, raised eyebrows amongst the gossip-mongers. Now this attachment was being exploited.

For Leonardo this accusation bore immediate connection to the infamous court case of his youth. The sodomy plot that had been rigged against him and two others by envious rivals. Dismissed three times in court, it nevertheless was a reference point for malicious interpretation of his manner. It challenged his sexual character.

And then buried alongside this note a revealing letter, clearly written by Leonardo when he was but twenty-five, so why does it lodge here? Another note of sickness?

Florence, January 12th 1477

Marco, friend:

I am glad that last year has passed, for it has grieved my soul considerably. Never shall the mischief of Jacopo Saltieri be clear of my name. Who put him to this test of my virtue we cannot tell, but it was clearly designed to bring me down before I could fully establish myself.

There are a number of candidates, but no certainty. Nor did the courts, in the end, find any proof of his allegations. The *tamburo* was filled with lies beyond casual licence and di Tornabourni can only have been the real target.

Yet we are besmirched for life, with a result in our favour, a mark of innocence, but the records stained with our names, and our families impugned.

L.

Tamburo. The over-zealous post-box that citizens of Florence could use for accusatory notes against others. A convenient way of having fellows arrested that one did not like. Set up to attract evidence of common fraud and social misdemeanours, they failed the test of truth, and became reservoirs of false grievance. The accusation was one of sodomy, placed at the door of Leonardo, two friends and the above mentioned Lionardo di Tornabourni, on the body of Saltieri. The latter quite possibly hired as a complainant for money.

The Officers of the Night and Monasteries kept a night watch in those days on social behaviour, and were responsible for hearing the case in April 1476. But this produced no verdict, and a further hearing took place in June, again ending without a judgement.

For a third time the case was heard, but with no real evidence the four men were cleared, possibly with some political influence being exercised by di Tornabourni's family, which was directly related to the ruling Medicis.

That Leonardo was writing months later and reflecting back on this stained year confirms he was badly shaken by these events and felt strongly abused. Perhaps that is why the letter to Marco (a fellow artist?) lodges in this private package. A confirmation of innocence intended to be displayed if ever challenged again.

"We are in life as the young child formed at seven, a casualty of Jesuit thinking, but trying to dispose of the pain of early adulthood. Then we are still learning and making mistakes." Clearly the incident left its mark on Leonardo - this letter preserved in his private archive to balance any stain on his character.

Perhaps too it accounts for his solitude, his reluctance to

put himself directly in the hands of a wife or fellow man. Rather it is in his pupils that he found the comfort of a family, and in Salai a special indulgence.

br. 38

Salai: Be not afraid of the critical words of others for they are not aware of the comfort you bring me. They service the needs of the studio, of our income and the pursuit of Flight; all worthy causes, but they do not share that inner love that rises above the commonplace.

Reflect on this, that your mischief, whilst reprehensible, is but of a trivial nature in comparison with the acts of support you give me when I am wounded. That the devotions of the doctor administer to my physical condition, but in you I find another solace, a more potent medicine for my true ailment.

At Amboise was the new poisonous note from the same hands that had brought him the tampered food? There is no certain evidence, but there is a riposte from Leonardo in his papers - a document he must have used at some point when the smoke was rising from this fire:

Le Clos Lucé, 12th September 1517

Those that persecute me on this base platform overlook one fact that is in the heart of my life.

Namely as an artist I am brought to sight the many forms of the human body.

Not least amongst these is that of the woman in her youth. The intoxicating aromas of the naked flesh, washed in rose water in preparation for a sitting, or even, at the day's end, the sweat of the swollen model, who has appeared still, but suffered under the power of the sun on her limbs, the moisture a coolant to the heat outside and the desire within.

Think clearly - can one be so fascinated by this beauty and yet inured to its attraction? Do they think that I have been devoted all these years to this sex and not touched its pleasures?

Such are the fools that accuse me now. They have no inkling of the stupidity of their call for my condemnation. Where is the proof of their claims?

And an annotation on this record, no doubt made when the petition had been rebutted at Court.

'Fear not Salai, for they know not what they do. There are much greater secrets than you hold yet to be discovered.'

XXX

"The Book. It is me."

These words Leonardo had imparted in private to Salai, when referring to the Book - a gift outside his Will. Yet some of its pages have found their way into this package, suggesting that Salai was careless or passed them on to Melzi much later. Possibly that some other hand intervened, sifted and sorted out those insights that might otherwise reduce the master's reputation? To hide them away. Or had death intervened?

Salai is reported as returning to Florence at this time, but these notes from Amboise prove otherwise. For would he have done so, unless to fetch an item of value - or to store the Book in a safe place proposed by Leonardo?

The reasons are not known. Nor is there any reference here to Baptista de Villanis, the other servant who is with Leonardo in Amboise. He may have provided cover in Salai's absence. His place in history noted only in the margin.

Making Salai the more significant. Maturing from the rogue, thief and unreliable youth into a loved companion. Soon to be entrusted with the leaves of the Book of Reflections, whilst Melzi, the determined pupil, had the fuller treasure house to put in order.

br.38

In life as in love, the closeness of another is the soul of meaning, the sharing of intimacy, the touch of harmony, the completion of passion. She knew that better than anyone, and sacrificed herself for it.

That would leave Salai and Baptista out of this particular equation. Maturina unlikely in this context to be a candidate, albeit devotedly carrying out domestic duties without a murmur, without demand. Was it Caterina, when she returned to be beside her son, in the shadows of the kitchen, the larder and scullery; almost invisible, not catalogued in the census?

And in that characteristic jumble of unconnected ideas that were so often thrown together on a single page - a note attached to this folio, but not part of it, stating that the next test of Flight was due, though the circumstances of this attempt are unclear. Evidence that Leonardo was pursuing vertical flight in one of the spiral drawings attached to the sheet. Perhaps the balance had still not been solved between the weight of the pilot, the timbers of his fixed-wing flying-machines and his power through the pedals.

codex volante. xxii

The flight of birds when they migrate is made against the movement of the wind not in order that their movement may be made more swiftly but because it is less fatiguing.

And this is done with a slight beating of their wings whereby they enter the wind with a slanting movement from below and then place themselves slantwise upon the course of the wind.

The wind enters under the slant of the bird like a wedge and raises it upwards during the time that the acquired impetus consumes itself, after which the bird descends again under the wind.

An addendum beside this graphic:

> The Dauphin and I had sat underneath a
> sycamore tree, the seed spiralling down in the
> breeze that shook these pods free from their
> moorings.
>
> Nature was resorting to the regeneration of
> the forest but I was observing their slow
> journey to earth, the surface of the wings
> allowing them to glide down, then
> momentarily up, before finally finding the
> moss within which they would be reborn.
>
> If four men were to pedal a craft with such a
> rotating wing above their heads would we
> achieve the lift that eludes us at present?

The result is not shown. The plotters at Court may have
been pushing for the next test before Leonardo was ready - a
tactic which would bring another failure to play into their hands
in reducing his reputation and favoured access to the King.

Instead all there is in the archives of the Chateau
d'Amboise for that month is a notation regarding the assembly
of the King and selected courtiers to witness a 'Sample of
Flight' on the hillsides above the river, but the precise location
is not stated, nor is it clear what occurred. It is dated 24th
September 1517.

> His Majesty and engineers attended Messer
> Leonardo and pilots at the experiment with
> direct flight. (Upwards?) It was not
> successful, the energies of the pilots exhausted
> before the craft lifted from the ground. We are
> not reassured in this matter, but ML is to be

further encouraged in this obsession for his own sake and that of France over its enemies.

XXXI

Towards late autumn it was the Chamberlain who increased his visits to Le Clos Lucé from the Chateau. A distance of no more than 500 metres, it nevertheless had become for Leonardo a suitable space between the Court - with its day-to-day machinations - and his manor house.

Le Clos Lucé earned itself a reputation as a peaceful zone, with gardens of contemplation, cool streams running through its sunlit glades and dappled woods and on down into the valley through the town to the banks of the Loire. Into this calm, the King's keeper managed to intrude on one petty excuse after another, both monitoring Leonardo's designs for entertainments or expressing a suspicious interest in the progress of Flight. No doubt he was treated with respect, but equally an internal cyncism.

'The Contessa displays an excessive zeal in matters Italian, as in your designs and works of art. She wishes to cover the walls of the chateau with these effects, and tapestries that annoint your Renaissance. It is all too much.'

This record - dated 25th September 1517 - confirms that the Contessa had been allowed back permanently from some temporary resting-place elsewhere. The King had exercised his prerogative and allowed her again to be at Court.

'Her enthusiasm is innocent. Art is what she knows well, has seen at home in Pavia. She has been trying to please the King.'

'Exactly, and trying too hard.'

'She is born of the period, she wishes to import progress.'

'Then she is overplaying her hand. We are most proud of our

French heritage and she should fall for that - and show it well.'

'I am not her keeper.'

'But aligned.'

'We simply come from the same area.'

'Tell her not to display herself so conspicuously on the battlements. The Queen does not like such provocative exhibition. We have peacocks for that - and can strangle them if they make too much noise.'

'She seldom comes here.'

'We know that she does, often enough to ally herself to your cause.'

'Then your informants are misjudging the situation.'

'My judgement is final.' Once again the Chamberlain could not resist picking up the latest design - for an improved bird wing - inspecting it casually, and then throwing it on the tiled floor, as he swept out. 'Your head is in the air, and that will do you no good, whilst we keep our feet firmly attached to the realities on the ground.'

But Leonardo had another woman on his mind, whilst the Chamberlain's visit had had an hidden agenda - the accusations of Leonardo's impropriety. Unidentified rumours, continuing gossip that something was amiss in his behaviour. Comments alluding to his past, assertions that nothing had changed, that the follies of youth had extended themselves even to this day, that Salai was but one of his acolytes that enjoyed manly bonding.

The following note appears, clipped to a folio from the Book of Reflections. A written response (the original now lost) to support a rebuttal of the polarisation of his sexuality. A copy of a note from the past.

br. 40

Those that presume I had no knowledge of

women lack insight to my interest. For how can I have come so close to those whose souls and bodies formed the study of my art, and not have been under the influence of their troubled gaze?

A woman has no place in which she can rest, for her mind is in torment with the duties of alliance and dalliance with man or motherhood and at no stage can she be at peace. I have shared that anxiety and been myself drawn into the blessing of its generosity and once in fulfilment.

And was not she the greatest beauty that providence brought to my canvas? In her I saw the mysteries of faith and the capacity of love with which she was so abundantly endowed. In that youth was a blossom greater than that of the May tree, the rose or any of Nature's flowers.

In the Spring of her life she served in duty to her lord, with a subtle power that was greater than he commanded over his people. Yet she took the risk of our loving, against all that she might lose - including her head.

For she gave such hours and attention to my work that the portrait welled up inside me and is my greatest study. Nor was it chance that this should be so, for in the seclusion of the studio did we two share those moments of attachment which sealed my own fate and desire to commit to her the fulfilment of that unrequited loving which was within our reach.

When I stood beside her the better to measure her form, was it not her hand that took mine and laid it across her slight breasts so that I should most correctly imprint their beauty upon the canvas? And without words, when I felt unable to resist the tilting of her chin to catch the light on her angelic face, was it not again her lips that brushed mine with teasing abandon?

Who is this, with a smile more enigmatic than her more renowned competitor - La Gioconda? Did the artist fall totally and physically in love with this subject? What year was this - sometime in the 1480s?

There are contemporaneous records that remind us of Leonardo's powerful physique and attractive disposition as a young man. He had a powerful bearing and would proudly wear an unconventional short pink tunic to set himself apart, not only as the artist, but as the distinctive thinker. And have historians misjudged the man, overlooked the feelings that he really held, preferring to take his masculinity and associating it with his own sex, fuelled by that one false accusation by Saltieri in youthful Florence, with the moss of suspicion accruing over the years of celibacy?

If he could not pursue his affection for this woman, how did he force her from his passion, how did he expend that pent-up lust? There is nothing in the public domain that says. He completes the commission and is obliged to move on, but does he leave his heart behind?

Does a man ever leave that once-in-a-lifetime love behind?

XXXII

It was the Contessa di Pavia who one day slipped through the cordon around Le Clos Lucé, adding unwarranted danger to Leonardo's position within the Court. Her attempts to draw him in as an ally had begun to annoy him.

'You must seek help from Messer Machiavelli,' he insisted. 'He remains your best ambassador, and can guide you back to influence in Florence or Pavia.'

The Contessa: 'But I have abandoned them for France and declined the marriage set for me there. They will not forgive me.'

It was the Queen, however, who took things into her own hands. The Contessa's show of confidence at the masquerade in unmasking herself at the foot of the King represented a direct challenge. The King's hold on the situation weakened by this action, details of what followed did not emerge for another century - in papers held at Pavia.

The Contessa had been allowed to return after a short absence 'resting' to her apartment in the east wing of Chateau d'Amboise, though her movements were restricted. With the King's permission she was given more time to plan a return to Italy. But she was dithering too long and this led the Queen to believe that he might install his mistress permanently at nearby Chambord, where the new castle was turning into a residence of immense proportions.

Queen Claude was to wait until François was away on military duties before she struck. A final warning was given and the Chamberlain secretly briefed. She then removed herself to Blois. But her comptroller fatally decided to execute the plan with his own course of action.

In the Contessa's apartment he delivered an instruction: 'Your future is not here. The possibilities have been discussed, Messer Machiavelli may conjure up a berth for you in Florence, but you must leave - under my supervision.'

'Can I be sure Machiavelli will help me?'

'He is your best hope there... as I am for you here.'

The Contessa's diary records that he leant up against her, as a threat and the chance to brush against her breasts. His garlicked breath fought against her perfume.

'You are to obey my instructions, to the letter. The order confirms it.'

But two weeks passed with no message from Florence, and the King was still away, when her fate was sealed. Late one night the latch on her apartment door was raised with only the slightest sound and the Chamberlain stole into the room, disguised in a simple black cloak.

'Now is the chance, the moment you must escape. Do everything as I say.'

'I am not ready, my belongings not finally packed.'

'They will follow. Leave them now.'

'But...'

'There is no time to waste. Others are commissioned to dispose of you, remove the problem, this very night. It is not a matter of choice. I am your only chance.'

The Contessa sensed this to be a lie, but with her options seemingly closed, meekly said: 'Now?'

'A lady-in-waiting in my debt confirms it. Without me she is nothing, her favours a price she pays. Together with information.'

The Chamberlain approached her with menace and blew out all the candles but one, enclosing them in near-darkness, the flickering indecision of night. Then in these shadows he began not to help but to caress her again, roughly.

'I want you simple. Without this flamboyant court dress, utterly simple for the journey, to avoid attention. As simple as my cloak, black as the night, like a commoner. If we are to pass the guards.'

'Which you will have bribed.'

'Not all are in my remit. You must be careful.' And impatiently, 'Now off with this finery. It is far too conspicuous.'

She faltered, knowing something was wrong, but his temper increased, 'Take the rest off, just do it. Disrobe yourself. I have brought you this simple habit, like mine. That is all you need until the inn, where others will take you on.'

'How will I know them?'

He did not provide a sensible answer, did not bother to reveal any details.

'Off with this glory, all of it, now. Tuck your hair in under the collar. Nothing underneath, nothing at all.' He picked up her blonde court headdress used at formal occasions at Court. 'You will not be needing this anymore.'

His instructions seemed contrived - and false - and at that moment he lifted his cloak to reveal he was naked underneath. In defiant stance he pronounced: 'I should be your king, your life depends on me!'; and without a further word, ripped the camisole off her. Impatient with sheer lust, he saw before him a chance, to avenge, to rape her, a last parting gift, an opportunity to take an unexpected reward. A plotted chance.

He tore the last stitch of clothing off the Contessa, but did not reach for the cloak he had proffered. Instead he picked up the blonde headdress and in a fit of perversity donned it, as he threw her onto the bed. Raising his habit, he lay upon her, spreading her legs as she fought him, before smothering her mouth in coarse kisses. As the latch of the door was silently lifted.

Then he became immersed in his own sexual release, the blonde hair streaming behind his waving head as if he was the Contessa on top pleasuring the man. Her suppressed cries and moans came from beneath, but seemed to come from him, riding above her.

In his mad surge he knocked the last candle over and

cast the room into darkness as the door was quietly moved ajar; a glimmer of candlelight from the corridor enabled two figures to creep in and approach the frantic coupling. Had he looked round he would have seen two daggers raised in the glint of the light from outside, but he had not heard the intruders and was oblivious to anything other than his sex. It cost him his life.

The assassins, believing the Contessa was in their sights, and deluded by the blonde headdress, were caught in a moment of indecision. However, unconcerned as to the identity of 'her' secret lover, they nodded to confirm their orders and plunged daggers into the back of the body they assumed to be the Contessa.

The collapse of the Chamberlain upon the body underneath evoked the gasps of death they expected to hear from their target, and instantly satisfied of their mission, made a swift exit. Glances were exchanged with others in the dimness of the passageway, the deed done. Then any light was snuffed out, footsteps receded.

In the Court diary for the next day the return of their majesties is recorded, and with very precise timings. The Queen made sure she arrived from Blois and retired to her apartment some hours ahead of her husband from Savoy.

The King: 'Why is the Chamberlain not here to meet me?' No answers.

Then to his Queen: 'Any mischief whilst I have been away?'

'Nothing worthy of discussion.'

Nor when the King went secretly to the Contessa's apartment later did he find anything suspect. But he did discover her tearful and tense, sitting on the trunk in which she stored her gowns. From the state of the room he assumed she had accepted the inevitable, and was packing her clothes.

'It is regrettable,' he quickly said, 'but Her Majesty will not have it. Return to Florence - or Pavia - whilst matters are restored here. Then we shall see what I can do to...'

The page in the Contessa's diary is torn off at this point. Perhaps in anger rather than by a witness later, as if she could not accept there would be no prospect of seeing the King further unless in Lombardy. He embraced her and they kissed, but for her these kisses were empty, those of separation, the reunion no more than a promise.

She sat again on the trunk when he had left. In stony silence, in fear of her life. For in the chest was the body of the Chamberlain, which she had struggled to hide. A body the Queen almost certainly had intended should be hers, a corpse that would be found in its bed. A life murderously taken, but with the King and Queen absent, by whom in evidence?

For the Contessa immediate problems. The body would rot and before long give off the odour of death. The assassins, or rather their commander, might be driven by curiosity to attend the scene of the crime, as soon as the King was distracted by Court matters. For a day, possibly two, the wrong corpse could be her own death warrant.

Then a rash diary entry:

> "I departed at night with all my goods and
> chattels under escort. Provided in secret by
> His Majesty. Inned near Chambord."

For the moment out of the way.

But to the Court she had vanished. To the Queen, who had immediately retired on a simple excuse back to Blois, the mistress had been disposed of, the discovery of her body eagerly awaited. The King maintained silence on the matter. He had the apartment sealed.

However, there is no further notation in the Contessa's diary, nor in the court archives for that month. Yet curiously her name is added in script to a reflection of Leonardo's in the privacy of this collection:

br. 41

The hope and the desire of going back to one's country is like that of the moth to light; and of the man who with perpetual longing looks forward with joy to each new spring and to each summer, and to the new months and new years, deeming that things he longs for are too slow in coming; he does not perceive that he is longing for his own destruction.

XXXIII

The Queen broke the wall of silence. At the next sitting in Blois, watching the artist observe her in that characteristic detail that makes the model feel naked, she began to drop questions into this silence and sought answers to the nature of Leonardo's relationship with women - and then in particular, with the Contessa.

'She has vanished, perhaps her guilt overtook her.'

'I have no knowledge of that.' A truth Leonardo could only offer, unaware that the Queen herself knew more, convinced that her plot had succeeded and the body disposed of. Except the Chamberlain had disappeared as well as the Contessa.

'She was of a mind to call on you, maestro, and seek your co-operation in her many manoeuvres, was she not?'

'We were of one country, but not of one mind. I take care not to interfere in Court matters. I am past it, besides the artist must be free of politics, clear in his conscience and sight.'

'I trust that is so. I would not want such mischief to bring you down.'

'I do not need the weight of intrigue.'

'Have you seen her?'

'No.'

'She was here...'

'The last time was over a month ago. Can the Chamberlain not vouch for that?'

'He has effected an absence. We await his return.' The Queen was keeping her powder dry, whilst the real questions stacked high in her mind. 'I shall trust your position in these matters. Keep your distance at Le Clos Lucé and I will not trouble you. Now put a brave face on my condition in this portrait, it will be the record of my strength in this time of danger. A picture of calm is demanded for us women. We cannot be shown to be the weaker sex.'

'I hope your patronage stands firm, Your Majesty.'

'You do not understand the fairer sex, maestro. For all your art and inquisitive nature, you prefer the company of men.'

'I have eyes that can look into...'

'No, I fear not. One can sense these things clearly. The artist may touch upon the surface of a woman's body, but not always connect with the soul.'

'I have...'

'It is the inner tremors that we experience, in day to day matters. We are pragmatic you see, since we are obliged at a young age to defer, to be the bounty with which lords barter in exchange for further position. We are the baggage of man's intent. Is that not so, Messer Leonardo?'

'I have tasted the fruits of my labour, to have gained...'

'But not that inner reward which is the passion of the night.'

'My work is of necessity for the day...'

'When all can see your actions. That is when we observe, but do not play out our fantasies.'

'I have known...'

'Not the guts of the issue, the fire that comes into the belly, unexpected, instantaneous, uncontrollable. That is what you have missed in portraying women.'

There was no answer from Leonardo. He could not let the truth slip. But it was not the Queen who figures directly in two other letters that Leonardo has in this package. Two folios that are set aside, one wrapped with an outer cloth, an unbroken seal at its throat.

On the cover of the other, the introduction of a letter that has gone missing:

Caterina mia, tempo fuggito, ritorna

Perhaps this was simply a request from afar, the distance of absence over years, a lifetime. For this note appears to marry with a record in the public domain:

The return of a certain Caterina to his home in Milan in the summer of 1493. (This note is dated May 10th and must be the trigger to action that occurred in July).

Caterina... mia. My Caterina, my mother.

For attached to the cover is this note:

> "My mother was to find her last peace with me. Not in the care she was able to pass on, for I was now in the position of strength, her weakness evident. She would refuse to sit idly in the chair, for the routine of her life in the countryside of Vinci had disposed her to remain busy all day. She could not relinquish the duties of the household, so she served to make my quarters more agreeably tidy, despite the attention of my pupils in this regard."

No doubt in reality the pupils lived in the mess of a studio on the ground floor, outside her domain, but Caterina defied her years and chose to work silently away in the kitchen and sleeping quarters.

> "She would go to market two days a week and gather that produce which she could tolerate on her bent shoulders. I watched her performance, reluctant to offer a help that would be declined. She wanted to be of use, and the greatest value she brought was her presence, for we had been separated a lifetime and now had precious moments to fill that void."

'Too late.'

'Never.'

'We can sit by the log fire in the cold evenings of winter and muse on what might have been. With sorrow and regret acknowledge the vagaries of life and the politics of position that have kept us on different paths across the years.'

'Your father did what he felt was best for you - and me. There was no prospect of my gaining from our liaison.'

'But in that moment he loved you?'

'Or found his passion running away with him.'

'Leaving you behind.'

'As he had to. I did not expect more. The year you were to be born, he was married to Albeira, a notary's daughter, but sixteen. I did not compare. He did not look back, nor visit the countryside, as his obligations were in the city, the madness of Florence.'

'He helped...'

'He accommodated my situation. I was to be the wife of Buti del Vacca; Piero, or as he was known, Accattabriga. A furnace worker at Empoli. I accepted my fate... but not the release of you after at two years.'

'I was nearby, in the fields of Vinci, with...'

'Your grandparents. Yes, safe in their care, and the better for it. It was no easier for me to recognise that.'

'It is too late to change the record.'

'Too late for anything.'

'You are here now. Home at last.'

A codicile, written on the back of those reflections, relates to Caterina. One would not guess he is referring to his mother.

br. 43

I took Caterina in for two years. An absolution conditioned by mercy and forgiveness. She only wanted to serve, and I allowed this

waiting in the wings, the duty in the kitchen,
as she only was at ease there.

Her illness was not fully evident at first and
she deceived me on this until the coughing
and weakness in heart became too evident.
Even then she would not accept a chair in the
room with guests or pupils, afraid their
conversation and their interests would put her
at a serious disadvantage. As would mine.

For one year she served, for the next and last
she lay infirm, in a declining state, refusing any
luxury or extravagant medicine. She wanted to
rest, to die. Foolishly I let her have her wish.

In a notebook in the public domain:

Expenses of Caterina's burial:

For three pounds of wax	27 soldi
For the bier	8 soldi
Pall for the bier	12 soldi
Carriage and erection of cross	4 soldi
For the bearers	8 soldi
For 4 priests and 4 clerks	20 soldi
Bell, book, sponge	2 soldi
For the gravediggers	16 soldi
For the dean	8 soldi
For official permission	1 soldi
Total	106 soldi

Off the page, a lifetime's regret?

XXXIV

The Contessa at Chambord, however, was the one now contemplating death. Her own and that of the Chamberlain. His body weighed heavily upon her mind and the trunk in which it lay in an adjacent locked storeroom. She adopted the role of an anguished widow and the innkeeper left her alone to mourn, unaware of the murderous goods within his house. He had received generous payment in advance on her arrival and a clear indication more would be given if he kept his reserve. The staff were told to keep their distance and normal cleaning was suspended. The 'widow' would come to dine only when it suited her. A bowl of fruit was already in the one room of substance in this country inn.

Even with all these precautions she had to make a quick decision on the disposal of the body before its odour leaked from its prison and became impossible to ignore. The porter might expect to be allowed into the storeroom at some point and it would arouse suspicion if this duty was resisted for too long.

The Contessa began enquiries, apparently innocent in nature, but based upon the need to bury her 'husband' who supposedly lay in a crypt not far away. These conversations were conducted at arm's length and through a succession of unconnected labourers, undertakers and others so that, as each was not in the end used, the trail of information was broken, until she was able to employ in a secretive deal four men from a remote village who were unaware of the original need.

She met their gangmaster in a hired carriage at a clearing in the woods beside a village some distance from Chambord and told him a quite different story.

'My maid had a most unfortunate situation. Her lover fell foul of her father's anger, the boy being totally unsuitable in that man's opinion. The young couple persisted in their affections and met frequently in the fields. But her father discovered them and a struggle ensued, in which the father in his rage struck a fatal blow to the head of the young man. Even though he was strong as an ox, he collapsed and died at the feet of the daughter. The body has been entrusted to me for burial since the scandal cannot be admitted in the village. It is a matter that requires your total discretion.'

'Where is it now?' The gangmaster had asked.

'I will arrange for it to be brought to you here in three days time. Then you must fulfil my instructions to the letter in return for a most generous settlement.'

'I promise.'

'There will be nothing of value in the chest, just the body of this most unfortunate young man.'

'We would not want to interfere with...'

'You would do so at your peril.'

'He is infected in some way?'

'The father believed so, and did not want his daughter affected.'

'So be it. We shall do our duty.'

To broker the deal she lay before his eyes a jewel of worth quite outside the man's imagination.

'This is your guarantee that this business shall done. The full payment will more than meet your needs.'

'Indeed.'

'And your silence in this matter.'

On the following day she obtained further leather straps from the ostler at the inn and laboured to pass them around and under the trunk in order to add to its bonds.

On the night before the collection of her trunk, she warned the innkeeper of her plan to move some of her possessions and that a carriage and cart should be available for her use the next day. Two strong men would be needed to lift the main item of baggage from the storeroom. Another jewel passed hands discreetly. He said not a word.

139

A page from her diary, found years later is included in this package:

Chambord, the fifteenth

There was no one who could share my burden. RF had gained me this escape, but I remained in a prison of my own indecision and of the circumstances I could not determine.

I awaited news of his assistance, but events must be preventing any admission or communication. The silence is terrible. His touch is no longer on my breast with its insistent but reassuring guidance. How long can this go on?

What if the trunk should be opened once outside my gaze, can these devils be trusted?

There is little else to do but wait and clear my being of this evidence and hope that RF can win me a fresh presence when the crisis has passed.

P.

This pathetic entry is in itself dangerous evidence, the link with the King (Roi François) barefaced, albeit in a document she would not expect to see the light of day. In her misery she needed to write out of her system the greater realities – that she would struggle to return to Court and her favoured position.

Her scheme went to plan, and the gangmaster met her

carriage and took the goods from the cart. She walked off at some distance from the loaders with him and covertly gave him a bag of jewels, gaining once more his secret obligations in whispered tones.

'In this bag is your reward. More than can be in your mind. Take it and share with your minions but they must trade them in complete discretion at some distant town, so as not to raise suspicion.'

'I understand.'

'You must choose a site for burial in the most dense and remote part of the forest, for this is to be an end to the affair. Do you understand?'

'I do.'

'Can your men be trusted.'

'I will see to it.'

'Then be done with it and securely.'

XXXV

On the 10th October 1517 Leonardo took a heavy fall as he stepped off the terrace at Le Clos Lucé. The impact was softened by the lush grass of the lawn, but it left him badly bruised.

'More in mind than body', he insisted to the doctor, hastily summoned from a call at the chateau.

The King became increasingly attentive to Leonardo's condition during the autumn of that year and extra resources were admitted to Le Clos Lucé. Night watchmen were added to patrol the gardens and terraces lest there be the slightest intrusion. A doctor was brought in to lodge at the house and be on hand should the ageing master become afflicted. Guards were posted on flying-machines under construction. Strict royal instructions dictated that the Court should not impose upon the artist in residence, and François himself attended Leonardo as frequently as possible.

The two men sat side by side on the terrace, when the sun lent warmth to the day. The impact of the printed word on the wider population had become a subject of interest to both. To the King it hinted at a loosening of the strings of power and potential dangers from a more educated and collaborative populace. He knew more significantly it was beginning to erode the power of the Church.

To Leonardo the marvel of typesetting, as yet clumsy in many respects, nevertheless soon gave the thrill of new knowledge from a diversity of fields reaching him with much greater speed than had ever been possible. He had lent his hand too in illustration to his friend, the mathematician Luca Pacioli, with the preface to the *Divina Proportione*, a symbol that was to become an iconic reference point for future generations.

Around this convivial pair the gardeners continued to enhance the spirit of place, laying a mosaic of boxed flower beds, with fragrant roses at their heart; oaks were planted to outlive them all, and wild shrubs tied to the walls to soften the landscape and make it a haven, not a prison. A new dovecote was attached to the outside gallery.

br. 46

Gather the experience of those before you and the truths with which they have endowed us. The inner man is the inner boy, older but with the first threats to his existence still lodged in his outlook for all time.

If he loses one parent at the start of his life, and when that is his mother, he shall not act as under her instruction, but will miss the guidance she could have impressed upon him and will wander rudderless for many years.

If also the second parent is distracted by his profession or embarks upon another wife, then the young man will want to carve his own path and outshine so as to rebel against his mother's absence.

So was I inflicted, and reason not that I could have been a greater success, for I watered my talent at a half empty well. Only the rush of inquisitiveness focused my attentions on those areas of man's advancement which will matter in the future, as knowledge changes our ignorance.

Di Piero, *dispero.* Where were you, other than at arm's length? Introductions to the

workhouse of Verrochio, but quickly leaving
the scene to pursue your own privileges.

Amongst your thirteen children was I
invisible, detached from the retina of your
perspective? Or did you see my own
advancement as my best security and relax
your interest? You never said.

The rest of the folio is missing. The mother - Caterina. Di
Piero - the biological father who helped but farmed the issue out.
Leonardo had been forced to build his own career from talent
alone, earning commissions initially from the ruling families
whenever he could persuade them to part with their ill-gained
monies. Once his reputation had become established he took on
too many projects in his anxiety to sustain himself – only to fall
into the trap of failing to finish much of the works.

Only now at the last was he in the hands of a patron that
imposed no conditions other than an enthusiasm for
manifestations of the genius' art. Only now was Leonardo able
to give his fullest attention to Flight, and endeavour for that not
to fail. "Whilst I can still see the horizon".

But a greater accident than on the terrace came, not on
that final cliff, but on another to the east of Amboise; not only
Leonardo was placed at risk of death but also the Dauphin.
The Court records place it in late October 1517. With the
'future' of France - the Dauphin - knocked senseless to the
ground, the emergency was to be taken extremely seriously.

A further test flight of Leonardo's latest flying craft had
been the subject of the exercise, and clearly the Dauphin was in
the middle of proceedings, taking advantage of the absence at that
time of both the King and Queen. Although only very young, he
had already assumed the attitude of a prince-in-waiting, built on
confidence not arrogance.

'We should not delay each stage any longer, maestro, for

you yourself have said we are advancing knowledge only one step at a time.'

'But we must not make such gains at the expense of our men.'

'We have plenty in the basement of our ownership to use as we please.'

'Yet not to dispose of so lightly.'

'Invention is our need. We shall lose many more on the battlefield than here if we are not armed to the best advantage. That is why Flight is so important.'

Leonardo's craftsmen had assembled in the morning at the stable workshops of Le Clos Lucé to survey the new apparatus. The structure of the latest flying machine had been simplified. Fewer struts now made up the body of the machine, and these had been mathematically placed by new equations from the drawing-board of Leonardo, and together with tighter binding of the fabrics along the wings, these created more rigidity and strength but with less weight.

'We are nearer the final sum, are we not,' the Dauphin had questioned.

'Perhaps so, but we still risk the life of the pilot.'

In fact, there was a new level of confidence in the workmanship, and an air of excitement amongst the candidate flyers. No more prisoners were forced over the cliffs of Amboise, not least because they had shown such a loss of nerve at take-off that they were deemed unreliable in determining the true chance of holding the craft in space under their management.

'They have nothing to lose, but give up even on their faith immediately the first cross wind blows them off course.' Leonardo preferred courageous experimenters to these half-dead dummies. The volunteers now came forward.

On this occasion the first of the new breed of adventurers drew lots to chance their luck on the advanced craft. Georges Gallen's name appears in the day-diary as the opportunist who was willing to place his life in balance with the golden ducats promised, though his wife was not allowed to attend the trial.

The gathering of machine body, the wings, the undercarriage of pulleys, cranks and levers had to be loaded in specific order upon a train of flat carriages for transportation up the winding lanes to the flying site on the hillsides above Amboise. Even though this route avoided the town centre, nevertheless a crowd of curious citizens began to attach itself to the inventor's train, and this procession added to its number as the horse-drawn carts came to the clearing in front of the woods.

Whilst the team made the final assemblies of the parts, Leonardo appraised the weather conditions with his advisers – and the Dauphin. The latter's self-appointed role was to challenge any view that the conditions might not be favourable enough for the test.

'The wind is easing,' he said as often as another suggested it was increasing.

Many clothes, handkerchiefs, towels and ribbons were held aloft by a succession of 'advisers', most managing to contradict each other's forecast.

'I shall make the decision, maestro,' the Dauphin intervened. 'We must not let this defeat us. I thought you said we needed the breeze to assist us in this venture – just as the birds manipulate the air in their favour?'

Leonardo was caught between his contentment that the principles of Flight were now better understood and the reality that all the hypotheses were still at a very early stage. 'It is not as simple as that.'

Indeed, even as the wings were taken off their carriages in preparation, the wind took them as sails upwards, fighting the grasp of the men to hold onto them. At first such struggles brought amusement, but Leonardo soon realised that the fine balance between the powers of the pilot and wind were delicately balanced.

After an hour of assembly the flying machine was ready, and only the weather cast doubt on starting the trial.

Gallen had put on the harness that would bind the craft to his body, and he began to exercise his arms and legs to bring himself to full readiness. His eyes firmly faced forward, steely in their determination. 'Tell me when it is safe to go.'

Leonardo said nothing in response. He knew that safety was not a certainty, in fact the least likely outturn. He had been brought to the scene in a sedan because the fall on the terrace had left him with a sore ankle. Now he sat – in pontification – in a wicker chair, looking this way and that, holding a cloth up to the breezes.

The Dauphin initially waited at his side, willingly supporting the inventor's right to choose the moment of departure, awaiting the signal for the pilot. But impatience took the better of him and he moved over nearer the craft, as if this would help him judge the opportunity for release better.

> When the bird finds itself within the wind it can sustain itself without flapping its wings, because the function which they have to perform against the air requires no motion.

But the breezes blew with irregularity and it became difficult for Leonardo to make a decision. Equally there was a chill in the air that made a prolonged trial inadvisable. However the pilot was ready and his impatience grew as the wild gusts seemed to die away. A steady midday breeze settled in.

Then the decision was taken. Leonardo and his key adviser felt conditions were right – to take a chance. The pilot was keen.

However, unnoticed by Leonardo, the Dauphin had lost his patience.

'I want to be the first to fly,' was his constant refrain, and as if to assist the pilot at take-off, had in some way managed to hold onto the undercarriage from which the pedal gears were operated, defying the very logic of weight versus power at the centre of the equation Leonardo was trying to solve. Making this attempt with an even lighter craft than before not in balance, and though the wind at that moment is noted as strong against the bluff of the hillside, his hidden actions challenged whether the lift would be sufficient for extended motion.

> When the bird passes from a slow to a swift current of the wind it lets itself be carried by the wind until it has devised a new assistance for itself.

'We must ensure the balance is right, in test with the pilot. Your father will not permit your life to be sampled in such a gamble,' had been Leonardo's standard response to the over-keen Dauphin.

The drawing of this craft exists. The struggle the pilot had is self-evident, lying down, facing forward, as a hang-glider, with a pedal and rope mechanism behind him to be propelled by his feet to flap the wings up and down through a series of cogs and gears in imitation of a bird.

> When the bird moves with impetus against the wind it makes long quick beats with its wings with a slanting movement, and after thus beating its wings it remains for a while with all its members contracted and low.

The trial had proceeded on the strength of the wind, the pitch of the wings, the theory of Leonardo, the carpentry of his craftsmen, and the courage of the pilot. None of which was to be sufficient. No sooner had Leonardo released the pilot with a wave of a cloth which the wind blew horizontal, than the pilot ran down the slope, slipped his feet into the sleeve and began pedalling furiously.

For a moment the craft looked as if it had taken to the air, before the invisible force of a downdraught played with the man's ambition. At that moment, in an act of folly, the Dauphin, running alongside, held onto the base of the undercarriage and ran with his arms extended so as to add thrust and power to the craft's momentum.

But the pilot could not control the craft and it twisted sharply on the wind and swung back directly towards the seated inventor, with the Dauphin entangled in its struts. Its wing knocked Leonardo from his chair and swept the attendants to the ground. The Dauphin was dragged along making further attempts to halt the machine's progress.

He only succeeded in having himself knocked senseless, and the spray of victims lay scattered across the hillside, with the craft broken into as many pieces as people it had savaged, and the pilot concussed.

For a moment there was chaos as the attendant craftsmen saw their skilled work break into a hundred pieces. As the wind blew in fresh gusts, man and machine became entagled in a rolling ball of cords and splintered wood, until the mass found its own weight and lay in a heap before the horrified spectators.

Somewhere in the pile was the Dauphin.

No one had thought to bring a doctor. If it had not been for a hunting party *á la chasse* coming upon the scene shortly, the injured might have become the deceased.

Leonardo was also concussed and the medical report shows he was borne back to Le Clos-Lucé with the Dauphin as a matter of urgency. The latter however was not seriously wounded by the experience.

'At least we took off, and for a moment I thought we flew!'

'And nearly lost our lives,' Leonardo felt obliged to add.

'It was fun.'

'We are tackling a more serious subject.'

'I'll tell my father you did your best.'

'He will not like to learn of your involvement.'

'I will tell him that only the strength of the wind

prevented us from success, and that we should try again as soon as possible.'

'He may not be so keen.'

'I am keen. I am the future. You must succeed – for me.'

Leonardo remained in bed for two weeks, and was still in pain, when the King returned. At his bedside: 'There shall be no further trials of this ambition lest under my direct command. You nearly took my son's life - and yours.' Soon that was to be God's choice.

XXXVI

Panic set in amongst certain of the courtiers, when weeks had passed since the Chamberlain's departure from his post. No explanation could be found, nor could the King find an answer to his enquiries. The Queen stayed silent, but was the most confused. Where had her man gone?

Further conspiracy theories surfaced, yet everyone was reluctant to put their thoughts into the open, for fear that Artus was plotting some devious plan to sweep them away. His brother Jacques was summoned from Geneva and deputised in his absence. He demanded a review of everyone's movements and motives. He tortured, as an example, senior courtiers - selected at random - to unearth the plot. No one declared any involvement, some died in the attempt to maintain their innocence.

The darkening days of winter hung heavily over the Chateau d'Amboise and the town. No one felt safe from interrogation, no logic prevailed over the inquisition. Queen Claude called on Leonardo, and provoked her commissioned image-maker.

'You have not finished my portrait yet, maestro. Time is passing'

'My hand is weakening, the effort troublesome.'

She then noticed a scant outline of another woman amongst the sketches lying to one side of Leonardo's desk. He had written 'Pavia' against one.

'The Contessa is still in your sights, Messer Leonardo?'

'It is an old sketch, of no further application.'

'The ink is dry but barely aged,' she challenged. 'Do you know what happened to her? It seems a curious mystery that she and the Chamberlain became lost to us at one and the same time. Can you explain it?'

'Your Majesty, it remains a puzzle.'

'I suspect some know more. The King is most displeased to have lost his comptroller. His brother is less effective. The

Court lacks direction in many matters of state.'

'I remain intent on my work. It is enough for my concentration.'

'I sincerely hope so. It would not do to be embroiled in our politics or support lost causes. We must presume she is dead, then?'

'She appears to have abandoned us.'

'I insist on the completion of my portrait. You must give it more time. It is to feature on the wall outside the royal bedchamber, a barrier to any recall of the Contessa, where I can keep my eye upon the entrance, if only now to ensure she could not bother His Majesty.'

Nor serve as a ghost, Leonardo noted, after she had gone.

> Life is a fiction, in which we must all participate. The public face of acknowledgement, the screen of happiness, whilst hidden are the inner truths.

There is no trace of the Queen's painting having survived, certainly not in Amboise or any collection in the public domain. It may have not been finished, or possibly lost in the effects of the travelling circus that was the royal court. Events were to deny its purpose anyway. A ghost can haunt a palace at its own discretion, walk the corridors with impunity. Unless manifested in a grand assembly, when too many witnesses are to hand. A mistake the Contessa was to make.

But at that time Leonardo smelled failure on another front - Flight. His ultimate ambition. In the pursuit of Flight he was moving beyond the practical, crossing a threshold into an unknown space, in which the questions were endless.

'Where do we go next?', he has noted on one sheet of drawings of complex flying craft.

'Only God can answer that,' Melzi had retorted impatiently as the day's work once more came to a contemplative halt. 'And we do not know His will.'

XXXVII

King François increased the frequency of his visits to Leonardo. Not so as to suggest that the great man could expire at a moment's notice, but rather so that he could monitor the aged genius' health. At the slightest indication of frailty (which always annoyed Leonardo) he would summon his doctors and discuss the optimum medication that might resolve the situation. This posed a conundrum - how to advise a man who had explored more fully than any other the inner workings of the human frame.

"Don't make me pass that vile liquid," was a constant refrain, and he was not above remonstrating with any doctor who showed the slighted weakness in his confidence, when administering advice. Leonardo knew full well that most of the palliatives were the result of guesswork, rather that proven performance, and a look of nervousness on any attending doctor was sufficient to bring about a firm refusal to take the medicine. All his life he had been strong, and only the passage of time was wearing his limbs down.

"That's all there is to it," Leonardo insisted, "and none of your damned potions will cure that ill."

The King would sit by his bed and read through Leonardo's notebooks on anatomy, as if searching for solutions to the incidence of some weariness in a limb, or some abdominal pain. The result was more often than not a diversion into a study of the soul.

'Where lies the core of our being?' the King asked.

'In the invisibility of our creation. Not so much in the heart, for I have shown this is no more than a pump, which supplies the movement of blood in sympathy with our breathing to maintain existence. The soul is more elusive. We can sense it, we know we have it, but where has God hidden it, and how do we find it?'

Where indeed? Leonardo's extensive illustrations of the

inner muscles, sinews, arteries and veins revealed to all the inner structure of mankind, a curious assembly of skin and bone that sheathed a twisted mine of gut and entrails that, on observation, seemed to be quite an absurd collection of elements to form humans; a race that had somehow risen above the practical and developed the emotional. From the Church's point-of-view each revelation stole another of its clothes - or rather the costume of fear that relied upon superstition and ignorance.

As 'science' began to probe the mysteries more effectively, and the Renaissance gloried in the Arts, attention moved away from the benchmark of the Papacy. The printed word was relaying the new knowledge wide and far, and together with the extravagant sale of hollow pardons, a whole wave of freedom arose for the individual. The popes indulged in seduction, the proliferation of their bastard sons and daughters, their placement in positions of power, and the delegation of favours, but there was light at the end of the tunnel, and Leonardo was amongst those that had lit the flame. In this regard King François supported his desire for experiment, and the search for Flight. From his position of strength he could afford to face a more open future.

'You must not give up too soon, Messer Leonardo, we want you to succeed and bring our use of the ether to fruition. Stay alive, and prosper with what strength you can muster, we need you.'

There were times when this strength ebbed, and the old man would retire to his bed for days. His spirit was willing, but the body weakened and chilled. When the royal presence had left, Maturina would stoke the fire afresh in his bedroom, and limber up the stairs with new supplies of wood. Then she sat discreetly in one corner, awaiting orders, knitting quietly, listening to the breathing slumberer, attentive to any irregularity.

'I am not long for this world,' Leonardo admitted, and though she was well aware of the possibility of death, Maturina was shocked to have the truth spelt out. She kept her head down, but worried for her own position. Long separated from her family in the course of his service over many decades, this had left her dependent solely upon Leonardo and his instructions. She had no confidence in the plans of Melzi or Salai, nor saw any prospect of service with the Court. In Florence there might be no one to accept her. She had paid the price of devotion to a single cause.

On bad days Salai took turns to watch over his master. He too had bent his whole life to Leonardo, from that fortunate moment when he had been picked out of obscurity, mischief tolerated, and his affection indulged. Was he the prodigal 'son', forgiven all his waywardness? Or can there be detected a closer role, an intimate service?

Le Clos Lucé, November 1517

> You bring me much that is of comfort, dear Salai, and at the same time much that is of anxiety. Your touch is firm and kind, your skin smooth with the flower of youth. As the hide of the horse is gentle to brush yet capable of keeping out the winter's cold, so yours can warm the spirit with its grace - and its favours.

This note is appended to a sheet of the folio. Why was it written when spoken words would have been much more appropriate? Was Leonardo adding texts to confirm where his affections lay, so that - in this case Salai - would be not be abandoned, and receive his dues under the Will?

Leonardo knew only too well the price of disappearing patronage. He had lost all those who had commissioned works in Florence, Milan and Rome through that particular failure of his - the unfinished project. The murals still at cartoon stage, the frescoes yet in sketched outline, the images dripping so soon from the walls where his new mix of oil and paints had proved disastrous. The Last Supper flaking from the under-plaster within months of its completion. The evidence of failure was there for all to see - and he felt it more than anyone else.

'Salai, they will not forgive me, and now I cannot finish through ill health and tiring limbs. It has all ended in failure.'

Then in this folio an earlier message from Salai. Why would he be writing to Leonardo, if not from jail? A note of apology, scribbled with the benefit of an intercessor?

> Maestro, a thousand pleas for forgiveness. The pleasure of wine turned my judgement to disadvantage. The work of licentious fellows, who portrayed themselves as friends of yours and applied their enthusiasm to our indulgence and its excesses. Release me from this confinement and I shall repay your francs many times over.

The archives show no response, but it can be assumed from other incidents that once again Leonardo would have bailed out his mischief-maker, their companionship releasing the inner tensions hidden in the shadows. But who is to judge, when so much else was achieved? What offence is there in the laying on of hands, Salai nurturing that side of the man that Maturina and others could not answer?

On the reverse in Leonardo's hand, alongside a sketch of the human form, stripped of its flesh:

> Your body answers me many questions. From the surface of its smoothness, the flexibility of a limb, the rigid tension of the lingam, the release of passion that cannot be controlled.

An anatomical drawing that illuminates the structure of sinews, muscles and the workings of Man's extraordinary architecture. Leonardo amongst the first to analayse the inner workings of pain others took as a mystery, answered then by herbal remedies and leeching rather than surgical mastery.

Melzi was aware of inner passions between Leonardo and Salai but was not to know Leonardo would place his Book Of Reflections in the hands of the 'youth'. Matters clearly came to a head in the winter of 1517 -1518.

Melzi: 'How long, Leonardo, can we put up with this man's nonsense?'

Leonardo: 'He will make amends and I shall tell him once more to put this behaviour behind him.'

'But will he listen? Or exploit such generosity until your dying day?'

'Would that I died with him content.'

'But he is a poor influence in the household. The others cannot ignore his bad language, his stupid pranks, above all that he makes no serious effort to master his art, and yet you spare him all obedience.'

'He lacks their talent - for drawing, painting, yes. But he infuses me with a candour and enthusiasm they lack.'

Melzi: 'It is hard for them to understand.'

'His special gifts?'

'There is always gossip.'

'And they shall have their gossip, whilst I enjoy the touch of a madcap, the odd one out, the outsider.'

'In which you see a touch of yourself?'

'In which I see myself. You, Melzi, had a choice, an opportunity in life you took. Freely with both hands.'

'To pursue the arts with you, Maestro.'

'Nobly, and one based upon your talents. If you had no such capacity, no self-esteem, would you have charted such a proper course? We know little of the world or its rational explanations, aside from human frailties. The absurdities of the human spirit and how it plays with our emotions. You cannot say one man is right and the other not.'

'He will bring disgrace upon you.'

'It is a risk I embrace.'

'What explanation can I give to the others?'

'There is none to be declared. They must learn to be tolerant, in respect for me.'

'A respect in danger.'

'So be it.'

'But, Maestro...'

'No, Melzi, you too must be tolerant. This does not interfere with our relationship. We are on a different plane and concerned with higher achievements; your place is not undone by anyone. The matter is quite simple. I love him for his candour and the raw touch of the younger inquisitive man. So be it.'

The winter rains drenched Le Clos Lucé that year. It was one of the wettest for decades and hampered testing of the flying machines. This exercised the mind of Leonardo, and frustrated his ambition to give Man freedom of the skies. His vision was clear, in that whoever could first master this art would have the overseeing advantage on invading armies or forces attacking a castle or fixed position. He foresaw the value of aerial reconnaissance in all types of close encounter. A capacity for short flights would be sufficient in many cases to protect an army, to allow for tactical gain and the imposition of surprise on the grounded forces.

Meanwhile at the King's insistence his tank was being built in prototype form, though it was found to be unwieldy on the rugged terrain of the day; its rotary motion enabled fire to be directed on all sides, but progress across the battlefield was clumsy. 'All I want at this time of life is peace,' he pressed on the King's advisers who sought to expand his armoury of inventions.

But as for Flight, though he understood the principles of lift as a result of his extensive study of birds, the winter storms with their gusting gales left no room for mistakes and the pilots never managed more than a few metres before their craft twisted out of control and struck the ground. Two died in these attempts and lay on Leonardo's conscience.

'We should attempt no more flights until Spring.'

Then a record of the paralysis in the doctor's winter log. The medicine man had given Leonardo a herbal potion, but with what belief is not declared; all types of remedy were applied to keep the fingers moving across the sketchpad.

A second instruction is to Maturina to strip an onion of its outer leaves and rub the white flesh into the skin of the palm and fingers. There is no prescription for such action. Rather the belief that this would harden the skin, not make it more supple. Perhaps it is an unction from early magic and mystery, later lost in the advance of science. But peeling back the leaves is the same as attempting to find the man. The inner man, buried beneath the successive layers of his correspondence, well out of sight. Encoded, hidden behind the silver of the mirror.

Until later the third folio within the package became more intimate.

XXXVIII

The prolonged disappearance of the Chamberlain had developed into a witch hunt. His twin brother, Jacques Artus brought from the snowbound cantons of Switzerland had a 'personal guard' to implement the vigorous inquisition. His countenance carried that same dark brooding that imposed fear in the victims of interrogation. A sketch of him exists in the chateau's archives, attached to his licence to operate freely to expose the abductors or murderers of his brother. There are notes on the victims of this misplaced investigation.

Louis Marmande, the Under-Captain of the Guard was thought to be interested in assuming the Chamberlain's position, and under torture a line of reasoning to this effect was extracted:

> 'I confess that on December 2nd (1517) I expressed an objection to the further employment of Swiss guards to the maintenance of order in the Royal Household at Amboise. I accept that this questioned the authority of the Chamberlain in respect of responsibilities outside my remit; that I should not have challenged the structure of command, nor indicated I would take action myself to support such changes.'

This early confession is signed with a hand that is far too firm, a sop to the progress of investigation. Then the pressure had not built to the frenzy of inquisition that followed. This document was an initial sweep of candidates brought into the mysterious equation. No doubt there were others who suffered pressures of a threatening nature, an arm-twist here, a thumbscrew there, as the random nature of

160

the search widened. But in the absence of any clear motive amongst those questioned, the mystery only deepened. There is no indication that any suspect left the Court, there were no defections of a section of the Guard, nor sudden absences from the courtiers or hangers-on.

The only other person at the time that had removed herself was the Contessa, and no one put any complexion on that, other than she had rightly heeded the dangers of her competition with the Queen for the King's favours. Throughout history mistresses had fallen out of the line, were kept always second to royal succession, had to be dealt with or forsaken. No one looked towards her movements as anything other than expected, and this allowed both King François to keep his secrets, and the Queen to be glad of her riddance and stay mute.

In this void, the inquisition became more frantic, and suspects were subject to a second round of pressure, of more agonising torture in the cold dank cellars of the chateau. This wave of persecution is seen in a second confession drawn out from the Under-Captain only two weeks later. This time his signature is barely legible, the ink running from the page in a mix of blood, staining the document for ever with the anguish and pain of his misguided persecution.

> 'I, Louis Marmande, now confess that my first and willing *(sic)* statement was not true in all respects, and did not fully state the actions I took to advance the cause of France in protecting its own. I beg forgiveness from His Majesty for this error of judgement and accept my fate and full responsibility for the abduction of Jerome Artus.'

This confession became useless book-keeping, in that the scrap of blood-drenched paper on which it lay so transparently as an act of force, did not answer where the body lay, since Marmande had no idea himself; as for the resultant searches of the chateau grounds, the town's fields and close countryside, the banks of the Loire - none of these bore fruit.

Indeed the more searches, the more the evidence in favour of some other conspiracy widened. King François took the ironic step of organising *'une grande chasse'*, with hounds across the lands to the west of Amboise in what appeared as a logical sweep of the territory in which the Chamberlain might be found, perhaps the victim of an accident out riding, or when on some royal duty of his own connivance. But nothing was found, and peasants denied any sightings of the courtier. No one realised that the King did not extend the hunt to the Chambord estate, and no one was in a position to question him.

The Contessa understandably kept out of sight, in disguise and silent at this time, for she is not mentioned in any record linked with the investigation. How she must have concerned herself with the situation can only be guessed. Her one secret action had been to dispose of the body of the Chamberlain in the forest of Chambord, the diggers bribed; otherwise her life was empty, pining for a message from the King.

In her diary, found much later:

> It was to be a long stay of execution. No word could he bring, no courtier to be entrusted with our secret at this time. Each day prolonged with sorrow.

> The pretence to the innkeeper that I am a grieving widow of some courtier is manifest in my true loss and a simple disguise to these ignorant peasants.

RF cannot see me but I live for a change of fortune, of heart that can bring me back into recognition, detached from the disappearance of Artus, for what is there to attach me to that death?

1518

XXXIX

But the Contessa's diary does not tally with a note here for was it the King himself who made the next move and threw caution to the wind on his return journey from some diplomacy in Paris, resting at Tours? Then late at night did he set off in plain cloak with two trusted guards for Chambord going to the Contessa's lodgings and dismissing them for the night, arranging for their cover in the morning? Overlooking the spy within the inn's staff.

"As determined by your Lordship, I noted all that passed:

Chambord 14th January 1518

'He entered at midnight, the place then covered in darkness, there being no flares to light the entrance. I had heard the noise of horses' hooves, which we were not expecting. I saw a man detach himself and, as with prior knowledge, enter the annexe within which the lady held her privacy.

He made a play of the lady's surprise at his presence and, sweeping her into his embrace, kissed her at length with evident knowing. His manner was not of a simple gratification however, and he took her to bed with the most considerate forecaring, so much so that I had to wait one hour before they were in deepest passion and could listen to the matter of their subsequent exchange.

She: 'I have missed our loving. You must imagine, sire, that it is most contentious to be isolated here and disadvantaged.'

He: 'It has to be so - until calm returns to the chateau, and those who seek to have all Italians removed have exhausted their suspicions.'

'Can you promise me that soon I can return?'
'It is impossible to be sure. You must be patient.'
'Show me that you care, make love to me again.'
'You know that I do.'
'Prove it once more.'

There was no doubt that they were active in lust, for two hours passed before their engagement ceased and quiet followed. We were surprised to see the guards gather at dawn and collect him at the stables for their onward journey."

Signed: J. Beauchamp

Was 'he' a royal go-between or the King himself?

This dangerous report however must have travelled too slowly through hands to reach the new Chamberlain in time to act, for the Contessa was to reappear before he - and the Queen - could deal with her at a distance. So who held it in the meantime - a courtier too frightened to pass it on, or a servant fearing his own complicity in the act?

XL

Meanwhile the witch hunt continued within the portals of the Chateau d'Amboise, but inevitably without result. The complete protestations of innocence became irrefutable and Jacques Artus's anger and brutal treatment of any servant or courtier under suspicion forced King François to issue an order for the matter to be placed under general review without inquisition. An act seen by all to be a prudent course.

So the matter was on hold, not least for Leonardo, whose

quiet existence at Le Clos Lucé had been swept into the ever-maddening hunt. As an Italian, he remained suspect, but seemed untouchable. Though blind vengeance might dispose of him.

'He has no reason to hide here,' he said to repeated visits from over-zealous Swiss guards. 'Search as you wish, but do not destroy the models of Flight, my paintings or books in your pursuit of evidence.'

To Melzi: 'This madness must abate, before we all die in the mire of conspiracy.'

Salai: 'Innocence is our ultimate guardian. Ser, we have both been wrongly accused in the past and we shall be saved from further query in this matter.'

Melzi to Salai: 'Your convictions are for well-known felonies. Expect to be included in any list of suspects.'

'This is beyond my competence, Melzi, and you know it.'

Leonardo brought the matter to an end. 'Salai's errors were minor demeanours, foolish, but mere incidents.'

Melzi: 'Perhaps Jerome Artus is on a foreign mission and will return with some alliance or matchmaking.'

But the silence greeting this optimistic vision may have said it all. No one had any clues to the absence of the Chamberlain, and many may have been glad to be rid of this oppressive master-at-arms. A conspiracy of its own silence that masked the real situation.

At this time Melzi himself was despatched on a mission to Milan. The details are not clear, other than his absence is evident in Leonardo's notes. The fading genius wanted Melzi to accept dictation of his Will and Last Testament. The question of mortality hung heavily in the air, not least at Leonardo's constant prompting of his weakness.

The King became his second doctor, diverting from more pressing matters at Court quite willingly to attend Leonardo's bedside. François interpreted his deal with the old man for daily conversation as a contract not to be broken even by illness, and certainly not by infirmity. His encouragement was a tonic alongside the quackery of the doctors, who in turn felt obliged to administer potions and lotions as a sign of their skill and value, though everyone of them in private saw no indication other than old age and the rigor of paralysis that continued to affect Leonardo's gifted right hand.

It is most likely that Melzi's assignment in Milan was to retrieve final payments or funds still left in the banks, to collect the taxes of life from the few remaining patrons that owed Leonardo balances on their projects.

'Bring safely home what I am due so we can reckon the final balance and dictate the terms upon which it shall be apportioned.' This innocent task, however, may have been a cover for a more incautious act. That Leonardo wanted Melzi out of the way for a while in order to reason with Salai without interference.

Melzi would not have stood by whilst Leonardo succumbed to the wiles of his younger miscreant, forgiving his confinement in the local jail, and then by default to forgive him all.

'Salai, I want you to learn from me, from my own mistakes', Leonardo has noted on the cover sheet attached to this reflection:

br. 49

I say this in all humility, that the wise old man has the benefit of a lifetime's errors, but is no better placed to advise the young, who wish so eagerly to repeat those mistakes.

Respect the touch of partnership that is between two, and resist the foolhardy that jeopardises such love and affection. For, in the

> gutter of life, disease and disdain will weaken
> that bond for ever and the young repentant
> will have left it too late to recover that which
> he once so casually assumed, and which was
> his protection.

This admonition would have come as no surprise to Salai, but indicates an attempt by Leonardo to restrain his wilful *ingénu*. Is there a sense of the frustrated patron in all this? It would be ironic to think so, but again the bonding between these two may have held the streak of madness characteristic of such liaisons. Or is this analysis a presumptive judgement? The fact is that Leonardo found in Salai a source of contentment that no other pupil, friend or courtier could muster. It was a private affection, perhaps affliction, that served him to his own satisfaction, and debate of it was not to be tolerated from others, not even Melzi.

There is no written answer from Salai. His only evidence was the plea from jail, the one time a letter of apology seems to have been necessary. Within himself, he knew that Leonardo would forgive him, and more significantly present him with the Book of Reflections, as proof of their liaison, their love.

> 'Master, the leaves of the young tree bud and
> form each year in total disregard for the
> dangers of wind, rain and storm. So it is for us
> to meet the challenges of life with enthusiasm.'

Baleful philosophy from an incorrigible mischief-maker, who knew the length of rope with which he could play without hanging.

'But what will you do when I am gone?' Leonardo annotated on a page from the Reflections.

No doubt Salai had thought such an eventuality through, because he would be disposed of once death had taken Leonardo, with no security of tenure. Maybe that realisation was the motive behind his master's gifts. A small house in Milan. The Book of Reflections that was to be kept secret, but *in extremis* would have a value to later historians, for which payment could be found. Except that Salai either must have lost the Book or sold it on later as the terms of Leonardo's wish allowed. Or perhaps another adjudicator chose only these pages which, in private, could be kept as a personal memento?

To imply the rest of the Book is out there buried in the archives of some museum, just as the remnants of the Codex Atlanticus lay on Madrid's dusty shelves?

br. 51

The source of one's inspiration is curiosity and when that enquiry begins to fade, so does oneself. There is much to be learnt before we give in to the expectation of death, and we should be encouraged to persist in this ambition, as without that quest, what are we in service for on this earth?

In February 1518 Melzi returned from Milan with the outstanding funds of patronage and the final audit could be dealt with. It was the last full year that Leonardo was to see, and the records show it had started with a severe winter.

Snow blanketed Le Clos-Lucé for a month, and whilst this painted a pretty picture and gave amusement to young snowballers and skaters on the ponds, it did nothing for old bones, and the cold brought Leonardo's work to a halt. Further tests of Flight were to be delayed until the Spring.

It left time only for reflection, on what in life had been, and in death what might be.

br 52

Think not ill of me. What you see now is the failure of the body, not the mind. Much has been achieved, but the weight of all our enquiry and skills in this period will soon be overtaken by the advance of new sciences that shall make our work fall into insignificance, and we shall be forgotten.

I shall be measured only by what lies fixed on paper, and my dreams will remain as sketches whose ink fades with the passage of time until no discernible weight can be attached to their worth.

XLI

There was a second fire at Le Clos-Lucé in March 1518, and again it was Leonardo that started it. In his artistic and inventive lifetime he had been disorganised, with papers accumulating in sacks and boxes; these were carried on mules as he sought fresh patronage. Now this compendium of dreams lay around his study in untidy piles, being sorted with Melzi's help, into folios with a cohesive context.

It was one of these folios, its loose sheets laid one upon the other, that drifted on a sudden breeze from the table towards the burning timbers in the fireplace. He himself had moved out of the bedroom to discharge his bowels and saw the emerging smoke too late.

However by throwing the bowl of slops into the courtyard he had drawn Maturina's attention to the unfolding crisis and she gathered other servants with buckets of water to drown the flames already licking at the tapestried wallcoverings.

The event is identified on a page that has been singed down the middle, burying part of the sienna-inked text under brown scorch marks. Melzi has dated this 23rd March 1518 and marked it for disposal outside the catalogue of hope.

Le Clos-

> The attempts at Flight are doomed
> persevere one more time to
> optimum the weight of the wings
> who can press the gears more
> if across the rear struts
>
> Many birds move wings as swiftly
> they let them fall. Such are the
> and birds like them.

There are some as the doves that
more swiftly when they lower them
raise them. We must learn them.

Why has that stayed in this private package? Was Melzi
trying to make sense of the great man's mountain of
memorabilia, extracting the personal log, the few sheets that
left a door open or revealed a few inner truths? Or maybe
because the reverse of this sheet had a further dedication, a
note of gratitude that the fire had not taken more than half a
page of his work, not burnt his clothing, nor taken his life
before his Will was known.

'Messer Leonardo *vivat*. In God's mercy we trust.'

King François was the first to visit Leonardo after this
incident. He was not convinced the poisoning, and the series
of accidents befalling Leonardo were not plotted, though he
had no proof. With the Chamberlain missing, everything was
suspicious, the Court in disorder and no one could be
trusted. The King had returned from some military diversion,
but found time to attend the old man. The details are not
clear, but there had been a campaign that settled the
battlefield for the time being, and the town's records list a
procession down the high street of Amboise, directly under
the battlements of the chateau.

A march-past of a thousand horsemen and two thousand
foot-soldiers back to barracks, surveyed from the castle walls
ceremoniously and in safety. Though the town - and more
importantly the Court - was distant from the actual field of
battle, it was a reminder that life remained cheap. Something
that could be disposed of in the moment of political change.
Wars fought between city states through mercenaries. Religious
enemies still being burned at the stake. Murderers hung, drawn
and quartered. Fortunes as well as life itself made and lost on
the whim of patronage, as Leonardo knew only too well.

Melzi: 'Take better care, master, and restrict your

174

ambition, so as not to tire the very life out of you.'

'There is still much to be done,' Leonardo's simple answer, often repeated.

Maturina introduced new rituals into his daily life to protect his weakening health, insisting on bringing his breakfast in bed, stoking the fire, bathing him with essential oils each evening. He was still admired by the new wave of artists, decorators and craftsmen that François had gathered to his burnishing court, but needed protection from the strays of political envy, the time-wasters of nobility, who sought to attach some of his bright light to their cause. And those who sought to dispose of him.

'Melzi, it is time we addressed my Will and Testament, is it not?' But the Will was not to be actioned at that point. Typically events deflected his attention. Salai had gone missing again.

The younger man never quite mended his ways, yet Leonardo kept faith with him; but could others at Court measure such curious loyalty from a distance? He served as the leavening spirit, the unknown factor, a surprise in the package. In him the free spirit that Leonardo still craved. Imprisoned throughout life by a relentless pursuit of knowledge in a dozen fields, the great man may have wished for the liberation Salai found without any sense of responsibility, a cavalier attitude to those higher in society and more gifted in talent. Salai brought no particular talent other than to amuse and please his master. As Leonardo noted once - about Salai?

br.54

The sole relevance of life is the love of another. All else will come to be explained empirically, by the proper allocation of scientific investigation. In time there will remain no other mystery than why two people - often of

contrasting favour - will find in each other that
bond which no other can rightfully see.

There is the hope that I shall not be denied
such reward, when much else has fallen dead
on the page. You brought me that luxury of
surprise, the undemanding gift. I ask little of
you in return, other than you guard this small
legacy until such time as the forces of
circumstance justify its placing on the record
of our lives.

For within will remain what we shared alone,
and none shall touch that with gossip. The truth
will stay in our comfort and never be lessened.

Leonardo's hand is upon this script, mirror-written,
doubly encoded subtly with a linear re-arrangement of the text
that has taken time to unscramble. Yet the lines run across the
page in the neat hand which expresses his determination.
Ordered, unlike so much else. When was this written - some
time in the past or at Amboise?

If it refers to Salai, then it is in contrast to the adjacent
folio. Salai is again in police records as found in Tours, astride
a gutter in the poor district, sozzled with cheap wine. The
contrast between his cloistered position at Le Clos-Lucé and
this back-street did not serve Salai well. There were no
explanations, as is often the case with drunks.

'I cannot remember what happened,' his plaintive excuse.

'We have important work still to attend to,' Leonardo noted
in the presence of Melzi, when the renegade was summoned.

'And time this man pulled his weight,' Melzi's critical aside.

The dedicated Melzi felt that attention should be in his
favour, and there are signs that this was so, most clearly shown
in the bulk of the estate, the core of works, being passed to him

for retention and cataloguing. Francesco da Melzi had indeed proved his worth, becoming an accomplished painter in his own right, with the encouragement and training of his master down the years. The Virgin of Light in the Oratory chapel at Le Clos-Lucé a testament to his talent. The tall form of the Virgin extended high on the mural, dominant in a strong red tunic beneath her cloak, the holy child in her arms made deliberately small in comparison. The powerful holding the weak. The infant to become more significant to the world, but for the present too young for influence. Her halo underscored with its rays of hope spreading either side, contrasting with the grey storm clouds of life encroaching on her divinity.

As Leonardo became weaker, the tension increased between Melzi and Salai, cast together yet required to be tolerant of each other. Just as Leonardo and his fellows had been arraigned falsely on a charge of sodomy in Florence, so the accidents that befell Salai were acknowledged by Leonardo as shared experience, based on the random chance of lowly birth, positions on the edge of society. Or was there more to it than that?

The familiar portrait is of a great man, white beard flowing from his intent face, stern, accomplished in so many skills. But does he let us see within? The tormented failure, the rebellious spirit damped down by respectability. The missing element in Salai. Was his outward life a fiction too? Did Leonardo only print what he wanted others to see, to form the images that can be tolerated, the criticisms that can be easily accepted?

XLII

The Contessa, who had remained in hiding, engineered a meeting in a tavern in Tours, concealing her presence other than to the one man in France she felt could be trusted. Leonardo had expected to meet a designer for a castle there. He was amazed to see her, and in his anger at being tricked, has sketched an outline of her features beside these notes. Faithful image or deliberate exaggeration, Leonardo draws an anxious face, with wrinkles of concern, as if her skin had aged in a matter of months. He saw her beauty had slipped like a mask since the chateau entertainment. She told how she had managed to slip out of the royal chateau.

'I cannot wait at Chambord indefinitely. His Majesty sends me no signals as to his intent. His queen believes I have been disposed of. A servant has it that my name is never mentioned at Court. I am disowned.'

'There is nothing to be gained in hope alone,' Leonardo had cautioned. 'They are consumed with another mystery, the absence of the Chamberlain. It is unexplained and provoking enquiry as to a motive for his sudden disappearance.' The Contessa remained silent for a moment, hesitated as if to speak, but changed her mind and did not offer any evidence on this matter.

Leonardo continued: 'I will see if I can send a private message to Messer Machiavelli. Therein lies the best route back to society in Florence. From there you could regain position in Pavia, in time. They will not know of the conflict at Court here. A mule train can be arranged, but not openly by any of us.'

'I do not want to leave in disgrace. His Majesty will surely place me?'

'Nothing is certain, there can be no easy option. The Chamberlain, if he returns, or his brother, will deal with you most rigorously, if the King's protection is not ensured.'

Leonardo brought this meeting to an abrupt close, left quickly through the back door to the waiting carriage, angry once more he had been tricked into this rendezvous.

He did not know that the Contessa had already taken the gamble that later was to have disastrous consequences. She had dealt with the most urgent matters. The trunk, within which the Chamberlain's body lay, had been removed and buried. It had passed as personal baggage, when she had been provided with horses and a wagon to slip away from the chateau - the last orders that had been privately arranged by her lover, but the King was unaware of the contraband that had lain in this chest.

In later accounts some wags at Court generated conspiracy theories, however preposterous, that the Contessa and Chamberlain had eloped together - merely based upon their absence - a level of common gossip that dominated the assembly. In reality no one believed it, but the King, knowing better, let rumour build.

Into this silence fell the Queen's sense of triumph at her rival's despatch, which missed the truth, and was ignorant of the Chamberlain's position. She now worried that any line of complicity through him might work against her, though as an officer, he was disposable *in extremis*. The mystery was to remain for some time, and the Contessa leaves Leonardo's notes at this point. Until her fateful and ghost-like reappearance at Court.

XLIII

The early rains continually drenched Le Clos Lucé in Spring 1518. It hampered further the testing of the flying machines. This frustrated Leonardo's ambition to give the King - and Man - freedom of the skies. His vision remained clear; whoever could first master this art would have the overseeing advantage on invading armies.

'All I want at this time of life is peace,' Leonardo pressed on the King's military advisers who sought to expand his armoury of inventions.

But as for Flight the March gales left no room for mistakes and the pilots never managed more than a few metres of progress before once again their crafts twisted out of control. Three more died in these attempts and lay on Leonardo's conscience.

'We should attempt no more flights until early Summer.'

XLIV

The Queen remained puzzled. She had first returned from Blois expecting the Contessa to have suffered an end that suited her royal purpose, but when the apartment had been unlocked and searched, the object of the Queen's revenge had not been there, no body lying in a pool of blood on the bed. No one was there, the room had been deserted, her essential belongings removed.

The King continued to affect surprise and then consternation. Only the latter was genuine, for there was no logical reason why the Chamberlain had also abandoned his post, no duty elsewhere, no new alliance of which he could make sense. The treasury was checked, the Captain-of-the-Guard had been mustered. No one knew. It smelled of conspiracy, but there was no obvious motive. Hated by all, but feared the more, if he had taken flight, with whom and for what gain? Nobody had an explanation, no one looked guilty. No one thought to search Chambord, and the King did not suggest it.

Jacques Artus was now deputising in the post of Chamberlain as there was no sign of his brother, no discovery of a body, no witness coming forward with news for a reward. A steely silence lay over the Court. Everyone felt himself innocent but that the next person held a secret, yet each inquisition produced nothing but pained absolution. No one had the first idea what had happened to him, and the entries in the ledger reflect this paranoia.

All Italians in service or at Court remained under suspicion. Leonardo was tainted with doubt, but the distance between the chateau and Le Clos-Lucé separated him from further accusations.

'I have no time to spend on political ambition.'

It was the Contessa, however, who made the next move weeks later. In the disguise of a servant, she left the seclusion of her lodgings in Chambord, and mingled with the townsfolk to reconnoitre what was in her own mind an opportunity to re-establish herself at Court by a surprise gesture of reconciliation.

There was to be a Ball at the Chateau d'Amboise, and she had learnt of a most ingenious surprise by Leonardo for the King - a robotic swan device that "is to approach His Majesty at the climax of the celebration, and draw amazement from its gliding and imponderable action." A complex mechanical set of ropes and pulleys had been wound round a drum within this automaton, which could be put in motion down the aisle, and upon a given revolution would raise its lid, for a hidden maidservant to leap out and present the King with a gift of doves. An offering to restore a sense of peace to the Court. It was this maidservant, by some bribe, the Contessa replaced on the night of the celebration, whilst the swan was still stored away in a dark chamber to the rear of the main banqueting hall.

On the centre stage sat the royal family overlooking the revellers, dancing energetically to the music of lyres and mandolins swelling across the hall. Then at a given signal they lapsed into silence, and a score of trumpets licensed the parade of Leonardo's costumed fantasies, with wood nymphs, birds and butterflies amongst others, painting a bright Spring world before the royal assembly.

And last, as all these others lined either side of the aisle, swept into view the swan, fixed in its smile, serene in its movement, gliding effortlessly on muffled wheels along the surface of the stone flags, unhurried, gracious, silent, with no sign of how it was propelled. Finally it came to a stop in front of the royal table, and as its robotic nerve centre performed exactly to Leonardo's design, the lid lifted and out sprung the most beautiful nymph of all - the Contessa di Pavia.

For what seemed an eternity, but was a minute, the only smile in the great chamber was hers, fixed in questioning the King's reaction, awaiting the blessing he could bestow on her sudden reappearance, on her acceptance back, her due place in the Court retinue. 'I thought we had all seen a ghost,' Leonardo noted, 'and each of us examined our sight, checked our very heartbeat for signs of irregularity, but found none other than the evidence before us. She had returned from the dead, from the void into which she and the Chamberlain had disappeared weeks before. No one spoke.'

The Contessa stood her ground, waiting for the signal from her protector, staying in position as long as she could muster the strength of purpose, but as the look of surprise on the King's face turned to steel at one glance from his Queen, so the young woman broke from her fantasy and jumping from the robot under the crowd of disapproval, turned and took flight.

'We were paralysed, rooted to the very spot each of us stood, having no thought as to what to do,' Leonardo had added in the margin.

'Nor dared move for fear of association with the plotting of this mad act,' Melzi later penned.

The King it was who first turned to Leonardo. 'I trust this is not of your doing, not some misguided act of Italian conspiracy.'

'Not of my knowledge or desire, Your Majesty. The servant-girl who was delegated to fill this role was properly prepared and exercised. I cannot think how she was replaced.'

'This could only have happened with your blessing, Ser,' the Queen challenged.

'I can swear it was not of my doing,' Leonardo felt able to plead, 'she has ruined my invention and cast us all into suspicion.'

'We shall hunt her down and extract an explanation.' The Queen had taken charge.

The Ball was finished, the players departed. There was no more to be enjoyed after this sour intrusion. It was the third time a celebration had been interrupted by an alien body and only the lingering memories of the Dauphin's escape helped Leonardo's cause.

Though the Contessa attempted to slip out of the chateau

walls in the resultant melée, she did not get far, and was detained. There was no need for any trumped-up charge, her confinement on suspicion of the Chamberlain's demise writ large on the indictment. Now she would be interrogated at length, and there was nothing the King could do, nor be seen to be doing to stop such an investigation.

The questioning started the next day, and for this woman the only factor in protecting her from the worst forms of inquisition was the lack of general belief that she could have brought harm to the Chamberlain - such a strongly-built henchman. And sensing this, she sought refuge in professing ignorance of his whereabouts, or indeed the circumstances of his disappearance. 'A coincidence of events.'

The chateau records that month are concerned with the background to the Contessa's predicament and continued bouts of questioning; these sought to prise from her not only confessions of guilt in regard to the attempted abduction of the Dauphin, but every other recent mischief that could be laid at a foreigner's door, and specifically the disappearance of the Chamberlain.

His brother, Jacques Artus, made the most of these loose connections, arguing that she alone could be a common link, and at best was a spy within the camp. The mix of nationalities attending the Court meant that such a line of suspicion was not unusual. But as the frustration of the enquiry proceeded to produce nothing, Artus became more rigorous - and speculative - in his examination. An Italian servant was put forward as witness to events:

> I, Jacomo Vialli, being in service to the Court, in the manner of husbandry of the *prima sezione di cavallo* was in the stables, when I saw the Contessa di Pavia meet with strangers and order up the provision of horse and carriage for the removal of effects from the chateau.

This was but one day before she left Amboise without the licence necessary to so draw upon the offices of the equerry. The carriage was later found abandoned on a farm road near Chambord.

There is no further light shed by this witness in the records, and indeed he may simply have been primed to deliver this statement to a prompted writ. It served, no doubt, to prolong the investigation and pressure on the Contessa:

> "The carriage was taken for the purpose of exchanging goods that I wanted to bring to Amboise as a gift in respect of my hospitality, but it broke a wheel and had to be left in its place until a repair could be organised."

But was this a sufficient deflection from the truth?

'She is not to have a false *(sic)* confession wrung from her flesh and bones by excessive force, solely to furnish us with a plot of wrong conviction.' An instruction from the King?

But another unauthored note in this folio answers differently, and it is with Leonardo's file perhaps kept as a tally for his own protection:

'You must draw from her the truth, any truth, that will enable us to dispose of her in final solution of this problem'. This must be on the Queen's instruction, though the hand on the quill is sweeping and broad in its manly brushstroke. Artus would have needed some cover for such an act of distortion, but how the message went astray and fell into Leonardo's possession remains a mystery. As indeed did the true position that two conspirators kept - the King and his Contessa.

If she was tortured it may have only been in the manner of psychological pressure. A systematic examination of her motives, of her possible fate, if she were to be connected to the attempt on the Dauphin's life in the first place. Her true innocence and the lack of logic saved her from this line of argument. But the implications of the Chamberlain's disappearance were quite another matter.

The coincidence of timing of both their removals from Court made her the one platform upon which any case could be developed, and yet to everyone else there seemed no plausible reason for this. The inquisitors' doubts must have given her the final chance to avoid her own impeachment. But not her murder.

XLV

"Son, why hast thou forsaken me?" From the Bible or Leonardo's father?

These words lie in uncoded Italian on the outer cover of a sealed letter. The signature clear though in an uncharacteristically faint hand. Yet why should Leonardo resort to religious source, when he was essentially agnostic and without true faith - that is until the last moment, when breath was escaping from his worn body? This was a time when the Church was losing its omnipotence, wracked with its own deceits and extravagance, its monopoly on truth slipping through distribution of the printed word; the veil of secrecy that gave it power being lifted by those who were plundering trial and error to prove the mechanics of life.

There is a date on this envelope - 1484 - and yet the significance is not immediately clear.

"My son, why has thou forsaken me too."

Back in time, for these words are repeated on a separate message dated 5th July 1504, and the hand is not Leonardo's as it is addressed to him, and in a corner 'to be brought by the hand of Guiliano'. This messenger will be Guiliano da Vinci, the second surviving son of Ser Piero da Vinci, Leonardo's father and his third wife, Marguerita di Francesco di Jacopo di Guglielmo - and the deliverer of a fateful message - the news that their father was seriously ill and his life fading.

'On the ninth day of July 1504, Wednesday, at the hour of seven, died Ser Piero da Vinci, notary in the Palagio del Podesta, my father. He was 80 years old. He leaves 10 sons and two daughters.'

Succinct, cold and factual.

They were both in Florence at the time, and yet the need for a messenger, and the brief recording of the subsequent event give clues as to Leonardo's state of mind at the time - and an inner torment. For there is more distance in this brief call-to-arms than the width of the city they shared. There was a chill in the air that kept the son away from the man responsible for his presence on earth; the ice of their relationship came because Ser Piero had long ago abandoned him in preference to his legitimate sons. The gulf between them had widened irreparably, and only staring death in the face had prompted the father's final call.

Leonardo was already at the height of his fame, and working on a fresco for one wall of the Great Hall, facing another by Michelangelo - a formidable challenge exciting the whole population. So was Leonardo simply too busy to have time for his father? A succinct assessment, cold, but not factually correct.

His father was actually seventy-seven years old, the day was a Tuesday not a Wednesday, and not all the children mentioned still lived - Maddalena his step-sister having died in childbirth in 1477. Leonardo later amended some of these details, but there is more to these errors than pressure of attention. And why has he kept a second forsaken note in this portfolio of memories and reflections?

His mother had come into Leonardo's care at the end of her life, and he accounted for her meticulously in the funeral expenses, but the father is finally dismissed to the recesses of his mind.

Perhaps that is why in his lifetime he felt unable to expose his inner feelings; they were too raw, hidden under the veil of his success. These letters and extracts from The Book of Reflections may be a truer measure of his real thoughts.

br. 58

Then it was that I felt the futility of life. My father had reached such heights of position in the councils of Florence that he wanted for nothing - and sought nothing from me, either in learning or contentment.

I am as a lost son, ultimately deposed in neglect at the expense of so many others, unwarranted in the accounts of his affairs.

Is it God's intent that the child should grow to so stand independent upon its feet that love no longer is the hinge upon the lock of our hearts?

My work must continue here as the contract demands, but at this time, with the passing of his life, the power of concentration is weakened at the hopelessness of it all.

The fresco contract had been drawn up by The Signoria of Florence in May 1503, and the initial cartoon sketches of the outline of the chosen subject had to be completed by February 1505 if Leonardo was not to face the penalty of paying back the 15 florins each month this commission was paying him. He had chosen to feature The Battle of Anghiari - an extremely violent battle in 1455 between the Florentines led by Francesco Sforza and the Milanese commanded by Niccolo Piccinino. This representation of the developing struggle vividly reminds us of the torment that he could so dramatically portray - an exorcism driven by his own feelings within?

His father's death had been given this short postscript, and Leonardo returned to his work, to finish the cartoons on 28th February 1505, and reveal his imaginative gift to an admiring population. Yet his mind had wandered again and free of his father's presence it turned to that other freedom - the release that Flight would give to his patrons and Man.

The bird will beat its wing lower on the side to which it wants to turn, supporting itself with imperceptible movements of balance, following the drift of the wind and events in its favour.

XLVI

The body of the Chamberlain was unearthed on the third day of April 1518 in the forest of Chambord by a hound persistently breaking from the pack to investigate a sunken patch of moss-covered earth.

The town's archives record the discovery in full, identifying all the witnesses who had by chance stumbled into the picture. The hunt had not started, since the King, his huntmaster, the dog-handlers and a vast array of beaters and runners were assembled at the cross-picket in the centre of the woods. The tally runs to over one hundred souls in all. The one name missing from the roll is that of the Contessa, still under house arrest and inquisition. It is noted as an unusually cold day, with a late frost crisping the senses, and the provision of hot brandy as a stirrup cup the wakening call to the courage of the riders.

But even before this gathering had moved off the inquisitive hound had been joined by others until the whole pack was scratching at the soil in a fit of frenzy, as if searching for truffles, refusing to answer the call of the horn, forcing the attention of first the huntsman and then, through their persistence, the King himself. Jacques Artus had joined *la chasse* and was the first to see a large trunk slowly revealed as labourers found spades to dig up this mysterious object.

But was this discovery chance? In nearby Blois a family of local peasants had been discovered attempting to trade precious jewels amongst the market traders. These prized objects were so out-of-place they were originally considered fakes, but brought to the attention of the town's jewellers, were pronounced real. The peasants protested they had found the cache in the woods beside the road between Amboise and Blois, an explanation immediately doubted, for there had been no reports of any robbery, but with no evidence to the contrary they escaped the truth.

They must have been the gravediggers for the Contessa, these stones serving to buy their silence. But their 'discovery' had been leaked, when the gems were appropriated in Blois, ironically by those in the Queen's service. The betrayal of the wooded area in which the jewels had been 'found' led others to try and find more and disturb the soil in various places. Heavy rain and water seepage must have lowered the ground, bringing the trunk nearer to the surface - and now within the scent of the hounds.

The jewels were held in the Queen's chateau in Blois, a day's ride away, their provenance unrealised; she had never seen these gifts that her husband had discreetly bestowed on his mistress. The Contessa in turn was unaware of events, and most significantly Jacques Artus did not have cause to identify the unmarked trunk as her property. Consumed as he was with revenge, it did not occur to him that the knife wounds in his brother's back would have been inflicted by a woman, the force dictating that of professional assassins. The Queen in turn was saying nothing.

All this can be pieced together with Leonardo's evidence - information that Artus lacked at that precise moment, surrounded as he was by mystified royals and servants. He was left alone with the torn body of his brother and silence.

The investigations were pursued now with recklessness, every person is booked with their denials - a heavy tome in the archives stretching to three hundred pages. But not a clue that reliably came from anyone's lips. Then the net was cast wider, particularly amongst those at Court from foreign lands, catching Leonardo's household again in its sweep.

'I fear, Melzi, this madness will overrun us and we will all be cast into the dungeons of despair with this *homo desperatus* driving stakes through our hearts in pursuit of the murderers.'

Melzi: 'We have nothing to declare and thus nothing to fear.'

Salai: 'Nor me, sire, I can vouch that I had no hand in it or knowledge of the jewels.'

'Your time for such escapades is long past.' Leonardo had leant on his arm in reassurance. 'We no longer put your face in the frame for these transgressions. Nor did we have cause to bring down Jerome Artus.'

Melzi: 'We best keep our station at Le Clos Lucé and concentrate on our studies.'

But Jacques Artus called on Leonardo and insisted he attend the body of his brother.

'You are an anatomist, I am told. Tell me what you make of this, what sort of person could have inflicted such a blow?'

'I am not a doctor. My enquiries were into the inner workings of the body...'

'Searching for the soul?'

'To discover how this mess of entrails, flesh and skin can form into such a talented animal.'

'But not one that can save its life so easily?'

'Your brother must have been surprised by these assassins.'

'He never took his eye off an enemy.'

'Perhaps his foe came directly from behind - that is the cast of the daggers' entry.'

'But how would he be caught off-guard?'

'Unless this occurred at night. He is dressed only in a shroud.'

'How would he come to be in the forest?'

'I cannot begin to imagine.'

'But that is your skill surely, to see into the darkness and bring us light?'

'I can see no more than is before us.'

Jacques Artus turned the body of his brother over, the ghastly pallor of the rigid face a shock to them both - perhaps to shake Leonardo into some admission.

To Melzi: 'At that moment I had a terrible premonition that the assassin or assassins would be discovered, and that it would prove to be someone close to our household. But I could answer truthfully I had no evidence as to who had robbed and murdered him.'

Melzi: 'There were too many candidates. None had a good word to say for him.'

Salai: 'He was a mercenary and died as such, a hired hand in danger should he ever drop his guard.'

The Court struggled to pin the blame on anyone. That same day Leonardo felt an irregular heartbeat, and the King's doctor came promptly but could not diagnose the ailment other than the stress of events and coming under Artus's suspicion. He left a balm beside the old man's bed, but Leonardo ignored this potion.

'Read to me Salai from my treatise on Flight. Time is not on my side to conquer the skies. We must attempt further tests this summer when the new craft is ready, or I may never see the horizon conquered.'

codex volante. xii

Above the horizon the birds drift with an ease I cannot muster from my craft. Trial and error will bring us to the heights between Man and God, and more shall be revealed once we have that vantage point.

The craft must be as light as balsa, for the motion of the wings must be driven by the pilot in imitation of the birds we observe. Man has to be the engine that sustains the power created by the muscle of the animal that so readily demonstrates this competence.

Only then shall we be free from this ground upon which States battle each other endlessly. We shall own the secret mechanism with which

to ensure peace across the land, sitting beside the
judgement of God in matters to prevent war.

Then too I shall be at peace in another place,
whether in the heaven so daringly presumed
by religious orders or in some haven beyond
our present knowledge.

Someone - Melzi or Salai, one would suspect, has written
in the margin 'Wherever it be, maestro, they shall award your
service to Man with the comforts you deserve.'

The doubts of Leonardo reinforce a life-long distrust of
the Church and its preachings. He had seen the wanton exercise
of power over the ignorant masses, a leverage that protected
their position against the dawning of science - but for how long?
Knowledge increased doubt rather than reduced it, and no one
was more involved in the revelations of science than him.

'I cannot disprove God's existence, but I am uncertain as
to his presence. For what is there other than Nature to warrant
his presence.'

But Jacques Artus claimed God was his authority, and
despite finding no obvious candidate for his brother's murder,
condemned three of his own Swiss guards to death for failing
to protect the Chamberlain. This sacrifice achieved nothing
other than to fill a space in the register. He knew it, the King
knew, the assembled staff realised it. Life was still cheap and in
the accounting the poor held no station.

'The King has put a stop to this persecution,' Melzi was
able to report to the still bed-ridden Leonardo in the daybook
for 27th May 1518.

'You are more precious to us than any other,' King
François was to observe on one of those visits that became
more frequent as he watched the weakening genius fight on.
'Be strong, as you have through life, and we shall suspend you
in perpetuity in our affections.'

But after the King had returned to the chateau above the town, Leonardo was to comment: 'To conquer death is not to be a miracle that any of my studies will provide. Rather I would account for the survival of love beyond the grave as the one gift that one generation can pass to the next. Thus shall life be perpetual and the desire of man to extend the soul that maintains our species on earth, with or without God's blessing.'

Yes, Father, why hast thou forsaken us all?

br. 59

A son should consider the life of the father and lay less blame than at first imposes itself on his anger. For we all start with an inheritance but no knowledge of how to best use it.

If we then set ourselves aside and fail to consider the lessons that have burnt themselves into the father's soul, we shall miss that most precious of jewels - the cause of love. For he will have loved the son at conception or birth and would only deny this if shame or anxiety prevented him.

And so shall be repeated the mistakes of each from one generation to the next, with births in succession but only a thin cord of love that can tie the bonds firmly together.

In this cause have I, Leonardo, fallen short and with pain kept my silence for too long against the evidence that lies within my knowledge and that of my chance mistress.

196

Salai, when you return to the house in Milan,
as surely you must on my demise - with the
goods I have granted you - do not make the
same mistakes as I.

This is not the first time in these excerpts from the Book
of Reflections that Salai's name has been on the page, but the
other fragments are footnotes of philosophy from Leonardo's
endless quest for knowledge, the experiments with machine
versus Nature, Man against God.

XLVII

But it was the Contessa who surfaced again. She had been released from the quarters in which she had been kept, whilst the investigation into the Chamberlain's death went unrewarded.

However she was confined to the chateau grounds and watched over as she walked the gardens and battlements. This release appears to indicate no connection between her actions and those leading to the discovery of the Chamberlain's body had been established, and she was just one of the many candidates in this matter.

Later, the Court records show the truth - that Jacques Artus was playing a devious game, and that he hoped she would reveal a missing connection by contact with a courtier or attempting to bribe a guard and send a message to some co-conspirator. He had created a false sense of security with this shot in the dark, and by keeping her under pressure he felt that any temptation to make such a mistake could prove fruitful.

Instructions to the keeper of the watch:

> Keep her under clear direction. She may walk the battlements but not step beyond such boundary, nor may she enter the gateways and seek escape. A daily report is to be made to me personally in this regard and a record of all suspicious contact advised.

This lonely figure became the talk of the townsfolk, who could observe her silent pacing of the battlements from the street below. A tall figure, dressed entirely in black, she was seen to be widowed from the King's favour, and their stares only served to drive her further into her ghostly self - plotting what form of escape no one knew. For refuge she took to praying endlesly in the tiny chapel of St. Hubert embedded in the battlement walls.

Queen Claude: 'Why has she been shown this courtesy, when the matter is still not determined? I do not wish to have her in my line of sight when I am at Court.'

Artus: 'It can meet our purpose, Your Majesty. Patience serves us well, with a chance we shall get to the bottom of the mystery, if she is involved in my brother's death.'

'My instinct tells me she is.'

'Indeed, but proof is our right to action, if the King is to be satisfied.'

'I shall be the one to determine this matter'.

So it was to prove.

King François meanwhile showed more concern for the life of Leonardo as May continued with an unusually late frost. He stayed other court matters and adopted a fixed routine in which he attended Le Clos Lucé in the afternoons, when the old man would be dressed and taking the air in the gardens. Sometimes the Dauphin insisted on being in attendance.

'There is a chill in my life, as well as the air, Your Majesty.'

'Leonardo, We shall preserve your talents with all the warmth you need. There is still much to be done and more that we can learn yet from your investigations.'

'I have only the energy for Flight.'

'That in itself would be enough, and I shall authorise the next test as soon as you are able to attend the field.'

The Dauphin had interjected: 'Flight is to be your greatest achievement, Ser Leonardo, and I will be one of your first pilots. The first successful craft will be in royal ownership to command the skies and control our enemies with surprise and as necessary - menace.'

'I am weary of war.'

'Your battle machines have helped us preserve an uneasy peace.'

'The flying craft can be a powerful arm in our cause,' King François had insisted.

'Melzi is making the preparations and will advise me.'

The stables of Le Clos Lucé were converted to use for the construction of flying machines, to keep the main studio for works of the more aesthetic arts. The painting known as the Mona Lisa had been damaged with a strut of wood affecting the paint of the background. Overpainting soon was applied by one of his pupils - perhaps Francesco Melzi himself - at the insistence of King François who had purchased the picture.

'Your health is our first priority, Leonardo. I shall burden you less with demands upon your philosophical studies.' The King handed him a bible: 'Consider the faith in God that brought you on earth and to this place. In Him trust, as we shall, that you recover and fulfil your powers.'

After the King and Dauphin had gone, Leonardo had set the holy book aside. Even at this point he was reluctant to accept Christian beliefs. Nature was the external force, but now mechanics demonstrated more essential truths. Religion buried its people in a fog of myths, written long after events, interpreted to the advantage of its church, and not always in the spirit of goodwill; it was fighting the advance of widely printed knowledge, and was lashing out indiscriminately at all challengers. Leonardo still doubted its authority.

The doctor's records detail Leonardo's waning health. Simply stated they record fevers, potions and lotions applied; and costs, as if the life of this man could be judged simply and accounted for as a burden on the treasury. These notes remain in stark contrast to the unlimited affection of the King. But the person who was in closest attention is not mentioned in the records. Maturina is constantly at his side, taking the medicines to his shivering lips, applying the oils to his body, unashamedly massaging the weak limbs back into life, concentrating on the creeping paralysis in the right hand. She is listed as his 'personal maid and kitchen-woman' yet held a more privileged position of trust through his authority.

Salai comments: 'She was the rock upon which his life hung, though we also wished to believe we held his vigour in our hands. As for me, the master endowed me with special favours and required me to attend his body when Maturina was asleep or in the town to gather goods. For this I am grateful and the bond between us grows ever stronger, allowing me to repay his trust when I so clearly did not deserve it.'

br.61

In the son is the image of the father mirrored, not in each action that can be accounted, but in the spirit and vigour that drives the heart on.

For the son may choose a different life, in contrasting colours to that inherited, so as to set apart his individuality and claim an original talent or personality. And may act in total contrast; stupidity for wisdom, dishonesty for integrity, so that these actions deliberately disguise the parenthood so that none shall guess the essential truth, even when they are in close company.

Such is the strange and complex nature of Man. The sperm shall keep the father's oils, but the son shall brush away the evidence and paint a quite different picture. In this regard are we disguised without the awareness of others.

Melzi, Salai and Maturina appear to be facing the end of Leonardo's life with equanimity. In 1518 he was in his sixty sixth year - the rigours of a hard existence normally brought death much sooner, whether through war or pestilence. Yet as the shadows lengthened Salai was to be in the light of Leonardo's heart.

XLVIII

The Chamberlain's decomposing body was kept in brandy spirit to preserve its ghoulish form, whilst the inquisition fell into disrepute. Then the body was laid in a lead coffin and sealed. The investigation had achieved nothing.

Jacques Artus took the split cloak from the body, cracking his brother's limbs to release it from the *rigor mortis*. A seamstress had to sew up the slash in the back of the garment and was commanded to embroider a crest on it so that he could wear it sometimes as an overcloak, as a badge of office. She was not allowed to fully repair the tear as Artus wanted everyone to see evidence of the wound as he strutted around the Court. It was his sign that the killing would not be forgotten.

But only one person had a conscience - the Contessa. Now kept firmly under 'house' arrest, she plotted ways to escape, for the King was unable to show her any favours, and her future here held nothing - except the risk of death. The letter is in this package that she had wanted to smuggle out to Machiavelli - she may have known he was due to visit the Court. Whether he ever saw it is doubtful; it is more likely that it was intercepted or witheld by a member of Leonardo's household, in whom she had trusted.

Ch. du Roi, 18th July 1518

> Ser M: I cannot remain in Amboise any longer. The darkness is closing in on me and there is no one that will show affection or assistance in my position.
>
> You promised to help me when it might be

necessary and now that time has come. I need to remove to Pavia and seek cover with my family again, and make amends for my desertion. Will you warn them and seek their indulgence?

It will be necessary to arrange matters with those we both know to trust in Amboise, for they alone can engage the favours that will release me from this prison.

I entrust this deed to your imagination and powers and request the most expeditious solution; I will provide dues from his Lordship in Pavia on my safe return. I await the signal.

Maria di P.

There is nothing extant in Machiavelli's diaries either to prove he received this message, and its presence in the folio suggests it never left the town, and was almost certainly held at Le Clos Lucé - perhaps with the intention it should be burnt – once the 'body of other evidence' had been buried.

For indeed it became the time for the Chamberlain's funeral; a procession that made its slow way down the chateau ramparts, disgorging through the narrow portcullis entrance - a passage barely able to take the cart, draped with a scarlet cloth, upon which the coffin lay.

Swiss guards, pikes at the shoulder marched either side, before and after, the clatter of their boots on the cobbles and the creak of the loaded wooden wheels the only sounds as the procession moved down the High Street amongst the silent townspeople. Many servants had been afraid of the Chamberlain's powers to hold them - under false pretences or to blame for any accident of fate. They shared a sense of satisfaction that someone had found the courage to kill him before he accounted for them. But now his brother brought up the rear, protected by more of the Swiss mercenaries he too employed. *Plus ça change.*

The cortege turned by the riverside towards the Church of St. Denys. The breeze off the River Loire blew the cloth around the coffin as if the man inside was making moves to lift it off and reappear to haunt the watchers. Then the procession turned into the heart of the town to Le Place St. Denys and halted at the arched door of the church. Here the King waited, dressed simply in black, to provide a final blessing on his servant.

The service was short, attendance a minimum, the record showing only the guard of Swiss mercenaries and a handful of Court officials. No doubt the latter felt they could not stay away. The Queen did, staying in Blois, no explanation provided, but with other actions on her mind.

The King did not stay for the burial. Called to some unspecified and urgent business he left the last rites to Jacques Artus and delegated courtiers. Some believed he had taken the opportunity to go to the Contessa's apartment and fix her escape, but she is accounted for in the next day's log, so this was mischievous gossip.

The town's archives record the funeral with an appendum:

> The town was unusually quiet, with much reverence for the departed and the wish of all to observe the sacrifice of Our Lord Jesus and retain in their worship the life he gave for the world.

> There being no cause for celebration, the bells were not rung for Evensong, and choirs in St Florentin and St. Denys sang their hymns without accompaniment, the purity of their voices befitting the solemn occasion.

Yet later that night two bodies were found on the road from Blois. Assassins coming back to claim a further reward for their silence? Only the Queen would know that. The following day she returned from Blois with the express purpose of pursuing Leonardo's portrait of her for the antechamber to the royal bedroom. It was not quite finished.

'I think, Ser Leonardo, that you might never finish it,' she reminded him, 'and your reputation that preceeded you in this regard might be proven true.'

'It will be the last painting of my meagre collection; age has seen to that - and this dread paralysis that loiters in my right hand.'

'The world will not condemn you.'

'Twenty paintings in forty years is not a record of which to be proud.'

'The pursuit of perfection is a squanderer of time.'

Melzi, who had been to hand: 'The master has been occupied with too many diverse spheres of interest for his own good, Your Majesty.'

'Indeed, but this picture will be treated with respect if it is to be the last.'

This portrait and its position was not the only thing hanging on the Queen's mind. With Jerome Artus laid to rest, this was the day she put in hand the final disposal of the Contessa. The smile on her face in the portrait is noted in the Court diary for the day: " it being agreed that it was not so much enigmatic as satisfyingly pleased". Leonardo may have lent her a warmth that was only on the surface. He was not to know the anger and retribution boiling beneath that cool exterior, the revenge that was to sweep the Contessa off her feet and into the emptiness of space.

Since the investigation into the Chamberlain's death had brought no exposure, the Contessa felt, with his burial, that her position would improve, and with less cause to keep her confined to the chateau, she could have the King's sympathy at least to obtain a safe passage for Pavia. She accepted now she had no alternative but to leave, yet without a direct word from the King, she remained extremely nervous and grew rapidly thin as food hardly ever passed her lips.

'I cannot be burdened with food, when it is the last thing on my mind,' she had thrown at the servant delegated to keep her quarters.

Indeed the guards noticed that the once proud figure had thinned to such an extent that the lavish gowns which had shown her off to such advantage no longer fitted, and as they fell away loose from her skeletal frame, so she had replaced them with high-collared black dresses, as if she was in mourning, or had a premonition that another death hung in the air. Foolishly she did not believe it would be hers. She was allowed to take the air on the battlements twice a day under the watchful eyes of the Swiss guards and for these airings she wore bright red, however, to project a sense of confidence. She became a lone figure, prayer book in hand, for others dared not show her any affection lest suspicion fell on them too, or they might be presumed to be message takers. In fact this licence to walk the boundary remained exactly that, the trap to see if and with whom she might communicate, and thus provide a lead.

In truth she was only eating fruit because the threat of poisoning was on her mind. It became in her nightmares the most likely way she would be eliminated, with no outward trace of its administration. She could be deemed to have suffered from her own starvation. Either way she faced the threat, and in her increasing anxiety, made a fatal mistake. That of entrusting the one maidservant she felt would keep a secret.

The note was discovered by a guard who pretended to be in love with this maid, having solicited her affection and brought her to his bed. The note fell out of the pocket of the girl's dress when he passionately threw it off her. He took her forcefully and impatiently before, his lust satisfied, taking up the note and examining its contents.

xix.iv.xix

To the hand of M. With God's grace provide
me with horse and companion to take me from
this place to the border of France. I shall pay
you tenfold for this service and jewels shall be
further reward from my family in Pavia.

This maid will show you the turret from
which I can be lifted. Dusk will see me still
apace, when the guards are least vigilant and
changing watch.

M de P.

This note was all the Queen needed to spur herself
into action, while someone else dealt with Leonardo.

The poisoner's art was much feared, and rightly so. With
constant rivalries and envious jockeying for position at Court,
its impact could never be overlooked.

'Never let it be underestimated as a risk to all our lives,'
the King himself advised Melzi, in consideration of Leonardo's
welfare. This comment may have been made much earlier on
the first occasion that Leonardo had appeared to suffer from
malign preparation of his food, when Maturina was absent for
some reason. But now, with the anxieties at Court over the
Chamberlain and the Contessa, a fresh attempt was made to
alter the balance of royal favours.

The details of this new attack are contained in a
number of documents and records in the archives, and a
rebuff in this package.

'Do not begin to consider I had a part in this,' Jacques
Artus was quick to say, when paying his respects to the sick
man in Le Clos Lucé.

But after he had gone Salai comments: 'Who else had either the inclination or authority to instruct another to threaten our master's existence?'

The event was a dinner given by the King for a new *assemblage* of artists and masons, whom he had gathered to further glorify the Court, the Chateau d'Amboise and the massive structure being built at Chambord – already much more dominating than the pretence of a hunting lodge.

These craftsmen had been drawn from all corners of Europe and the young blood of the Renaissance to bring adornment and colour to a Court that was intended to outdo those of Italy and give France a greater glory. No expense was to be spared and residence was being granted to an increasingly large number of artists.

'Most of whom would like to be recognised as of the new wave,' Melzi had pointed out to Leonardo, as they sat on the terrace under an unusually warm Spring sun. 'The more to be envious of you and the influence with which you dominate the King's conversation. They would rather a line was drawn in the sand, and a new era promoted, in which you would have no part.'

'Nor want it.'

'Ah, but until you are off the scene, clear of the map, you stand first in line in His Majesty's thoughts, and are thus a bar to their importance.'

'They have nothing to fear.'

'They believe they do. Any one of them would wish to take your place in the King's affection – and commissions.'

'They are foolish.'

'Dangerous.'

'I have seen no animosity.'

'Exactly, their deceit is why they should be watched,' Melzi added.

'They are unnecessarily impatient. Time is on their side.'

'Greedy and impatient. They need you out of the way.'

'They should be more concerned with each other's motives.'

'But clearly someone is still focused on you.'

At the dinner, held in the Great Hall of the Chateau d'Amboise, this rich variety of artists sat in a square of tables, the design of the placing so as to render all equal. The babble of conversation, the clatter of musicians centred in the open square between the tables and the constant rush of serving men and women may have been the factors that cast the poison into the wrong mouth.

For Angelo Fabrizzi, an accomplished draughtsman, whose architectural talents were being implemented at Chambord was sitting next to Leonardo in companionship. Other Italian craftsmen were seated opposite, each tunic producing in identity a colourful display of the individual city state colours. Here in deepest France were represented Mantua, Ferrara, Urbino, as well as the more familiar Florence, Siena and Milan.

It was after the seventh – and main - course that Fabrizzi took on an ashen pallor, and began to choke intermittently as he digested his meal. The poison must have been embedded in the strong flavours of the sauce, hidden both from inspection and taste, and by its portion slow acting though no less potent.

Fabrizzi felt the need to excuse himself, and in the noise of the banquet was not missed as he slipped away, clutching his throat, aided by two strong assistants holding him upright. Those watching suspected an excess of wine. It was the next morning that his manservant could not rouse him, but thinking that overindulgence was the cause of this lethargy, did not further attempt to wake him, until noon, when the obligations of attending an afternoon conference on design with the King, forced him to shake his master's limbs. Unsuccessfully.

The King was amongst the first to be aware of his death, since he had summoned Fabrizzi to this meeting, and when the assembled artisans discovered the news, there was a sudden chill in the air of their expectancy. No one dared speak first, for fear of appearing to know more than others, or seeming defensively concerned. There was no detailed memory however of events behind the serving scenes of the night prior, for such a mass of servants could not be reliably monitored. Jacques Artus was immediately to the fore in impressing an investigation, but even he knew it might prove fruitless.

'Who amongst us should plot such a thing?' he asked the King rhetorically, not expecting a meaningful answer.

'Someone who wished to have Fabrizzi out of the equation.'

'An envious craftsman? Which amongst them would benefit most?'

'Carlo Monte. His assignment would increase significantly. But Fabrizzi's obligations are – were - already onerous.'

'Bring Carlo here at once.'

The young Italian was summoned from his lodging in the town centre, the locals watching this diminutive architect be swept up to the castle between a force of pikemen. The look of amazement on his face a clear indicator of his innocence.

'I know nothing of this, Your Majesty,' he said with conviction.

'Nor why anyone else should gain by it?'

'We all have more than we need to satisfy your designs.'

It was then that Carlo mentioned that the portions had been exchanged – at Leonardo's request.

'For what purpose?'

'He does not eat meat. The portion was very large as well. It was quite unfit for his appetite, and his preference.'

'He has taken to eating vegetables and fruit only?'

'By habit, though he will not always decline meat in front of Your Majesty's offerings, so as not to offend. I believe I saw him take one taste of his generously filled platter, but immediately realised the presence of strong meat and the rich sauces. He glanced around at first in some embarrassment, but seeing your attention was not upon him, he seemed to me to transfer his plate by persuasive invitation for that of Angelo, who in politeness agreed, his plate being more suited and smaller in substance.

'And what did you see further?' Artus intervened.

'No more than the rest of us, when Angelo appeared to choke and falter, and was assisted from the room in some disarray.'

'From wine or gluttony?'

'Neither would I venture. He has been a good and skilled companion of those of us from the states of Italy. As craftsmen we were in healthy competition, but bonded, and never had cause to treat him with doubt. I never saw him drunk, even in celebration.'

The King rose from his seat and cast his gaze over all those present. He saw no mischief there. 'It is clear that someone who intended the poison for Messer Leonardo is too impatient for his departure from our presence. Artus, you must pursue your investigations with vigour. I will not have such a curse put upon him – or me. For he is my brother in ambition and still alive with ideas even at this stage.' Then the King paused at a window and looked to the south east side of Amboise through the wide windows of the castle as if seeing some apparition.

'You said Messer Leonardo took a first taste, Master Carlo?'

'Yes, Sire.'

'Then he too could have consumed some of this poison.' To Artus: 'Has anyone checked this morning, is there any news from Le Clos Lucé?'

A carriage was immediately prepared at the chateau entrance, and in moments the King and Artus were borne down the short distance to the manor house. They travelled in silence, no doubt with different fears and expectations.

But Leonardo, Melzi and Salai were gathered on the terrace observing new designs for the flying machines with carpenters and weavers, who were absorbed in the implications of new variations in the wing patterns. The arrival of the King and Chamberlain in a cloud of dust drew their immediate attention and when the arrivals hastened over to this studious group, it was Leonardo who first spoke.

'To what happening do we owe this honour, Your Majesty?'

'To a check of your condition.'

'I am well, and this brief burst of early sun has lightened our mood and sense of well-being. The designs...'

'Then God be praised.'

'For?'

'For keeping you from harm. Have you not heard?'

'Nothing of consequence today. We have been fully occupied.'

'Then you – Messer Leonardo – do not feel any misgivings, any ailment?'

'A slight stomach ache, but otherwise I feel as well as can be expected to meet the challenge of these machines.'

'Damn the machines. I mean have you suffered any illness, any cramp in the stomach, any pains in the head, the throat...?'

'Nothing has passed my lips that...'

'Could have poisoned you?'

'Nothing, Sire, that I am aware of. I thank you for the entertainment last night, it was much enjoyed.'

'But not by Fabrizzi.'

'He may have taken too much wine.'

'Someone took his life.'

'I cannot believe it.'

'It is so, and we believe the potion was intended for you. Did you exchange dishes as has been reported to me?'

'Yes. I apologise. The dish put in front of me was too generous, too strong for my palate.'

'Do not apologise. It saved your life.'

'At Angelo's expense?'

'Indeed. Some jealousy or envy of you, we do not know. Artus here is looking to find the culprits.'

'Why poison me?'

'Perhaps because you outlive the average. Whilst you are still here in my commission, some doors are closed to others.'

'They will not have long to wait.'

'There is no hurry to complete these works – or your life.'

The element of treachery hung in a silent air. The sun

softened the coolness of the Spring day. The craftsmen stood beside the table with the new drawings. Some held scrolls in their hands as if frozen to the spot. In the raft of artists, artisans, designers now assembled at Court, amongst the sweep of courtiers and favourites, someone held a grievance, but no one could see the obvious candidate.

'What matters is that you are safe, Leonardo. Proceed with your plans. We must test Flight again soon. These threats to our life remind us of the need to gain advantage above all others, if we are to fight successfully our enemies – and those within.'

But as the evening light faded early and cast a chill into the stone of the manor house, so the colour drained from Leonardo's face. Maturina was the first to notice as she banked up the logs in the fireplace of his bedroom.

'Master, there is a yellow tinge to your pallor, if I may say so. The look of jaundice, which surely is not possible?'

At this comment, Leonardo acknowledged, as if he had needed an independent prompt, that he did not feel well. Not the hints of age, but rather a more pronounced sickness in the stomach, and that his confident responses to the King earlier in the day now seemed premature.

'Shall I bring you something or call the doctor?' Maturina said nervously.

'Give me some milk to absorb the acid.'

'Hot?'

'No, cold, and quickly. I feel nauseous.'

Maturina wanted to call Melzi or Salai first, but one glance at Leonardo showed a sudden paleness in his face, and she fetched the milk as a priority. Then she helped Leonardo into his bed, arranged extra blankets to ensure his warmth, before going downstairs to raise the alarm.

Salai it was again who elected to stay beside his master's bed through the night, once the doctor had been and gone, having administered herbal remedies to work against all known toxins.

'He's guessing as ever,' Leonardo said to Salai on the man's departure. 'He's a quack.'

'But the King's delegated physician.'

'That doesn't mean he knows anything of substance. Just a little more than most herbalists. I wouldn't be surprised if his potions were as dangerous as any substance that has been introduced into my food at the banquet.'

'He is obliged to treat you or face the King's wrath, and loss of position.'

'I'd be better trusting my own judgement.'

'Who might have attempted a move on your life?'

'Salai, there are many that are envious, but fail to understand I do not care for such jealousy. Not now that my work is done.'

'We have not conquered Flight, maestro.'

'No, but may be close to resolving even that.'

'Which is why we must keep you in good health.'

'Poor Angelo.'

'He had a good future ahead, many commissions waiting back in Florence.'

'He felt better staying in France with the King's patronage.'

'A reliable bastion.'

'He has been more than generous to me.'

Salai prepared his bunk across the room and wrapped himself tight in thick blankets. As the old man's snoring began, he was reassured rather than annoyed at its regularity, a persistent music that metronomed sleep, and by its presence indicated the continuation of life. If the damage could be held at a stomach ache only, there would be a fresh attempts at the challenge of Flight, and that he knew would satisfy his master's sense of achievement.

'Not that anyone would doubt him, if flight proved impossible,' Melzi countered, when Salai briefed him in the morning about the night's safe passage.

Jacques Artus paid a courtesy visit that next morning. 'To

satisfy his curiosity on a plan gone wrong?' Melzi observed quietly to one side.

'Or to determine the crime under investigation?'

'To falsely accuse some minor servant and hide the true culprit?'

'Anything is possible,' Salai interceded, 'at a Court with so many positions to be fought for.'

'That is why the poisoner is preferred. If successful it is an instant despatch, and can be executed from a distance, third or fourth hand.'

'The test will be whether any candidate is found at all. If not, we can be sure Artus had a hand in its commitment.'

But Jacques Artus was still pursuing a guilty candidate, for he sensed conspiracy everywhere. His brother's murder weighed heavily on his mind. He saw treason in everyone at Court that held any position of authority or privilege, and challenged them all with his inquisition. His behaviour became increasingly erratic as he pursued his quests mindlessly. For he knew he had not instigated this new threat to Leonardo. That meant dark forces other than him felt they had the room to manoeuvre events.

Artus consulted the Queen, but she kept a cautious counsel and retired to Blois, to absent herself from the King's frequent questions on the poisoning.

This allowed the King to make one more visit at night to the Contessa in her apartment, overruling the guards' standing orders, gifting them an incentive to keep his movements quiet. But someone was watching, taking notes – perhaps with the chance of greater reward at their exposure. When the time came.

But did that moment come? For this spy's report would have ignited the flames beyond jealousy if they had been revealed at that point. Whereas they have found their way into this package, maybe never seeing the light of day, locked ultimately in Pavia at the Contessa's home.

Chateau d'Amboise. 3rd August

"RF came to the apartment at midnight, the Queen at Blois and the Court at sleep. The guards, recognising him, even though in the simplest of cloaks, sought instructions, for the Chamberlain's orders insisted on no entries or releases from this room, but being reassured by his superior authority of his right and intent, were ordered to open up, as RF had the purpose of conveying orders regarding my future. At the same time their silence was to be guaranteed on this matter under threat of consequence."

And attached with a ribbon to this, a further note in the hand of his mistress, clearly written the next day to be hidden immediately in her belongings.

"I was fearful of the subtle release of the door bolts, for is it not at night that prisoners are taken and despatched without the light of day upon their elimination?

To my temporary relief and happiness it was the King, and in a warm mood. I could not contain my pleasure, nor his need to express his most forcefully, for only with me was it that he now found satisfaction. Every word he spoke I remember with a tenderness that followed his first urgent plunge into me. That energy I understood, and the loving I was now convinced could yet save me from this detention. It suddenly seemed possible that this

217

nightmare might finish and I should be restored
to my place of favour and able to lead a free life
at Court. However his words were opaque."

'There remains too much commotion at Court. You must
stay here further. Ser Leonardo has suffered an attempt on his life.'
'And is harmed?'
'By fortune not. An exchange of platters saved him from the
poisoner's fix. It was by sheer luck that the toxin did not reach him.'
'But who took his place?'
'A fellow Italian, Angelo Fabrizzi, an architect. He was
seated next at the table, and knew that Leonardo would not
want the dish of meat.'
'And we Italians are suspect again?'
'Not so by me. They form an essential army of talent for
my designs.'

> "Then I knew that I could not plead my case. We
> made love through the night, testing each other
> to the extremes, sensing that this might be the
> last union. He left before the first light of dawn,
> but I did not stir, the emptiness of the room
> filling me at once with horror and I did not leave
> my bed until the warmth from our bodies, so
> fiercely kindled, finally ebbed away, taking my
> spirit with it. I had a great sense of foreboding."

Later that day two servers from the banquet were detained
in the town barracks. Whether the Captain of the Guard knew of
any guilt is not recorded, nor are their screams under torture, for
such treatment was commonplace when panic measures sought
someone to blame at any cost.

These two unfortunates probably had nothing to do with the
poisoning, but they were the last identifiable handlers of the plates
from the servery, that could be connected with Leonardo's table.

In this air of suspicion the great swirl of artists and artisans was prohibited from leaving the town for days, until the impracticability of this restriction showed as work on the various royal schemes ground to a halt.

Leonardo's condition improved, the tincture of toxin with his sampling taste of the dish proved too small a dose to have a greater effect than the stomach pains he had endured. Indeed he brightened noticeably in response to his close call, and was freshly invigorated to move on the completion of the new flying machines.

The stables in Le Clos Lucé became a hive of industry and experimentation as different glues were tried to stretch the fabric of the wings, and the lighter wooden struts were ingeniously dovetailed to save even the weight of copper nails. The pilot volunteers had been reduced to two, based upon their fitness, agility in managing the harness that strapped them to the craft, and their endurance on the pedalling of the sample gear ropes and pulleys that the great mind continued to design.

'Shall we ever get your machines off the ground?' Jacques Artus felt obliged to ask, knowingly provoking Leonardo, hoping perhaps that some slip of information might fall from the anger of the old man, which could bring sense to the loss of his brother. But such enquiry led to nothing, because there was nothing to admit, yet the defiance only served to prolong the Chamberlain's suspicions.

'I will root out the culprits for sure.' Yet Leonardo could see only doubt in the man's eyes. No amount of torture was going to reveal the assassin, unless Artus struck by chance upon the guilty.

The Contessa kept her counsel, no longer was she the subject of enquiry, unaware that her fate was already sealed. She could not see the King, but walked the walls when the brief allowance to do so was tolerated. Courtiers kept their distance, and walked in the opposite direction if chanced upon. The bribed guards kept their money.

The Queen in turn occupied herself with plotting, out of sight, but clear in her mission. There should only be one woman at the head of this empire.

XLIX

The summer of 1518 was proving particularly hot. Periods of intense heat were broken by frequent thunderstorms, which cleared the air and filled the hill streams that ran through the gardens of Le Clos Lucé and down into Amboise town and onto the dried riverbed of the wide Loire.

Leonardo had the opportunity to relax on the terrace and regain some of the strength that had ebbed away in winter. His physique remained firm but activity betrayed the inner draining of the muscles that once bent iron rods with ease. But this calm was broken by an unusual incident that gave rise to suspicion and intrigue. It is noted in the archives, where the informers at Court relayed their accusation.

The Dauphin was at the house, as were the pupils Francesco Melzi, Salai and the servant Baptista de Villanis, and they had taken the liberty of using the cool streams to bathe; these had been dammed in the wooded glades within the gardens to provide pools of sufficient depth to swim and paddle. It is not clear whether the Dauphin was proving the latest advance in the inventor's swimming aids, for the informant devoted his report to another aspect of the occasion:

> 'The male members of ML's household had brought the young Dauphin to this pool, secluded as it was, and hidden from the sight of the house. They had taken to removing all their clothes and affected to be swimming, but I am informed the character of their actions was far from simple.
>
> It is understood that, in Ser Leonardo's presence and with his connivance, acts of lewdness were encouraged, and that they not

only played roughly with each other but
incurred the interest of the Dauphin - being
entirely inappropriate for his disclosure and
contrary to the principles with which he
would be held in the future.'

Clearly Leonardo was present, and this author considered
him in charge and responsible for the actions of all. Equally
obvious is that this report was motivated by a desire to reduce
Leonardo's position. No doubt the King was absent for such a
claim to be staked at all, or the lodging of this complaint was a
snatched opportunity to touch a raw nerve - the memory of that
incident in Leonardo's youth in Florence where the sodomy
charges had been laid againt him, and his sexuality arraigned.

To Salai an enclosed address:

"Salai: This new falsehood must be refuted; my standing
in these matters has been stained for too long. In this record is
their answer, but it cannot be exposed until after my passing,
and that of Cecilia. Protect this with those of the Book, until
such time as there shall be no pain inflicted."

Attached is a document, heavily sealed with wax. Broken
into, it provides this confession:

'Take note that the most wonderful emotions
were created in me by this young woman, who
gave of herself to me in secret, when she was
obliged to her Lord. She endangered herself.
I, by my inability to resist did fall into the same
chasm of love, the stronger for its chance that
we might neither survive its exposition.

Cecilia Gallerani was but sixteen, and already
given in promise as his mistress to the Lord
and ruler of Milan. No less than Il Moro -

Ludovico Sforza. Tender of years but with a unique beauty that swayed him in his judgement, and I in my recklessness.

For as I painted her - at his command, to which all my projects and commissions now lay - so the normal attraction between artist and sitter became overwrought with a greater passion. Not the familiar, the proximity that arouses the senses, but a deeper affection that broke through and began to capture our souls.

Never did the danger of this situation evade us, for this was the very time her Lord increased his attention and was providing her with gifts of residence in the parish of Nuovo Monasterio, together with jewels and funds to extend her commitment to the enjoyment of his service.

Yet his demands were of a more basic nature. A persistent desire that was rough in its handling of a young body, barely defined enough to take his plunging greed. She would return from his bed with sore limbs and bleeding body to find rest sufficient for the next round of her obligations.

As I painted, so I covered the tracks of his imposition, for the face you see is not that which she wanted to present to him, but the image she offered to me; the love she handed to me within the walls of her room. The ermine is his badge and the clue to his ownership, but not the possession of her, for that now lay with me - in that period of intensity that reveals all in the introduction of two lovers.

Yet we knew that her Lord held her in his grasp, and should he discover our love, would destroy us both with one sweep of his sword. Into this foolishness we cast ourselves and made of every moment what we could and in the darkness of our embrace touched each other's soul in a manner only truth can define.

For four months did we bring this passion to its fullest expression, unwritten then for fear of death, now vouchsafed in the briefest record of memory:

14th March

This day Cecilia first held the ermine in the frame of my portrait, and when it attempted to free itself, leant towards me and our limbs entwined as we struggled to contain its flight for freedom.

Then it was that she looked up at me from her proximity, with a flash of her eyes that dared not show more at that moment, for there was an irony in our wrestling with this emblem of her Lord and master. Yet when I had contained the animal and caged it, she burst into laughter to say: 'My Lord cannot hold me either in capture, since I have not learnt the full possibilities of life.'

4th April

We had often left unsaid the reality of our position and the demands of her master, yet she brought me a small figurine as if to tempt my touch upon her hand in which it lay, presented. It was a phallus of ancient Greek origin. She looked at me for my assessment, but there was none I could rightfully give, without laughter. I took it from her grasp and kissed her for the first time, and she made no move to free herself from my attention.

25th April

We met in secret outside the city in the garden of a friend's residence, but as soon as we touched, we knew such evidence as it may provide would not be kept from informers. We kissed briefly as if meeting by chance, but returned to our homes chastened by this foolishness.

3rd May

This day we consummated our love. It was the most perfect of my life, in which I gave of myself without restraint, and she too, until falling asleep beside me, mocked me with the words that touched on our fate: 'If he discovers us, I shall die content.' I answered faithfully, but knew this could not last.

20th June

Her face in this portrait is done in the image of my love, and there can be no excuse to demand her further presence. We finished the day in one last surge of passion that left its mark in the heart of my mind for all time. I knew I should have to now reach for the remainder of the portrait and finish those lesser details in which I had little interest. The anger at my incapacity to deal with her further was a bitter poison.

This document reveals one other mystery. The broken seal, if remarried in its two parts shows the image of a salamander in its impression. The emblem of François I. Did Leonardo confess this record to the King to allay any fears as to his actions with the Dauphin? Did François become the trustee of this information and hand it to Salai on the will of Leonardo - for it has found a home in this miscellany of fragments? There is no further mention in the archives of the accusations.

L

Leonardo, renewed by the summer sun, determined to tackle two last ambitions. The first was the final solution to Flight. Some premonition however urged him to act on the other - the necessity to prepare his Will.

Whilst the carpenters sawed and bent the light woods to the exacting demands of Leonardo's designs, and the weavers formed fabric to cover the wings, his inner group focused on their master's sudden obsession with drafting the Will.

Salai has annotated one page of this first draft with some sense of pride; he was standing in for Melzi, whose role was dictation. The latter must have been sent on some errand, or maybe had been excused the work on this section, which covers himself as a beneficiary.

'Is it right, master, that I should share in such an important task?', Salai had asked.

Leonardo insisted: 'Time is not on my side, and I am often abed; I cannot stay the execution of the Will's purpose. Be diligent and write clearly, so Melzi can complete the text on his return. He will need to complete the final copy for the notary Borian.'

In what we can assume to be Salai's handwriting, part of Leonardo's first dictation:

> Item. The said Testator gives and bequeaths to the said Messer Francesco de Melzi, being in agreement, the remainder of his pension and the sums of money which are owing to him from the past till the day of his death by the receiver or treasurer-general M. John Sapin, and each and every sum of money that he has already received from the aforesaid Sapin of his said pension, and in case he should die before

the said Melzi and not otherwise; which monies are at present in the possession of the said Testator in the said place called Cloux.

And he likewise gives and bequeaths to the said Melzi all and each of his clothes, which he at present possesses at the said place of Cloux, and all in remuneration for the good and kind services done by him in past times till now, as well as in payments for the trouble and annoyance he may incur with regard to the execution of this present testament, which however, shall be at the expense of the said Testator.

Item. He desires and orders that the said Messer Francesco de Melzi shall be and remain the sole and only executor of the said will of the said Testator, and that the said testament shall be executed in its full and complete meaning and according to that which is here narrated and said, to have, hold, keep and observe, the said Messer Leonardo da Vinci, constituted Testator, has obliged and obliges by these presents the said his heirs and successors with all his goods movable and immovable, present and to come, and has renounced and expressly renounces by these presents all and each of the things which are to the contrary.

For Melzi it was inappropriate to write such gain to his own benefit. He was to be sole executor of his master's treasure trove and have the power to deal with these effects without restraint. Leonardo knew however that he was entrusting this holding to

227

the safest of hands, for Melzi came from a noble family with money to hand. Indeed his pupilage, with only 300 ecus a year, had been an act of willing sacrifice against fortune-hunting amongst the legal system of Milan.

Melzi's greater concern was the hapless task of cataloguing this inheritance, spending days, then weeks, sorting the thousands of pages of manuscript, the sketches, essays, into codices where he felt the individual theses best fitted or complemented each other. Some were easier than others to classify - treatises on painting, hydraulics, machines of war, anatomy, the four elements, the powers of Nature - these could be indexed and the sheets glued together in hard covers. Others, insights into the structure of birds' wings, mechanics (a subject not of Melzi's own understanding), the tales and allegories, and the studies of art were often confusing, absorbing months of analysis, even with Leonardo on hand to identify the scraps of paper.

These folios were later to carry signs of the cutting knife used to form collages of data and illustrations, where he felt best appended. The notebooks, some small in size tend to be the exception and complete, but the movements of the inventor from one city to another broke up this library of logic.

In comparison, the effort of Salai on this one day of drafting, seems to have weighed heavily enough on him for a separate record: "I am not certain I fulfilled my duty to the master."

'Salai, you will have your own reward. The Book of Reflections will be your inheritance, so that what lies between us remains within your own possession, and that knowledge is to be used wisely whilst it can affect those around us. But in time you will be free to gain from it, long after I have been forgotten.'

'I will remain better with the house and garden within the walls of Milan you have granted me. I shall have enough in remembrance of you, sire.'

Leonardo: 'Think hard on this - the inner man is more important than the reflection others see in the pupils of their eyes. For the skin covers the flesh of which we are temporarily made, and deeper inside yet is the core of our persona, the secrets we wish no others to discover.'

'Yes, master, words that we have exchanged in the warmth of the night.'

"Trouble and annoyance." Melzi's view of Salai's efforts in his master's service.

Melzi had come full circle. Vasari records that as a young man dying to become a painter himself, Melzi had a fascination for The Last Supper, and often went to see the fresco in the refectory of Santa Maria delle Grazie. Like everyone else he realised it marked a sea-change in revealing reality in a painting rather than mere imagery or symbolism. With other admirers he dwelt on the use of perspective to draw in the eye and have it focus on the figures who sat at the table, proud of the background, inviting one's participation in this dramatic occasion.

Is there a loneliness in the figure of Christ that is an insight into Leonardo himself - the pain of living with fame amongst so many, yet drawn within a shell of detachment? Christ is the protagonist, occupying the focal position at the table, distanced from the apostles, the wide gesture of his arms, eyes looking down and inward. Is that how this old man saw himself? Is that why he did not keep a diary?

King François' predecessor, Louis XII had wanted to lift this fresco from the wall and conduct it to France, so enamoured was he, and only practical considerations prevented him. Whereas Francesco, 'gentleman of Milan', was only fifteen when he had engineered an audience with Leonardo through his father Gerolamo Melzi, captain of the Milanese Militia, and sought acceptance as a pupil. In this bright handsome youth perhaps the older man saw something of himself, and so the attachment made, Melzi was never to leave his service.

'Never has my service been of the slightest burden. Nor is it now, as we prepare your Will without enthusiasm, since it reminds us of our own mortality.'

But the Will was set aside as Flight took over their attention, and the Queen closed the books on her contract.

LI

Queen Claude visited Leonardo at Le Clos Lucé on 16th August 1518 to formally reveal the portrait worked under the old man's fading talent. In the past his commissions had been started yet seldom finished as he diverted onto other projects, but now it was a question of frailty. The portrait was to be the final barrier against the interned mistress ever regaining her position and access. To be doubly sure the Queen was also to be the instructor of her death.

'The portrait is finished, Your Majesty,' Leonardo was able to pronounce. His condition had improved and he was up and about to greet her when her carriage arrived. There is no record of this painting surviving and it may have been destroyed in the civil wars of the eighteenth century, when the Chateau d'Amboise was variously attacked or abandoned from time to time. Though the core of the chateau survived all assaults, one section of the upper chateau was reduced to rubble in the Revolution to render it more of a residence than a keep, and it is most probable that pictures of royalty were burnt at the same time.

From other sources, it is known Claude was not a beauty, and indeed Leonardo's own struggles to make what he could of her limited looks, is at the back of his slow progress. She admitted her failings too, but conscious of his declining powers wanted him to finish, and nagged constantly.

'It makes the best of me shine,' is her only recorded comment.

She was unaware however that Leonardo had resorted to his pupils for this completion. Perhaps they were employed to fill in the background, the details of her dress after he had concentrated on the face and those windows of her soul - the eyes.

Melzi's pompous notes: 'The school (of pupils) is to finish this study before Summer's end, lest Her Majesty exerts an excess of time and effort on the master. It is our duty to weigh the strain of this exercise and deliver it up in full regard before the due date.'

Portraits of that era are concerned with lavish clothes and regalia in reflection of the grand court that François I was building. Before his reign the Court was made up of a relatively small number of people, but he was to expand it dramatically, and Leonardo had been one of his first appointments. An enviable position that might explain the curious number of 'accidents' that seemed to befall him. He had too much attention from the King for many courtiers.

As for Claude, she had been a daughter of Louis XII and Anne de Bretagne, and arguably in the right place at the right time. Anne had established in Blois a feminine entourage of young girls whose education she personally encouraged.

She created an order of knighthood - La Cordeliere - especially for them, which rewarded merit and virtue. This distinction had such an excellent reputation that foreign princes came here to seek wives. Maybe some of that luck had attached itself to Claude with the capture of François I's attention and hand. Luck in itself was the difference between fame and fortune, life and death. A second folder in this package that was sealed most securely testified to this. It must have been written in around 1482, yet lay unbroken in the package. To this talisman of love was attached another lock of hair. A different colour from the first, straight and soft to the touch. Cecilia.

"The most dangerous day of our lives was the 23rd April – my 28th birthday, celebrated with her that I loved with an intimacy allowed by the work in hand – the development of the portrait for her Lord and Master – Ludovico Sforza, Il Moro – no less. My patron, who ruled Milan unaware of the increasing bond between his young mistress and the assigned artist.

The proximity of our bodies and my admiration of her beauty had stolen common sense from me initially and then from her as I probed the very detail of her mouth, lips, the structure of her bones and well-formed cheeks, the nape of her neck, the gentle curve of her breasts, the fingers of her hands. In every feature I had the excuse to close in and lengthen the time of my observations. Indeed until she would brush my attention away with an embarrassed laugh.

Absorbed each sitting in more of her youthful blushes, in the tender handling of the ermine on her lap – the young animal wriggling to free itself from this unnatural containment – I passed on from artist to admirer, all the time wrestling unspoken with the reality of her existence, mistressed to the most powerful man in the land, when only sixteen. Preferred above all others by the very man who controlled all our destinies.

Yet we began to touch each other, not in accident, but knowingly, with a willing sense in spite of the sparks of danger such intimacy created, until unwittingly we had moved on from friendship to a desire to be holden only to ourselves whilst we shared the enclosure of my studio, and shut the world outside for an hour or two.

And throughout this liaison the ermine wriggled between us, the potent symbol of Il Moro, the clue planted in the portrait to remind the world in perpetuity to whom she belonged. Then this day, by my own connivance the need for the animal was excused, as I professed to focus my painting on the fabric of her dress, which to me was but mere decoration to set below the enchanting face I had completed and was the sole area of fascination in my thoughts. This focus had allowed me to stipulate no interruption, whilst I needed to adjust materials as my brushstrokes progressed, and I allowed no visitors during a day when this young woman might need to change her clothing. So I engineered our solitude and revealed my true ardour to Cecilia. For no longer could I resist the longer touch, the closer brush with her bright face, or the temptation of her lips.

In this reverie did we finally enjoin and embrace tightly as she stood up to receive my arms around her and kissed longingly but without words, for which neither of us could muster any that would not remind us of the illicit nature of our passion.

Then my desire gained the better of me, and first lifting the rough smock that lay across her chest and shoulders to protect her clothing from the paint, I felt my hands unlace the top of her dress, whilst she remained motionless, allowing my delight to show itself, and without thought for her own position, let my hands take her small breasts into their care.

As I caressed her nipples with the soft palms of my hands, rather than the rough edges of my working fingers, so we became unaware of the world outside us and with each touch brought ourselves nearer to releasing our passion. Until heavy banging broke through our indulgence and we realised that her master was at the door downstairs, and before we knew it at the studio.

With no time to do other than bring the smock down over her open breasts, Cecilia attempted to recover her composure, but with tell-tale blushes upon her rosy cheeks.

Ludovico burst into the room, swearing at the doorkeeper, who had tried to refuse him entry, and set his eyes on the young mistress who was capturing his imagination. In his haste he did not see what I saw – the subtle clasping of loose laces that she brushed under the smock, nor when he went to kiss her did he lean closely against her, lest he too caught paint on his finery. That sliver of separation prevented him finding the truth, her breasts exposed.

'Well, Maestro, how long before the portrait is finished? You have done the most important elements, my beloved Cecilia, the ermine and the outline of her dress. Surely you can finish it quickly now?' 'Three weeks,' I had muttered absently. 'A week too long. I want to display it as soon as possible.'

Il Moro spoke with her, but my mind was in a fog of danger and foreboding. One embrace of her could have brought us to justice, finished my commissions, starved me of my career, even risked my neck. We had drifted into madness. But the very brazenness of our behaviour saved us from suspicion. The rosy cheeks admired as youth, his pleasure with the portrait sufficient to defray any inquisitiveness. Having made me agree a deadline, he rushed out with the same vigour he had entered, leaving us to sit in silence and gather the naturalness of our breathing. 'I am not free, Leonardo.' Nor, when she was freed all too soon as Il Moro's interests moved on, was she allowed her own choice in the matter, married off to Count Bergamo, with a house – but with what licence to love?

As for me, I say again, does one ever leave that once-in-a-lifetime love behind?

LII

Flight. Leonardo came to face up with increasing determination to this last challenge. He could be found in his chair on the terrace as Autumn approached, staring up into space - the very ether he wanted to conquer, the pathway in spirit he would be taking soon. Faith in God or not. Time was of the essence, the record incomplete without success in the air. A platform of knowledge for others to develop in the future. A gift to mankind.

br. 67

Consider what is best in your work and lend it to future generations so that many gain. Recognise your achievement and ignore the losses, which have worried you. They will disappear and not show in the reckoning.

If there were others who created the spirit in your soul, take that on with you into the next life, for there you will find them in comfort and the love that left you will be found.

Examine these works to the full extent, and consider them the broadsheets upon which my dues were settled. Leave me with the love of those I have encompassed in my soul, where I retain the beat of their hearts. Their support has sustained me.

And later:

br.68

Soon, in the passage of time printed words will reach the mass of people, and the mysteries of Nature, the universe and machines will bring the Church and politicians to account, so they no longer hold sway over others. Then I hope the world will find the peace that it aspires to. Proof will be the ultimate revelation that will make this clear.

A flight from life, but in that Autumn and Winter running into 1519 there is one more test of a new flying craft, and it was of a different design - the autogyro.

'We must examine the power of man to raise the machine upwards, without reliance on the winds to lift our craft. Gather the strongest men and train them to move the pedals with the greatest of energy to propel the turbine with maximum effect.'

There is a drawing of this craft. Within an outer frame two men are positioned on seats to pedal a set of gears that rotate a spindle at the top of which is a corkscrew device that turns a pair of small sails. It is not clear what materials these are made of, but a stiffened fabric is most likely. Leonardo has not annotated the illustration.

In the archives there is mention of a training schedule imposed on 'the most virile of our men', and this programme includes 'running up and down the steepest hillside paths with weights upon their shoulders', swimming tests across the Loire 'at the strongest flow of the flood water', boxing and wrestling.

'They are to be fed without restraint from His Majesty's kitchen, twice a day, three hours before their exertion.'

The absence, however, of a mass of records suggests that these heroic efforts may have been excessive, and other than the medical records in the town's hospital - 'Today another man took to his bed exhausted before he could qualify for the

test" - there is little proof of the regime being maintained.
The test itself is noted:

Chateau d'Amboise, 23rd November 1518

Messer Leonardo, being ill, could not witness the trials. His new craft of vertical design was complete and positioned in the main courtyard, so better to contain its movements within the battlements should it fail.

The two pilots, chosen for their proven strength, began to build a turning motion in the central spindle, as intended, and then raised the speed of the gearing quickly to the maximum of their ability.

For a moment there seemed to be some lifting momentum, but it became soon clear that this was no more than shaking of the light and fragile structure and that no amount of pedalling would conquer their weight and adherence to the ground.

The craft that had been first inspired by the fall of the sycamore 'wings' was left stranded on its base, and returned to the stables.

The onset of winter, and Leonardo's loss of vigour stalled his pursuit of Flight. He was not well enough to tackle the issue until the Spring, and a more immediate issue faced him. Completing the Will.

1519

LIII

Leonardo was now often to be found in the Oratory - the small chapel in Le Clos Lucé that had been built originally by King Charles VIII for his wife Anne de Bretagne, mother of Queen Claude.

In that previous reign Anne had lodged there from time to time to escape the oppression of the Court and seek the peace and quiet offered by this corner of Le Clos Lucé. She "went to cry the most painful tears a woman could shed" and to pray with her Book of Hours in hand. Contemplation here inspired Leonardo to work on his Book of Reflections.

The chapel is barely six feet square with an oak pew on one side set against the dark red wall and a prayer stand and kneeler opposite. The small altar table with its six slim arched supports stands at the end wall beneath a delicately stained glass window. This simple space is decorated with three frescoes that Melzi and the other pupils had embarked upon - The Annunciation, The End of the World and above the door - the Virgin of Light. Virgo Lucis - the original source of the manor's name?

In January 1519 Leonardo is recorded as giving thanks for his recovery from a bout of sickness that had confined him to his bed and alarmed his retinue - and the King. No chances were to be taken now with his health, yet no great medical knowledge existed to analyse the symptoms. If someone had been trying to hasten his demise through poisoning or other means, these risks now had passed. Whatever threat he was to the position of other envious courtiers, they could reckon that God would do their dirty work for them, and remove him from the scene before long.

'Fearful old age,' he had volunteered to the doctor, who looked baffled. 'Fear of old age, that is what troubles us. When we come near to its gates we hope to remain outside its greedy embrace.'

240

If he was praying now rather than hoping, the conversion was a late commitment. His obsession with matters of scientific explanation had led him away from the teachings of the Church and the manifest indulgences it threw so recklessly around to protect its interests.

The fact that he had at last persuaded Melzi to work on his Will may have eased his mind. Leonardo was deeply conscious of the support of Melzi, Salai and Maturina, let alone the selfless generosity of the King, who had provided this secure home.

The Court diary shows that the King had made a visit on the last Sunday in December prior to a simple service at Le Clos Lucé. It was a public display of concern, rather than one of his private visits via the connecting tunnel that ran down from the chateau directly into Leonardo's ante-study.

'We are here to pray for your continued presence on this earth, and for the maintenance of your advice and judgement.'

'Which I shall do my best to sustain, Your Majesty.'

But it was his Will that kept him occupied on those dark cold evenings:

> Item. He orders and desires that the sum of four hundred scudi in his possession, which he has deposited in the hands of the treasurer of Santa Maria Nuova in the city of Florence, may be given to his brothers now living there with all interest and usufruct that may have accrued and be due to the aforesaid Testator since the said four hundred scudi were deposited with the said treasurers.

> Item. He desires that at his funeral sixty tapers shall be carried by sixty poor men, to whom shall be given money for carrying them at the discretion of Melzi, and these tapers shall be distributed amongst the town's churches.

241

Item. The said Testator gives to each of the said churches ten pounds of wax in thick tapers, which shall be placed in the said churches to be used on the days when those services (of remembrance) shall be celebrated.

Item. That alms be given to the poor of the Hotel Dieu, to the poor of Saint Lazare d'Amboise and, to that end, there shall be given and paid to the treasurer of that same fraternity the sum and amount of seventy soldi of Tours.

He made time to remember those least well-placed in society, and often assembled for supper the chosen few he had come to call his close family, for during his whole life, his half-brothers and sisters in Florence had kept their distance, divorced from his fame. To his new family:

'In each of you is a special blessing. Each has played his part. But at the end of it all, what have I achieved?'

'Much, maestro,' Melzi had immediately countered, 'as Europa knows only too well.'

'Yet within me is dissatisfaction. For Flight is not yet accomplished.'

'But may be so - in Spring,' Salai had volunteered. 'The new birdwing in preparation will surely carry a man not only across the river but return him safely to the town bank. That would seal the achievement.'

'But not prove the ultimate ambition I have for this skill.'

Melzi: 'We have a storehouse of your work to act upon.'

'But not the means to power this invention. If we could store the energy that would take the machines forward - at speed and for distance, then we would be in favour with Man and God.'

'In whom we trust,' Maturina interceded. 'Master, you

must throw off this melancholy and observe what great achievements are in the records.'

Only Maturina was in the habit of drawing attention to God's role in life. She could interfere with Leonardo's reluctance to accept the Christian faith, whilst with others he became angry and aggressive towards the machinations of the Church and its exploitation of ignorance. She saw him at his most vulnerable, in the morning bath, when his bowels failed to function properly, in sickness or when influenza brought him down. She recognised the dangerous effect on him of even the common ailments. The once vigorous body, a subject of great strength and beauty in its day, was now open to attack from a wide range of maladies. The beard white as snow. Only the mind was as alert as ever, never at rest, stimulating thought, creating in the imagination yet more invention.

'Be cheerful, master,' Salai had insisted. 'The true weight of your achievements will remain beyond most men.'

'They are nothing compared with the love all here have shown me.'

The love that rises above duty - of the father - or that of sibling rivalry. The love that Caterina would have wanted to hold him in, with which she might have smothered him, as all truly loving mothers do with their first born son. Instead the void in which he had to play so much of his life.

'Each of you in turn has been a pillar of strength to me, in constant friendship and family. I have gained notoriety for the power to bend iron rods with my bare hands but no man is so strong that he can live without the comfort of love, and in you have I found that quality of existence.'

Melzi: 'We have been blessed in return with the gifts you have bestowed on us in using our meagre talents.'

'You, Francesco, have indeed followed me without complaint. It has been a long journey.'

'My draughtsmanship and colouring is now competent.'

'Great competence. I insist that you follow this path after

I have gone and command the respect of patrons.'

'First I have the task of arranging and codifying all your manuscripts. I doubt I shall have time for anything else.'

'A punishment!'

'One I accept in good grace.'

'And Salai, you too have travelled far.'

'From nothing to something, sire.'

'From a rapscallion to a member of society.'

'I am fully satisfied with my lot.' Leonardo took hold of a wine flask with his firm left hand and poured Salai a glass, then rested his hand father-like on his head before pulling the younger man's face against his chest. 'There is yet more between us...'

'To be granted, to be discovered?'

'To be kept between us. Now is not the time.'

'The Book?' Salai had unwittingly blurted out. If the others took note of this remark it may not have seemed significant, nor was it mentioned in the drafting of the Will. It was not the matter Leonardo had in mind, nor would the others have seen the letter from Leonardo to Salai in this package. That must have passed into Salai's possession at the last moment. Handed over by Leonardo in silent apology.

To Baptista - his other servant - Leonardo was bequeathing much of the furniture at Le Clos Lucé. 'It will serve you well when you move back to Milan on my departure. I shall think of you in this chair.'

'There is much time yet, master.'

'No, I fear not, but in this gathering I have found satisfaction.'

As the new year of 1519 began, so Leonardo felt a sense that events were moving faster to a conclusion for him. The act of drafting his Will added urgency to the *'last equations in life'*.

He ordered his craftsmen to progress the latest flying machine with a sudden haste, binding them to work through the nights, forming the wood, cutting and glueing the cloth to the lighter frame - one which seemed to defy the strength required to support a pilot.

codex volante.xxxv

The pressure of wind beneath the wings will outweigh that of the vacuum formed above, and will thrust the machine and man upwards, just as the birds achieve their lift so easily, without great beating of their sinews.

So shall man prevail when the winds are favourable, for without great effort can he ride the air waves and manipulate the currents of fortune that God provides.

'But what, master, if the sky is calm and fails that man, when he has already embarked upon the flight? What power can he employ to ensure his safety?' That was the conundrum - the power of man to keep the craft in the air and in motion, with direction and purpose.

'How can we control the machine to oversee our enemies in the battlefield?', was the King's question.

'Can God be relied upon to provide us with the currents to support our endeavours?' Jacques Artus, now fully ensconced in the position of Chamberlain, had interposed.

No one knew, of course, and Leonardo was merely extending theory in the hope that some balance would be struck between weight and motion to make flight practical.

'We approach success,' he reports in the court records for an early February day. Whether he either believed it or felt he had convinced anyone else, is not sure, but his spirit remained persuasive in this particular project, which had come to represent a matter of life and death. Perhaps he was thinking of his own success - or as his notes came more realistically to reflect - a sense of failure. Not just in matters of Flight, but in summary of everything he had achieved.

As a perfectionist, he focused more on his failures, the unfinished paintings and frescoes, the unresolved mysteries of anatomy, the function of the heart and blood system - much like this he felt had escaped him, leaving a deep feeling of frustration. Mortality was on his mind in these closing months.

Indeed the malfunction of his own body was beginning to annoy him. The paralysis in his right hand now prevented him from painting at all; it became a focus of his irritation. For so long this gifted hand had held sway over palette, paint and brushstrokes as his lines portrayed in faithful detail swans, horses, fish and beasts of the forest. Pages full of warriors, shields strapped in the face of danger, wrestling with enemies at their feet, waves of battlelines that introduced some great military machine; a tank or multi-barrelled gun appended almost as footnotes.

Then amongst all those sheets of weaponry are Isabella d'Este, Ginevra de' Benci, La Gioconda, Lucrezia Crivelli, and above all the beautiful and youthful Cecilia Gallerani. Love requited but stolen from him.

But now in 1519 the pages are full of new characters - the grotesques. How can these be analysed - strange images, drawn in intimate detail, each distortion of the face, twisted in unexplained anger, the head bent down over some unseen threat? Pages and pages of them, viewed from every angle, showing the pain of tortured souls.

> Man cannot survive his own decline and anger rises in old age at the imperfection of his body, which recedes before him in the mirror, allowing no discretion in the truth that no reversal of fortune will alter the harsh fact of his impending demise.

'Master, do not assume such misery,' Maturina interjected, as she applied the warm oils with which she sought to loosen the creaking limbs. This comment is noted in the doctor's record. The latter's name is lost with the cover, long since torn off by some negligent archivist. Perhaps it was a litany of false prescription, for what irony there was again in attending to a man, who had the greatest knowledge of anatomy, and the workings of the body. The doctor might well have been intimidated and subject to guessing with a range of herbal potions and lotions to help resolve arthritis and other ailments.

Maybe Leonardo saw in his mirror new lines of age, no longer hidden by the flowing beard, and translated this evidence into the images of the grotesques. Was he drawing himself, in exaggeration, or exorcising his feelings through what he knew best - illustration and chalk - rather than outbursts of anger and frustration against those around him?

Salai is known to have taken over more of the administration at times of sickness, working watch and watch about with Maturina. Melzi was keeping the projects going, as there was to be no let up in the imaginative sphere of Leonardo's mind, however weak the body. Salai, despite sources placing him already back in Florence, is revealed at the right hand of his master, repentant and keen to serve his last will.

LIV

The evening cavalcade on the 10th March 1519 was the last function at the Chateau d'Amboise for which Leonardo was to create an effect for the King. The theme was War and how to hold the Peace through strength. A display of power designed to show, with the backing of Leonardo's new battlefield machines, the opportunities they gave to surprise an enemy.

The commission for this extravaganza had originally been given some months before by the King as a parade of mechanical invention and so as to maintain a challenge to the mental powers of Leonardo rather than the physical. He knew that the great man's health was best preserved by the vigorous stimulation of an inventive mind. The theme was reflected in the military costumes which Leonardo designed.

Five drawings of these outfits remain in the chateau's archives, but the pencil lines of his still working left hand are less secure than the confident draughtsmanship of previous years. It is possible he delegated some of this work to Melzi or one of his other pupils. His authorship, however, is not in doubt.

The focus of his invention were guns of various sorts, providing new levels of accuracy and firepower. The centre-piece a carriage-mounted multiple-barrelled field gun, capable of firing across a wide arc to destroy a whole regiment on foot. This was to be the climactic piece of the final parade, to be fired from the battlements at the midnight hour before the assembled company.

'Two thousand guests, ten thousand candles and a hundred roast oxen' give some clues to the size of this event held in the chateau grounds. Implicitly the whole Court, the attending nobles from all over France and soldiers were to benefit from the feast as well, given this wealth of hospitality. There was excitement and celebration in the grounds of the chateau, with the dutiful mercenaries of the Swiss guard arranged along the battlements and at the portcullis gateway.

These events glued together rival factions and forced them to be of one obligation to the royal cause. The evening would bind together the Court in a display of common endeavour and allegiance.

The guests replete and the royal party seated, the illuminations began with the firing of rockets into the night sky, and the successive explosions of gunpowder bombs. Yet all these fireworks were shown as clumsy devices - frighteners -

but with no harmful effects, mere diversions on the battlefield and indecisive in their real effect on an enemy.

In contrast, this display over, the mighty effect of Leonardo's weaponry was seen for all its invention. From the walls there now was fired one cannon after another of the new designs that his mind had crafted. Battlefield weapons: dual lightweight cannons that could be manoeuvred readily and targeted at roving horsemen, multiple-barrelled guns that could master a whole arc of fire from a fixed position. These were reloaded quickly to demonstrate their versatility until the stocks of powder and ball were exhausted.

'You have moved us on in our capacity to defeat our enemies, Ser Leonardo,' the King admitted.

'But will they bring peace?'

'We shall hope to maintain it. And those lands we hold in our grasp.'

Only later, on retiring to bed was Leonardo to comment: 'I fear for the future, for our inventiveness only opens doors to new conflicts, to be fought all the more mercilessly.'

'Unless Flight can be the ruler, the maker of Peace,' Melzi had reminded him.

'Yes, that indeed is worth pursuing. The break in the clouds of war.'

It remained the final ambition, sought in the finality of life.

LV

In late March 1519, those close to Leonardo at Le Clos Lucé gathered even closer. Baptista de Villanis, his other servant, was despatched to Milan to collect some remaining funds. They cannot have been much, since his position was too junior to be of authority to the bank. Perhaps there were some private effects of special significance to the old man. It is the nature of the gift, rather than its size that carries the greater value, the emotional commitment to the inheritor.

Melzi had been instructed by Leonardo to work further upon the frescoes that would adorn the ceiling and walls of the little Oratory chapel. He needed to know these commissions would be progressed. They represented the late conversion to some form of Christian faith, imposed by the imminence of death. Melzi also was beginning to struggle with the mass of manuscripts, codices and essays that remained in chests and boxes in the studio and back rooms.

'You must ensure, Melzi, the binding of my works is pursued with vigour. I pass this burden on to you, as attested in my Will.'

'It is a weight,' his pupil had insisted, 'that I can carry. But it will take time, many years I fear, to collect them into their rightful order, for students to benefit from their wisdom.'

"They will ignore them, mark my words. Youth has its own agenda, and will not acknowledge the source of its inspiration, but rather claim it for itself.'

Salai had interposed: 'They will be inspired and we must provide them with the ammunition for their progress.'

'I doubt it. Raphael, Michelangelo - they are already in the vanguard of their patrons' new interests in sculpture, painting and portrayal of the world. I will be soon forgotten in the affections of those in power.'

These sombre reflections were borne on the wind of walks around the extensive grounds of Le Clos Lucé - wooded glades and ponds, fed from the local river streams off the hills above. To Leonardo Nature settled the mind, when it itself was at rest, when the daffodils and croci squatted below the great trunks of chestnut, plane and lime, and the shafts of sunlight found a way through the blossoming foliage of Spring.

Leonardo's melancholy was out of place in the freshness of the new season, and his 'family' sought at every opportunity to comfort and encourage him on. Everyone hoped that a further surge of energy would extend his life. They knew they would be lost without him.

LVI

Leonardo became preoccupied with his 'family' as the horizon closed in, and in Melzi's service is there the shuffler of these folios, has he set aside these pages that were the inner man? For the package releases a further revelation close to Leonardo's heart. The link between Cecilia Gallerani - "my most beautiful sitter", and the birth of Salai. Not a direct parentage, but the embittered and casual action of the young genius, when he had been 'forbidden' to embrace the love he had secretly declared for this young woman.

This folio is a confession, which Leonardo had coded and hidden away:

> A man loves truthfully once. Other loving is not from the same heart; that is conquered but once in its lifetime. If that love is requited but briefly, then the taste of it is never lost, and much account can be taken of its significance. Mine has lived with me always, private until this declaration be found after my demise.

The impossibility of holding Cecilia to me other than on paper led to actions that were immediately impetuous, borne of frustration and the recklessness of a younger age. For our brief expressions of passion were limited by the danger to our lives so evidently threatened by discovery.

I was thirty but acted as an angry youth deprived of his first romance. I lay in the arms of Anna - the first woman to offer herself in my misery.

I am not proud of this admission at a time others considered my solitude and lack of commitment to womanhood an intrinsic part of my nature. They did not see what was in front of their eyes, a painter, an interpreter of the soul. They simply saw the body of man.

Yet this mistake turned to advantage ten years later when this same woman addressed my doorstep and presented me with the truth of a child of our liaison.

Salai, forgive me for taking you in years after as another, rather than as a son. But it was your mother's wish that you should be safe rather than oppressed with the misfortune of our dalliance. She forswore me to keep the secret that she had you adopted by the family whose name you bear - that of Caprotti. Giovanni Pietro Caprotti from Orento was the master of the house in whose trust you were placed at the insistence of your mother - Anna.

She has reserved her own family name, lest
you feel obliged to pursue them for her guilt in
passing you to others. A guilt, much less than
I hold myself in disregard - for only now am I
allowed to put the record to that truth, and
able to give you the circumstance of your real
parents, Anna and I.

A different view from the reports repeatedly slipped into
the public domain:

'Giacomo - now by my choice named Salai - came to live
with me on the feast of St. Mary Magdalene of the year 1490.
The second day I had two shirts cut for him, a pair of hose, and
a jerkin, and when I put aside some money to pay for these
things he stole the money (4 lire) out of the purse; and I could
not make him confess although I was quite certain of it.' This
record comes from Leonardo's own manuscript C.

Vasari - that biographer of the great and godly - writing
almost fifty years later expounds the theory:

That 'Leonardo took for his assistant the
Milanese Salai, who was most comely in
grace and beauty, having fine locks, curling
in ringlets, in which Leonardo greatly
delighted.'

The lock of hair? There are two sketches of Leonardo's
that can be associated with or attributed as Salai. One portrait
of a young man with ringlets dated around 1504, expressing
attractive youthfulness.

The second drawing of a very similar youth is dated a few
years earlier. Strange that the youth is face-to-face with a much
older man, who has the exaggerated look that evolved into
Leonardo's depiction of grotesques. Yet looking at the pair, is
that an exchange of glances between father and son? The

father's knowing, the son's merely an innocent adolescent enquiry? 'Nutcracker' man and a beautiful youth.

Was there a tolerance with which Leonardo puts up with Salai's 'little demonship', the lavish indulgence he poured on him with tunics, jewellery, bows and arrows, silver brocade - all carefully listed in an inventory? A sense of paternal resignation, rather than outrage at the various misdemeanours? Challenging the supposition that Leonardo took the boy in as some form of sexual partner? Here may lie the true answer. From the man himself. From the father a second missive in clarification.

> Anna and I are your true parents, and the occasion of our loving has been the fountain of my love and understanding of you in your living with me all these years.

> Whilst others derided you, reproached me for tolerating your behaviour, accepting the sullen apologies, the repetition of petty larceny, these and much more - I have been dealing with my own demons and have not wanted to lessen the spirit in you.

> For that spirit has been my inheritance. I too was born a bastard and paid the price of limitation that this bestows on one's ambition. I could not suppress you in the same manner.

> You may keep these revelations to yourself when I am gone. I cannot demand a particular path. That shall be the weight of your own conscience and desire. There is no price I can ask of you. I have paid enough for of us both.

254

But in the love we have shared and the years been joined is the love of a father. It is my hope that you felt within the care of my heart.

That is why I have gifted you The Book of Reflections. For it is me. No one shall know me as well as you. If you keep its pages in the sanctity of your possession, then no one shall know the inner truth. That I leave in your hands, and without dictation as to its eventual use.

Ti amo. L. 24th March, 1519

Salai is portrayed elsewhere as the eternal youth, persistent in his mischief. Leonardo's own attributions in Manuscript C: *ladro, bugiardo, ostinato, ghiotto* - thief, liar, obstinate, glutton. But these failings matured into a more sensitive man over the years. Salai was about thirty-eight years old in 1519, still the comparative youth to his master, patron, father, but he cannot have received his father's confession, for there would have been further mention of it in those last weeks. There is none.

Perhaps because Melzi was the archivist, willed and entrusted with all the *codices,* the thousands of loose sheets carpeted with sketches of machines, illustrations of plants, the entrails of the human body and other miscellanea.

On the morning of the 25th, Leonardo had another fall, whilst crossing a path in the gardens of Le Clos Lucé. Salai was at his side, and cursed himself for letting the old man slip from his grasp.

'It is my fault you have injured your foot, master.'

Leonardo wanted to remain seated on the grass until he recovered his breath, but there was still a dew on the surface, and Salai insisted on raising him, whilst calling for help from within. Maturina quickly appeared and took the other side, so that they could pass Leonardo's arms over their shoulders, and without force, carry him back indoors.

'I shall light a fire, and bring a warm drink.' Sombre instructions shown in the kitchen diary: "Warm milk is to be administered to the patient." Evidently the cold snap had not completely vanished, and the arrival of fine Spring weather delayed. 'It is ominous that the season is so late this year,' Melzi commented, 'when the master needs fresh light and encouragement to lift the burden of his troubles.'

The doctor was summoned but does not appear to have arrived before the old man fell asleep in the comfort of an armchair. Life's own cure.

Leonardo's bedroom in Le Clos Lucé is relatively small, with the square four-poster bed and its heavy velvet drapes dominating the space. The large fireplace, whose wood fires caused those frequent accidents to the tapestries and his worksheets was the other noticeable feature. The room maintaining a close warm atmosphere, in which those intimate members of his adopted family cared for him. Once Maturina had completed the morning duties of slopping out, washing Leonardo and bringing him a first meal of the day, Salai would read from those texts and manuscripts, now becoming blurred in their author's own eyes.

'I see less, and without clarity of sight what am I?'

'Your insight, master, is the more important. Nothing will pass you by.'

'Much will now. I have done enough to fill the records, it is time for others to challenge their beliefs and by investigation take their message forward.'

Melzi was also responsible for reporting on Court and political events. Though Leonardo no longer had real interest in them, a sense of intrigue stayed with him. He liked to know but not participate, and Le Clos Lucé was the perfect distance from the Chateau d'Amboise to keep Court affairs away. Only the King had both the wish and determination to attend Leonardo daily when in residence. Matters of royal interest were passed first-hand.

The fall did precipitate a change in the household arrangements. The doctor was housed closer in the gallery wing, to be in attendance morning, noon and night. In the afternoons, Salai would undertake one other private task. Seeking explanations on drafts for The Book of Reflections:

br. 71

A man is spent when he has lost the will to learn, and it matters less with what he educates himself, than he exercises the mind. For in time learning shall reveal all life's secrets and man shall expose the workings of the body and mind so as to range widely in the universe.

Salai: 'And will we find God in this hemisphere, master?'
'Maybe. I will not live to see it.'

Not with time ticking away in the very room in which you shall pass on to that other world.

'We *shall* meet again and be in God's company.'

Recovering from the fall was important because of the planned next flight of his 'bird' machine. The young Dauphin could not resist pestering Leonardo to start the next trials, ignoring the old man's frailty, demanding that the attempt was proceeded with.

'Ser Leonardo, attend in a carriage, and see your instructions are followed. I will check your every word is executed faithfully.'

'But it is God's hand on the rudder.'

'Yes, maestro, but my father and I will provision earthly and heavenly powers to make a success of this invention.'

A carriage was prepared to take Leonardo as far as the track would take him to the hills, from which the flight would be attempted. Then a sedan chair extended the journey to the slopes overlooking the countryside and the river Loire far below, the sunlight glistening on the rippling water.

'A sufficiency of wind at least, Your Majesty; fortune may be on our side.'

Four soldiers were sufficient to drag the new craft on a sled to the take-off site. The wings had been taken separately as the hedgerows prevented the complete machine being moved through the winding lanes. Leonardo's chosen craftsmen had taken a whole day to assemble the structure, rigging the cords and fabric skin over the frames together with the pilot's gears and pulleys for power.

'The machine is much lighter,' Leonardo explained to the Dauphin, ' now there is a chance the equation is possible, that we can leave this ground and return to the starting-point. If the wind assists in this endeavour.'

'With God's will.'

'With divine intervention to strengthen our case.'

But soon after the craft, pilot and cast were assembled the wind got up to such a strength that all were blown about in an undignifed fashion. This did not worry the King, nor the Dauphin, but it made the flying attempt impossible. The pilot, strapped within the lightened craft was buffeted mercilessly, and the irony of his situation became evident to all. The possibility of movement in the air was clear, but its very lightness made the craft unmanageable. Only the birds above held sway in the gale.

Attached are the last words on the subject Leonardo was to dictate:

The vagaries of wind are in the competence of birds to muster the changes in their soft wings that render them still afloat and under control of their destiny. Not so with Man who as yet is fastened to rigid patterns of wing that limit his capacity to glide with confidence.

We must therefore learn further the construction of our craft, so as to flex our muscles through the pattern of struts upon which the canvas is stretched.

'We must hold off for a few more days until the weather changes for the better.'

LVII

Salai became Leonardo's prop in more than one sense. So the daily diary records. The walks are slowing and the younger man is holding up the weight of the older man, whilst they make painfully slow progress round the paths. Frequent rests in the shade on the garden benches are essential.

'You should not insist, master, on walking every day. It is not necessary.'

'It is vital to my mood.'

'You are making yourself more ill.'

'It is a diversion from the fussing of others in the house. I need more time to reflect on what I have achieved. Regrettably so little finished.'

This last phrase is scribbled across the corner of a sheet from the Book, that Salai must have later stored in this package:

259

br.72

In the reflection of a mirror do we see the hopeful face of the artist, staring onto a blank canvas, believing that inspiration will fill it in completion.

But many evenings that face looks drawn with emptiness, the goodwill faded and the tenor of its master shaken with anxiety. Will the brushstrokes ever fall again in proper perspective and grace the sitter? Will those images ever pass the scrutiny of the patron?

For the untutored patron never is disposed to accept in full the talent of the artist without whom novelty in expression would fail. The giver is taken, and for a small sum at that, so that the artist is for ever kept the more impoverished and at their service.

In the margin a later note:

Salai, make of these possessions what you will. My lasting thoughts shall not be my works, but those of my family - with Melzi and Maturina beyond you most loved. It is they who have given me the greatest comfort, but you the greatest pleasure. Let no one deny us that, even though I have failed you.

Did this message get through in the event *post mortem?*

King François was also deeply troubled by the dangers to

Leonardo's health. The fall and late chill in the air posed threats that would not discomfort others, but the old man was clearly faltering. He gave a stream of instructions as to the supply of wood for fires, extra provisions and required the doctor to report twice daily as to the condition of the 'patient'.

'Provide every comfort for Messer Leonardo,' he wrote in a private order to the new Chamberlain, ' he may not be with us for much longer. Nothing that he requires is to be denied him.'

Now there was a constant stream of servants from the royal household, bringing gifts and food to Le Clos Lucé. Much of it Leonardo could not consume. Indeed he began to take to his bed at the slightest sign of tiredness, or prolong his stay there in the morning.

'It is too much to attack each day with the vigour I once had,' his complaint to Melzi. 'I leave the work to you. I am tired of the demands of invention, there is no more to be added to the detritus of my papers.'

'Nothing shall be wasted or lost, maestro. I shall list the folios and place them in the libraries of art, engineering, mechanics, anatomy and others. It will occupy me for many months, many years; I shall hope that you remain with me to complete the task.'

'Do not presume. Every man has his time and mine is elapsing.'

'We are close to achieving Flight. Stay with us in that regard.'

'The King is looking to exploit its advantage over attackers, but I would rather he concerned himself with its potential to ensure peace. In the end we are all chasing the elusive airs of peace. That is how it should be.'

Not everything was as it should be. In fact very little was. The realities of Leonardo's condition were not lost on the doctor, his retinue or the King. The ailments seemed all of a sudden to cluster, and succeed each other in quicker succession, until his frailty was in the mind as well as the body. It was no longer possible to conceal the physical decline that had been staved off for so long. His right hand had become useless and could no longer hold a paper, let alone a paintbrush to make any gestures on canvas.

'Try again tomorrow, sire,' Melzi's encouragement, but Leonardo was not fooled.

'It is time to draw a line. Behind that line was the summary of my gifts on canvas. Beyond it is a void, which I shall not fill. That is that.'

'You have never allowed a collapse in our endeavours. You must not accept such a concession now.'

'Melzi, you and the other pupils have matured in your skills. It is time for you to take over the baton. Complete the commission I have given you in the chapel, then each and every one of you is free to pursue your own art. Learn from me, but be not of me, for in your own expression will new and better things come forth. We are soon forgotten; register your mark and take a place within the band of artists. Let your paintings be the lasting expression of your spirit.'

The records of these conversations are not pursued in this folio, probably because they were leading nowhere other than the inevitable. Just as family and friends sit helplessly around a dying patient in hospital with little to say even after a full life, so Leonardo spent increasing hours of the day in bed, with well-wishers attempting to raise his spirits.

'They are beginning to annoy me,' is scribbled in a note.

The doctor's hovering presence also upset Leonardo. He knew more about the fault lines in his body as a result of his anatomical incisions and resented the quackery.

'Let him look after himself, and not trouble me; my faculties worsen after his ministrations. I will call him when there's a real need but not before. Salai, you stay instead.' Salai extended the personal attention to his master's needs. Though he could not mend the man, he could comfort his spirit and tend to the limbs.

'There is a happy and satisfied look on his face when I

care for him,' Salai reported to both Melzi and Maturina, unaware at that stage of the special letter of admission the dying man had prepared for him. Maybe Leonardo could not bring himself to disturb the young man's contented position, with a seat at the table. The moment for a full confession, which could have given him knowledge of his true father - that moment had passed. Salai already had one back in Vaprio. To confess openly at this last moment would leave the 'man-child' in a fraught situation. Leonardo decided to not disturb the touch and affection freely given by Salai.

A cryptic note, in shaky script, no longer even in the characteristic mirror-writing:

Le Clos Lucé, 26th March 1519

Take no offence from my mistakes, dearest Salai, given their honest intent. For had I known at first what I was to learn later, I should have acted in quite another manner. I faltered in giving recognition to my actions and to you. That hesitation took me past a declaration that only now will I admit in another place.

What Salai made of this enigmatic note is not known. There is no record of a response. Were he to read it he might have assumed that the old man was beginning to lose his mental powers, imagining all sorts of disasters, misjudgements and errors that no one else counted as material. Salai might have guessed that 'in another place' meant a location - maybe in Florence or Milan even, where some papers might still be stored, and not given the matter much thought.

Whoever was charged with sealing and keeping this

valuable information must have fulfilled their duty - and perhaps a promise not to pass it on to Salai until some time after Leonardo's death.

Could it be that they held on to it for too long or that Salai returned to Milan before the treasurer had found the moment to give it to him? Did this person keep it, fearful of what it might say, and then intending to find the right moment or means, either move away himself or even meet some fate that left it in his house, or a drawer where some other person returned it to the owner of this folio?

There is no trail of evidence. It came into this package, still sealed, the wax untouched, no markings or uneven streaks of remelting. The implication is clear. Salai may never have seen this document. He lived again in Milan, unaware, oblivious to his true parentage. The (adopted) parents of his youth passed away - and kept their silence too? In his interests.

All he had was the Book of Reflections. Leonardo's greatest gift.

br. 75

Let me say this - that I have not been ashamed of my own birth, nor least my mother, who was taken from me; a duty that stole her love for me from the sanctuary of her soul. My father may have believed in the course of his actions.

But he was mistaken, for to strip a child of its legitimacy, whilst only a bar to the professions, is to sever that love which sustains the spirit in times of difficulty. Then to divide his favours and fortune between only those that were in direct lineage - that was to steal from me the worth of my share.

He undertook to guide me in apprenticeship, but as a duty, not love, and that he should so discharge his responsibility was an act I cannot forgive.

My 'created family' - you have been the source of all my satisfaction for you have given without demand, you have shared rather than taken, have been loyal rather than self- interested, and we have enjoyed the greater love for that.

"Cecilia, Anna, Salai - you are all gathered in one place, in my heart." Reflections in the mirror, key characters in his life, hidden in the shadows, where he wanted to shelter them from the public gaze. So much else was subject to scrutiny, but those he wanted to protect, he could only do so through silence. No dairies, no inner revelations - until now, in these final documents. Too close to the deadline.

LVIII

The end of March 1519 left a frosty landscape and mood in Amboise. Jacques Artus, fully confirmed in the post of Chamberlain roamed the corridors of the chilled castle, his beady eyes shining into every dark corner of both building and courtiers. A steely silence lay over the Court. Everyone still felt that those next to them held a secret, but every enquiry produced nothing. No one could explain the chain of events that had led to his brother being found in the forest, and the entries in the ledger reflect this paranoia. All Italians in service remained under suspicion. Leonardo was tainted with doubt.

'I have no time to spend on political ambition.'

As Melzi was back from Milan and all funds stored safely, Leonardo turned his mind to ensuring his house was in order before it was too late.

'Do not be so sure of your demise,' Melzi annotated in the margin of a brief sick note from the royal doctor dated 28th March. 'Two services of valerian a week to be applied.'

Leonardo's reflections become more intimate, more personally directed. Introspective and attached to those around him, rather than the world at large. He felt he had issued enough teachings, essays and treatises. 'Time, Melzi, to put my house in order, we must finish the Will. No more hesitation or reluctance on your part.' The final preface was at hand:

Le Clos Lucé, April 1519

Be it known to all persons, present and to come, that at the Court of our Lord the King at Amboise before ourselves in person, Messer Leonardo da Vinci, painter to the King, at present staying at the place known as Cloux near Amboise, duly considering the certainty of death and the uncertainty of its time, has acknowledged and declared in the said court and before us that he has made according to the tenor of these presents, his testament and the declaration of his last will as follows.

And first he commends his soul to our Lord, Almighty God, and to the glorious Virgin Mary,

and to our Lord Saint Michael, to all blessed
angels and Saints male and female in Paradise.

Melzi's final compliance with his master's wishes was
triggered by the illness that was taking a firmer hold; Leonardo
also despaired of events at Court which kept the Italians under
constant suspicion. There had been too many accidents of fate
for him to take any more chances. The horizon was closing in
and he felt its cold edge approaching.

> Item: The said Testator desires to be buried
> within the church of St. Florentin at Amboise,
> and that his body shall be borne thither by the
> chaplains of the church.

> Item: That his body may be followed to the
> said church of St. Florentin by the collegium,
> that is to say by the rector and the prior, and
> also by their vicar and chaplains of the church
> of St. Denis at Amboise, also the Minors of the
> place; and before his body shall be carried to
> the said church this Testator desires that in the
> said church of St. Florentin three grand masses
> shall be celebrated by the deacon and sub-deacon
> and that on the day on which these three high
> masses are celebrated, thirty low masses shall
> also be performed at St. Gregory.

Melzi: 'It is with a heavy heart that I undertake this duty'.
Leonardo: 'You will inherit what little I have, in reward
for your stewardship.'
'None will inherit your gifts of discovery.'
'Others will follow and develop the power to make the
machines work. Much of my design is still on the page; my
flying machines could be as tethered to the ground for all the

distance we have achieved. No, Melzi, you and I must accept the limitations of our talents and let others take advantage to their benefit.'

'We should try once more to obtain lift from the ground, and prove Flight.'

'We shall. I have the King's agreement to a trial of our latest craft. Once the weather improves.'

The sewers of cloth and the carpenters had been hard at work, weaving a lighter canvas and slighter struts from soft wood to create a birdwing that increased the chances of pilot strength overcoming gravity. There is a sketch of the new dimensions of this craft on the page and it is clearly lighter. But time was running out.

The doctor's ledger of 4th April 1519 states:

> On this day, the Master Painter and Court Adviser, Messer Leonardo da Vinci suffered a relapse of the workings of his heart, that put us all in fear of the worst.

> Yet I am able to report that the application of our favoured valerian stimulated the soul to his advantage and the alarm was met by his return to our attendance within two days. Praise be to God.

No doubt there was much relief, and none more so than in King François, who made immediate arrangements to attend Leonardo with a renewed frequency.

'Let vespers be said here at his bedside, whilst this malady persists,' King François himself led the responses and prayers. Melzi and Salai also took turns morning and night to ensure a constant watch, cooling his fevered brow with a saline solution. Maturina remained at her post in the kitchen.

Salai: 'Master, keep the future in sight and be of good spirit. We cannot afford to lose you yet.'

> Item: The aforesaid Testator gives and bequeaths to Messer Francesco da Melzi, nobleman of Milan, in remuneration for his services and favours done to him in the past, each and all of the books the testator is at present possessed of, and the instruments and portraits appertaining to his art and calling as a painter.

> Item: The same Testator gives and bequeaths henceforth for ever to Baptista de Villanis one half, that is, the moiety of his garden, which is outside the walls of Milan, and the other half of the same garden to Salai his servant; in which garden aforesaid Salai has built and constructed a house which shall be and remain henceforth in all perpetuity the property of the said Salai, his heirs and successors; and this is in remuneration for the good and kind services which the said de Vilanis and Salai, his servants, have done him in the past times until now.

> Item: The said Testator gives to Maturina his waiting woman a cloak of good black cloth lined with fur, a bolt of woven cloth, and two ducats paid once only; and this likewise in remuneration for good services rendered to him in past times by the said Maturina.

Reward sufficient for her position? Or would this faithful matron simply be returned to her family in Vinci and fall into the arms of her peasant family? And would she talk through the warm summer evenings about the great man, embroidering her simple living with extravagant tales? No portrait of her survives, not even in his notebooks, nor is there any sketch roughed out in these letters. She has fallen into the same void as her master, with those two ducats clasped between worn hands. She had acted as a surrogate mother, a reflection of his own Caterina, a substitute for the maternal love from which he had been separated. She provided the food that kept him alive, whilst his mind concentrated on the great projects. A silent witness to the machinations of genius and Court life in Amboise, maintaining her station. Underpaid.

LIX

The thief was named as Gian Marco Trivulzio. A Milanese in exile, a Guelph, who had long been dispossessed of his property by Ludovico Sforza - ironically Leonardo's old patron. He had been in the entourage of Charles VIII of France in the 1490s, and thus was not suspect when he came to present his consideration on Leonardo's sickness.

He had propositions for King François of assistance in resurrecting the scheme for the Water Palace at Romorantin, which Leonardo had failed to develop. His offer was couched in terms of solicitous charm and obsequiousness – not at that point unusual in those begging potentially profitable assignments, and ranged across whole areas of constructional service with which he hoped to further this favoured cause of the royal ambition.

Trivulzio inned his group of craftsmen in the town, and had obtained an audience with the King alone. The propositions were discussed at length, but to the King it seemed with a somewhat vague degree of detail, and the reason for this suggested itself when a mention of Flight took the talk onto a higher plane. Indeed the Romorantin proposals were too hurriedly let slip, as the conversation turned to this special project.

'I have built a team of engineers and craftsmen that could usefully assist the old man's attempts at Flight.'

'How did you know of our progress in that regard?' the King interrupted.

'We heard that his models had been brought from Florence. I assume he has not turned his back on that ambition?'

'The matter is in my interest – for France alone.'

'In which my hopes of future service lie.'

'I already have an abundance of Italian skills here. There are some at Court who say we are overprovided with talents from Lombardy and Tuscany.'

'I understand their pride.'

'Their concern. Whilst it is to my liking to have so many artists and artisans here, there is a reluctance to employ engineers, those capable of use on the battlefield – if they can be seen to be linked to an enemy.'

'I have been exiled, and favoured by your country.'

'But miss your true base?'

'I should want to help Leonardo.'

That Trivulzio broached the subject of Flight too readily implied that word was spreading on the possibility of successful flight. He had been based in Narbonne, some way to the south, healing his political wounds and slowly re-establishing himself in society with funds from his family, who wanted him kept out of the way of Milan, lest he corrupt their advancement.

'In what way can you help then?' the King opened, revealing nothing.

'In the engineering of machines. It is a subject I have come to educate myself in, and gathered skilled craftsmen to my side. There is much that will be soon done to improve our lives, mechanics that can move us around more swiftly, and take the strain of work from us in many ways, and most interesting of all in the manner of winged machines, if that can be conquered. I would like to impart our experience to Ser Leonardo.'

It was Jacques Artus as ever who smelt a rat. He discovered that the group in attendance of Trivulzio, waiting in the town, was an unusually large number of advisers, artists and craftsmen. He became concerned at the King's willingness to let this visitor and members of his team visit Le Clos Lucé.

'How can we keep an adequate eye on them all?' he asked Melzi.

'They will tire him out.'

'I agree, and will limit the number that can go.'

The group of four that did so acted strangely. Having arrived at the bedside, two of these men quickly stood down, affecting apologies for crowding in on a sick man, and expressing only the briefest of condolences, asked to leave the chamber and walk around the manor whilst Gian Marco made his concerns heard.

It was a twist of good fortune that Melzi sighted them looking into the stables and spending a lot of time in the area in which all the flying-machine drawings and designs were kept. He crossed the lawn and kept a discreet observation from behind an oak tree. Normally there would be craftsmen in the stable studio, but the latest machine was already completed and awaiting the trial that Leonardo hoped to execute, so they were absent at this time. It struck Melzi that the visitors were in the building for an overlong time and that they should have been more than satisfied with curiosity.

'Gentlemen, can I help you with any questions?"

'We were simply intrigued by what we had heard of Messer Leonardo's success in Flight. Were it to be true, if he did succeed, it would alter much on the battlefields of Italy and France.'

'He has not succeeded - not yet.'

'When do you expect the test to prove his propositions?'

'That remains to be seen. He is not well enough to

command the situation at present.'

'Do you believe it will work?'

'It is not for me to say. No one but him can design these craft or judge their capabilities.'

'Most interesting.'

The men drifted back to the manor house and waited in the entrance lobby for Gian Marco to finish his visit. When he appeared at the door, they turned to depart. As they did so, one tripped on the steps and from his cloak fell a roll of draughtsman's paper. On it Leonardo's designs. They were immediately arrested. Their death warrant is dated the 10th April.

LX

The attempted theft of his designs startled Leonardo. It was a shock to find the enemy on his doorstep.

The King's view was that this added urgency to the fulfilment of the great man's dream. Extra guards were placed at both the gateway into Le Clos Lucé and also outside the stable block which housed the drawings and models.

codex volante.cxx

> Wind pressure is not constant above and below the wings of birds. The vacuum under causes lift and it is this function that must guide the shape of our better design in the curve of our own wings and their cloth.

Then we might match the vigour of our pilot's strength to the greater effect of his craft's better design, and conserve his energies for a more prolonged endeavour in flight.

The issues kept mounting. Even the pilots lent their advice, constantly proposing modifications to the harnesses that might allow them to more easily use the flaps. They also offered advice on the gearing of the pedals and cranks, entering into the spirit of new equations being mastered in a struggle for success that had fired their imagination as much as Leonardo's.

'We are so near success that we must not waver in our practice or convictions', the leading candidate for the next flight stated firmly.

'Nor risk your lives unnecessarily,' Leonardo had countered.

The challenges began to be seen as a breakthrough, specific demonstrations that science was competing with God on new terms – and might win. Inevitably this raised anxieties amongst the Church and the King's religious advisers, but he was not to be deterred.

'God will approve of our actions. Control of the air will not only reduce the deaths on the battlefield, it will force those mercenaries and warmongers who too liberally set out to destroy other cities to pause in their rashness.'

No one dared mention his own passion for invading his neighbours. If they had, he would no doubt have pointed out his capacity to rule benignly and foster the arts and crafts so amply displayed in the Renaissance itself. In his time he was to design new museums and palaces, and set the Louvre on a totally new path to grandeur.

For Leonardo the bursts of energy that his team of carpenters and weavers applied to each fresh design were stimulating and distracted him from his own fragility. He was able to transpose the thrust of his ideas quickly since everyone felt an obligation to help him achieve the miracle of Flight.

By association they all felt part of a winning team and long hours were no deterrent, nor did they seek extra wages.

Le Clos Lucé became a hive of industry contrasting with the quiet airs it normally encountered. Instead of treating the craftsmen as a disturbance, Leonardo specifically encouraged them to work from the early morning to sunset, and found the sounds of planing, nailing and hammering sweet music to his ears.

'Their energy alone will make these machines fly,' was his flippant remark to Melzi.

'All the more power to their endeavour. I have never seen such industry from these workers. They are barely stopping for ten minutes at midday, when they have been used to a clear hour of rest.'

In recognition of his pained and useless body Leonardo drew a last set of grotesque figures.

> A man bent within his agonies is crippled and anxious to the extent that he cannot hide it. Observe the tortuous curve of his body and the grimace of his face and learn from these manifestations of his agony in the drawing of his condition. Fear not baring the truth.

'Master, you are becoming melancholy before it is necessary to do so,' Maturina had unguardedly observed when she found a great pile of these terrifying drawings on Leonardo's side table. She felt obliged to distract him from concentration on this subject matter, which she saw was an obsession with his own frailty. It had become a new tendency for the old man to delve into his stack of sketches and shuffle them into contrasting sets of figures. She could see, as Melzi too would when he pursued his obligations as his master's librarian, that there was a fatalistic progression from the cheerful images of youth at one end to the hideous and distorted creatures now slipping off the drawing-board.

Leonardo knew well from experience these grotesques were not exaggerations on life. It was still a coarse existence for those outside royalty and privilege. Many entered soldiery to earn their keep, but were often mutilated and joined the sick and wasted amongst the poor. The diseased also wore their sickness in clear evidence, and he faithfully drew their taught faces, their skinflint bodies, the women's haggard looks, their wretched clothes.

In his anatomical studies he portrayed the guts of men and women openly. In between the entrails of humanity however were brilliant sketches of the unborn child in the womb. Only the reality that this had been sourced from a death in childbirth brought poignancy to the illustration.

LXI

The woman's body was to be found at the foot of the battlements, her skull cracked open on the flagstones with the impact of a fall from over one hundred feet, the brain scattered, blood from her mouth staining the ground. The red gash on her face matched the brilliant cinnabar court dress she wore; the ruby jewellery that still sparkled from her throat remained unstolen by the first dawn tradesmen who came across the broken body. No one dared touch her, fearing association. 'Suicide, it had to be suicide', the first deduction.

In this secret package however a Warrant and report of its execution. Why does it exist? Perhaps the guards would not act without such a protective authorisation, maybe they or the Queen never expected it to see the light of day, or be purloined by a guilt-ridden member of the Court. It might have served as a bargaining chip for some later favour if threatened or stolen to order by one of Leonardo's retinue, with the intention that a message could be passed back to her family. A death certificate. Proof of her demise. Attached to it is the detail of her death. No suicide.

The Commander's report:

> Under instructions, and the release provided by the warrant, the Guard duly summoned four soldiers on the night of the 20th April and removed the prisoner *(sic)* from her confinement in the east wing and cautioned her to follow orders given to the full extent of their demands.
>
> That she should accompany the guard in the dark to the western tower and face her judgement. The prisoner refused to move, fearing for her life and began to cry out, such that we smothered her cries, bound and gagged her for the moment.
>
> In the struggle that continued she attempted to resist any movement from her quarters, and a blow was administered to her head to silence these protests. This only served to raise her alarm and it was necessary to pull the sleeves of her dress down over her arms to fully restrain the body. There were no means to place a night coat and hood over as instructed.
>
> On reaching the tower, we carried the prisoner to the battlement, a prayer was said, as instructed, to calm her - with no effect, and it became urgent to execute the plan of release from the wall as authorised.

In the town the Certificate of Death remains reported as 'suicide'. The Contessa's body was collected eventually by the poor people's undertaker, as only he put payment ahead of any other consideration.

Townspeople walked by on the other side all morning, gossiping discreetly, trudging past with a quick glance down. The muffled wheels of the hearse moved later through the narrow streets in silence, until the draped remains passed under an arch into the courtyard beside the cemetery of St. Denys. A short journey that was to end in an unmarked grave.

br. 66

Reflect on the body and compare it with the spirit. For what are we but a corpular assembly of parts that function to Man's purpose, but not God's will.

I have examined the body, but found not enough in anatomy to explain the whole, for the parts can be seen in motion, the sinews stretched, the blood in flow, but this knowledge is of itself insufficient.

The human body is shaped by its spirit, and the artist must penetrate deeper, expressing actions which suggest the motives that incite that person to act. Faces and gestures must reveal frames of mind, and the painter must reverse this process, and by constructing a body, give expression to its spirit.

And as man turns to the sun for warmth and

sustenance so do the plants of the forest and fields. A leaf always turns its upper side towards the sky so that it may better be able to receive over its whole surface the dew which drops gently from the atmosphere. These leaves are so distributed on the plants that one covers another as little as possible.

The rings on the cross-section of the branch show the number of its years, and the greater or smaller width of these rings show which years were wetter and which drier.

And in drawing man, the hands and arms in all their actions must display the intention of the mind.

A good painter has two chief objects to paint, Man and the intention of his soul. The former is easy, the latter hard, because he has to represent it by the attitudes and movements of the limbs. The knowledge of these should be acquired by observing the dumb, because their movements are more natural than those of any other class of persons.

Every action must necessarily be expressed in movement. To know and to will are two operations of the human mind. To discern, judge and to reflect are also actions of this mind. Our body is subject to heaven, and heaven is subject to the spirit.

Old men ought to be represented with slow and heavy movements, their legs bent at the knees, when they stand still, and their feet parallel and apart; bending low with the head leaning forward, and their arms but little extended.

Can anything have been missed in his observations? Leonardo lived ultimately with an excess of knowledge that he had himself amassed down the years, projecting conclusions, theories, essays. All this work, this driving spirit had prolonged his own life, accumulating years of vigorous activity, at least twenty over the average span.

Now he could set aside the life of the Contessa. Not of his retinue, but of his homeland.

For the Queen too, a clean sheet.

LXII

Leonardo's conversion to God gathered pace, and the clues become clear. One week after assigning his Will, the sense of his mortality had brought him closer to adopting the Christian faith. In the face of his 'scientific' enquiries he had never believed in the Church's preachings, as so much was clearly motivated by its need to hold power over rulers and the populace. Most of his inventions altered this balance; his investigations revealed more solid truths about the human form and the soul than any sermon from the pulpit, let alone Pope. The Holy See was a political wing, a random patronage of the ruling family, handed out with little regard for Christ or his beliefs.

This reflection is included in the folio, and is in the characteristic mirror-writing, so must have been written some time before he lost the means to write himself:

br. 78

Regarding Faith - is the question: upon what is it based? Is it the fear of the unknown with which we are born, or is it the creative invention of Man's agile mind?

Consider this - nothing written in the gospels is proven by experience of the world now. For where there was commandment, it has been broken with impunity. Where there was injunction to act at risk of peril, Man has survived to repeat his mistakes time and time again.

So where can Faith find its base? When the Church exploits its advantage to disavow the people, justice is lost and with it the confidence of all but its endowed attendants.

Fear will contain the many who face away from reality, but their avoidance cannot substitute for a true analysis of the world as Nature has built it.

In Nature we see the true powers of creation; for are the birds not innocent in their flight, do they not enjoy a freedom in the skies that defies Man?

I am not persuaded of God. The creatures on earth and its natural wonders have been borne of a wider universe of which we have yet an insufficient knowledge.

But Melzi records a change of heart:

28th April (1519)

> With the light fading on his horizon, he slept
> at night with the angels, and their communion
> seemed to press in on his own convictions.

'Master, I am glad you have opened your mind to the
possibilities of Faith.'
'Possibilities.'

br.83

> Preserve all that is best in your life and pass it
> on to the next generation with the wisdom that
> you have accumulated. Count your blessings
> and consider them alone, for the loss and
> dangers, which have assailed you, have passed
> and shall not show in the account.

> And, if like me, there were persons who
> created the magic in your being, take their
> spirit with you into the next life, for there -
> should God exist - will you find them again
> and the love that escaped you will be open to
> your longing.

> When I am gone, take my works and analyse
> them to the full extent that you wish, but
> consider them the daybooks upon which my

dues were placed. However, leave me with the
love of those I have enwrapped in my heart and
do not deny me the warmth of their embrace.

    The King now added his private priest to the assembly
quartered at Le Clos Lucé. On this last day of April, communion
was held in the tiny oratory chapel, and the first mention of
Leonardo taking the wafer and wine is noted. The Lord's prayer
was said, but to the Creed there was silence from Leonardo. Salai
mentions this fact in the daybook, as a particular resistance of his
master. "He did not agree he had yet accepted those beliefs that
should make him submit to this ordeal." But the King was
disturbed by this, more so than the priest who may have had his
own doubts hidden within. 'Leonardo, your God awaits you, you
must not disaffect Him now.'

    'Yes, Your Majesty, but I am not ready to meet Him.'

br.85

The ages of darkness are finished and the
printed words will pass across to the mass of
peoples in due time, so that the mysteries of
nature, the universe and machines shall
broaden knowledge to the point that church
and politician can no longer hold sway
through the ignorance of others. Then I trust
the world shall find the peace that it seeks.
Proof, not faith is the empirical truth that shall
make this possible.

    'You have painted a sufficiency, your works will be
acknowledged,' King François had insisted when Leonardo

retired to his bedroom that day. Leonardo made a sudden attempt to get up from the bed, but immediately fell back, exhausted with this simple effort.

'God has not shown me the mercy to regain my strength.'

'Rest awhile further, and await the warmth of the day, Ser Leonardo. There is time yet to be tempted with further invention. Flight is within our grasp.'

Maturina altered her daily routine as well. It was a major effort to rouse her old master in the morning, and she would call on Salai to help with the lifting and cleansing duties. Indeed Salai had taken to a couch in the ante chamber to the bedroom.

'There is no sleep. It is pitiful to see our master ebb away from the robust giant we knew.' Food was more difficult to consume. Maturina took at first to soups, rather than meats, as digestion became slower. As the warmth of Spring finally arrived and the frosty mornings disappeared she served cool collations, iced vichyssoise and fruit taken from winter storage.

The Court, used to Leonardo's commissions for balls or masquerades, missed his presence too. An understanding overcame the royal courtiers that they might not see him again walking the battlements with the King, rolled paper and chalk in hand, noting down some brief for another magical entertainment. Word spread through the town as well. People who had taken to walking at a respectful distance behind Leonardo sensed a gap in their ranks. He had always acted as one of them, rather than a royal, and for that they had adopted him with respect.

They had found him at the heart of every inquisitive interest, making some observation to illustrate the balance of wind and rain or commenting on the abilities of the birds to float so easily above them. He would explain their use of the breeze and updraughts on the hills to anyone who would listen. He was spreading knowledge - that source of wisdom which he felt would release ordinary people from the misguided magic of the Church.

The Court itself was loaded with the privileged few, their fortunes won by soldiering for the royal cause, or submission in service. But even to them Leonardo's discoveries were a source of inspiration, and King François used him as a touchstone for a greater assembly of gifted artists, designers, masons and builders, who converged on Amboise at the royal command.

The King was ambitious in extending the Court and his patronage of the arts. Chambord was taking decades to construct, but it would in time fulfil a magnificent dream as the largest chateau of its age. The thirty kilometres of walls around its hunting forest to form the largest estate in Europe.

'Leonardo has been the fuel for my ambitions,' the King said to visiting dignitaries. 'He inspired the dreams of the possible, and I never found him short of design whatever the challenge. The world will be a smaller place once he has gone.'

Indeed. Poor Melzi was to struggle for the rest of his life to assemble the ideas, the thousands of loose sheets into *codices*, only for them to be abandoned in lofts for a further two hundred years.

'Master, stay with us longer.' Melzi's desperate appeal.

But each day now there were alarms as Leonardo struggled to maintain his spirits. A flow of visitors called at Le Clos Lucé, but he did not want to see them; time to think was now more important than idle chatter. Whilst no new further invention fell onto the page, he became more reflective than ever.

br.87

> The human form is indeed a most mysterious body. It can be dissected and analysed and each member ascribed a place in the physiology, but the sum of these parts does not explain the whole.

For the indefinable spirit which creates and fortifies the soul is unexplained. A sense of preservation exists, but does not further the argument as to why Man should so desire to continue in the face of so much failure.

For myself I can reckon the strengths and weaknesses of my body and performance as an artist, yet nothing satisfies me in this regard. The praise of others does not count for my own judgement. Where they see success, I see failure. Were the records to have been kept with accuracy, they would measure little that has been good and much that has not passed acceptance.

'Not true, master,' Salai has observed.

'Bless you, my son, but your judgement is influenced by position, rather than clarity. My peers do not agree, and tout their work as evidence.'

'They are jealous.'

'But winning the commissions.'

'Your work is regarded with distinction.'

'Salai, much of it will be forgotten. It is on paper, but Melzi must order it, or it will become leaves on the rubbish heap in autumn.'

But had Leonardo used the affectionate term 'my son' deliberately, trying to build up to a last minute confession, the admission he was having trouble declaring? The knowledge written down and sealed in the Letter. He must have been afraid of its consequences.

LXIII

There is one letter each from Leonardo to Melzi, Salai and Maturina with instructions that they be opened in the event of his death. Thanksgivings he was unable to say in person; or which he preferred to be outside the public gaze of his will.

'He knew his time was coming.'

'Yes. His appetite left him and he knew what that meant.'

br.88

The life of anything whatsoever that takes nourishment continually dies and is constantly renewed; because nourishment can only enter in those places where the preceding nourishment is exhausted, and if it is exhausted it no longer has life.

And unless you supply nourishment equivalent to that which has departed, life will fail in its vigour, and if you deprive it of its nourishment the life is entirely destroyed. But if you restore as much as is destroyed day by day, then as much of the life is renewed as is consumed; just as the light of the candle is formed by the nourishment given to it by the liquid of this candle which light continually renews by swift succour from beneath as much as it consumes in dying above; and in dying changes from a brilliant light into murky smoke; and this death is continuous as long as the nourishment continues; and the smoke continues as long as the nourishment continues; and in the same instant the whole light is dead when it ceases.

Le Clos Lucé, 1519

Daybook for Friday 29th April

"Leonardo was attended by the doctor twice in the day and once in the night. There was increasing concern as to the vigour of Messer Leonardo, whose will to eat has departed him, and it was only with the greatest encouragement of his loyal household that he was persuaded to sup from the bowl of vegetable soup and eat fruit, sufficient to rekindle his alertness."

Melzi has added: 'Given the full life that the master has carried with such determination and invention, it pained us all to see another weaker being form within the once powerful body we had so much admired. On this day he did not at first recognise the King, who came especially to support his courage. This mistake angered him greatly and it was only the intervention and persistence of His Majesty that Ser Leonardo should not blame himself, that he was conditioned to be calm, and make a simple apology.'

The King stayed all afternoon, choosing to read to Leonardo from the latest advances in mathematics - the recent conclusions and equations of Luca Paccioli, with whom Leonardo had worked ten years before.

'His sums shall add to the advance of knowledge,' the faint approval of the great man.

'It is a persistent advance in which you have played your part well.'

Daybook for Saturday 30th April

"Messer Leonardo rallied, and the day being filled with the brilliance of the first summer sun, insisted upon removal to the terrace, whence he observed most particularly the small birds amongst the rose beds, and the doves in their loft."

He observed: 'There will always be life on earth as long as some have the freedom of the skies. Mark well their joy as they float so effortlessly upon the breeze. For they look down upon Man and his busy preoccupation with the minutiae of life, and wonder at our incompetence.'

Salai, who was charged with his care at midday, took Leonardo in a wheelchair, despite his initial protestations, around the large garden and along the winding paths of the woods within the boundary walls. They followed beside the river stream flowing gently over the low weirs to slow the current.

'It was of the greatest pleasure for the master to escape the confines of the bedroom and journey round this haven which is his natural refuge from the world outside. A remedy of greater effect than of the doctors hovering at the bedside. He was much relieved to be away from their fussing ministrations. We stayed as long in the garden as the sun persisted, before returning to the kitchen, where Maturina had prepared scones and a warm brew.'

Daybook for Sunday 1st May

"The night has not been good to Ser Leonardo. He is in much pain, but the doctors cannot specify the cause nor does he himself have a view. His analytical skills have deserted him, as has his capacity to take food, other than in the smallest quantity. The King was advised and arrived at noon, coming with despatch from Blois with Queen Claude, where they had been in discussion with the masons of the chateau, as to the large works of modifying the assembly chambers.

Maturina attended, whilst His Majesty contrived to restore the spirit which had flourished for so long. All others from the Court were dismissed, despite their sympathies, so that His Majesty could talk alone with his fallen genius.

"Towards evening, as the stars filled the night sky, Leonardo requested a reading of his observations on the earth and planets, to remind us all of our place in the universe - and how small our existence is."

> If you look at the stars without their rays, you will see these stars to be so minute that it would seem as though nothing could be smaller; it is in fact the great distance which is the reason for their diminution, for many of them are very many times larger than the star which is the earth with the water.

> Think then, what this star of ours would seem like at so great a distance, and then consider how many stars might be set in longitude and latitude between these stars, which are scattered through this dark expanse.

A darkness in the unknown heavens and this reading? Did he sense that night he was on the brink of departure, his intuition working fully but the body irretrievably weakened?

Daybook for Monday 2nd May

Salai, who had been sleeping close by in the anteroom was woken first by a cry from his master as dawn broke, and hurried to the bedside. Leonardo's hands were cold, and the breathing slow, but he massaged the limbs left outside the blanket to restore circulation.

"He was much relieved to calm his master, and called Maturina to bring some hot camomile to invigorate the system. This had the best of effects, and a brief smile was seen to pass across the face of Messer Leonardo."

'My son, you have not lost me yet.'

It was to be a short reprieve. King François came as soon as the morning assembly of the Court allowed, and once again was proud to sit at the bedside. He held Leonardo's hand and read from a book of prayer, with such persuasion that the old agnostic found himself in his final moments confirmed in the beliefs of the Christian message and acknowledged this conversion to his royal patron.

'God shall protect and care for you, Ser Leonardo, since He can forgive your doubting, and seeing what you have delivered of His mysteries and by bringing a greater light into man's understanding of His works, then He shall have patience with your soul and ensure that in the next life it flourishes as strongly as it has in this.'

'I shall trust in His judgement.'

In the afternoon, as the King read further from the bible, he felt the grip of Leonardo's hand weaken, and as the word of God spread across the room, the last words that ever passed Leonardo's lips rose quietly in competition.

'It is time for God to take me on that journey which I have so often anticipated. Let Him be in command of my soul.'

The afternoon guard noted that the sun went down as the life slipped from Leonardo. The King stayed for one further hour, in prayer of thanks for the great man, whom he had been privileged to sustain at Amboise.

'Ser Leonardo, you have fulfilled your duty.'

The silence of death descended upon Le Clos Lucé, and for days the body of its greatest incumbent was laid, resting in an open coffin, for his household to mourn. No one wanted to let him go, as the void in their lives would be so great.

Melzi, burdened with the weight of responsibility

dithered in his organisation of the funeral, until King François took charge. The service was to be attended by the leading members of the Court, and Leonardo was to be treated with full honours.

It is unclear on which day the funeral took place, but it was conducted with those 'items' in the Will respected. What Leonardo would not have known is that the long procession, headed by the King and Queen was the subject of all the townspeople's respect. They lined the streets once the flat cart, upon which the flagged coffin lay, had reached the bottom of the hill from Le Clos Lucé. Here King François and Queen Claude stepped down from their mounts, and walked down from the ramparts of the chateau and took their place at the head of the procession. The Dauphin followed immediately, carrying a small wooden model of Leonardo's latest flying machine.

Next Jacques Artus and the leading courtiers took station. In silence, apart from the crunch of the wooden cart wheels on the gritty cobbles, this ribbon of sad souls wended its slow way along the main streets to the riverside church of St. Florentin. The small church hosted the sixty poor men and the royal family, with Leonardo's household as the chosen few beside the priest and supplicants that could be accommodated within. The windows were thrown open so that the many remaining mourners outside could share in the words of blessing and gratitude for this life.

The wish of Leonardo to be buried in the grounds of the church could not be immediately followed - the reason is also unclear. Instead the body was placed in a vault until the burial could be honoured.

In the silent days that followed, three letters in this package that he wrote to Melzi, Maturina and Salai, were distributed. Melzi had been instructed to keep them until after his master's death and obeyed these instructions to the letter.

Amboise, April, 1519

Francesco, dearest friend:

This letter of appreciation for all your good works in my service is to assure you of my sincere gratitude. For you have never sought to count the cost to your own place in life, and have given all so that you might be with me in my endeavours.

This note shall reach your eyes after I am gone, and lest you feel remorse let me persuade you to bear up and be proud of what we have achieved together.

Ensure that you finish the frescoes in our beloved oratory, for Le Clos Lucé should carry your imprint as much as mine. I would not wish those that follow to be in ignorance of your talents, which I have nourished not created.

You have become the master of my works through the diligence of your study with me. By your chosen duty and my express will, you should deal with my papers as you think best.

Think not of it as a burden for your friendship is greater than that of a mere pupil and in finding favour with me I trust I have in turn given substance to you.

Man will criticise and seek to destroy what I have written, but you should withstand any interference. It is my wish solely that you bring order into the chaos of this residue, and that once so composed you may use these papers to such advantage as your judgement allows.

Be witness to the love and affection between us, now stated so that no one shall abuse you in any regard. For that family which left me to my own devices has had its small reward deriving out of kinship. But it is to you and Salai that I turned when affection was needed, and you met me with open arms.

There is one truth I have not admitted to, and that shall be at the discretion of Salai to offer up or keep to himself. If he appears to be troubled, then comfort him, but do not seek any explanation unless it is offered.

We live our lives in the open, and we have done so more than most in our travels in pursuit of commissions from Milan, Florence and Rome. But heed this, none of that is greater than that which we have shared in the warmth of the fireside here in Amboise under the safe patronage of our generous King.

My will is my last testament, and within it your instructions, but reckon more that you kept me company in the dark days and I account for this loyalty beyond all else.

Now you must pass the other letters to Salai

and Maturina. She will need your help for it to be read to her. Ensure their safe delivery and I shall be at peace.

Io Leonardo

Given in truth by my hand, April 1519 at Le Clos Lucé.

Letter to Salai

Le Clos Lucé, April 1519

By the hand of Francesco shall you receive this sealed letter, and it shall be yours alone to keep in the privacy of your heart.

For in this do I make a full confession. I shall accept your condemnation for not exposing the position between us before. The reason: my fear of losing the love that grew in nature between us. For how could I raise our affection more than it has already achieved?

In truth I utter the words - my son - in explanation and a love that has no boundaries. For before I met your mother I saw in Cecilia Gallerani all of heaven's angels, but that her innocence had been bought by the ruler of the day.

When it was not to be, my anger was such that I tore myself from reality and responsibility in frustration and took another woman to me in revenge for my loss. That woman, Anna, was your real mother and I her partner in your creation. As I did not know of my fatherhood, but in duty accepted it, I swore to her that I should look after you, keeping our secret from your adopted parents and binding myself to you.

In those years when none understood my tolerance of your improvident behaviour, I never spoke of this for fear it would displace you in their trust, and they be hatefully envious of you. In this did I mistake your welfare for mine? Forgive me for my weakness. It seemed prudent at the time. Now much has passed and we have enjoyed our love without restraint and I wish that you remember me without admonition.

Salai, should you feel cheated of your youth, take pity on my misjudgement, and count those blessings that passed between us, and those favours we alone enjoyed. Do not attach blame to Francesco, for he is only the bearer of these letters, and unaware of their truths.

Love has many expressions, but for you within me lies those of the greatest persuasion. I shall carry these to the next life and await you there, and wish for your indulgence.

Leonardo, pater.

Given this 12th day of April, 1519.

Letter to Maturina

Le Clos Lucé, April 1519

My faithful servant, Maturina

You have followed me with humility and service beyond reproach and my gratitude is expressed in the gift within my Will. At the King's direction, it has been commanded that you shall continue in service to the Court for as long as you shall determine, and have security of lodging at Le Clos Lucé, or the Hôtel de Dieu with your expenses covered to the end of your days, if you so wish.

Io Leonardo

Given this 13th day of April 1519.

LXIV

The relevant ledger in the archives for the week of 9th May 1519 is missing. The funeral is recorded elsewhere, but the only record of the last moments of his experimentation with Flight are in this package. Perhaps the archivist gave the book to Melzi to enter the technical details of a subject for which there was no knowledgeable scribe.

Or was the ledger stolen, by Artus? As an act of retribution, a mischief undertaken in the safe knowledge that the great man's influence with the King was no longer extant?

He could wipe the official record with impunity - and possibly in revenge for his brother's death.

This package however denies him that desire, for someone has gone to great trouble to describe events on the hilltops to the east of the Chateau d'Amboise - the very place where the previous attempts to Flight had occurred.

'Ser Leonardo was no longer of this world, but sensing that one more effort in the application of his new wings and gears might allow the pilot to break through with success, we resisted the protestations of others, and determining to fulfil his ambition, did authorise the test.

The birdwing construction was now much easier to manage, being of the newly imported balsa-like wood, a fraction of the earlier models, and there was more than one volunteer for the rite of passage.

The caravan of attendants and many townspeople, sufficiently warned of this gallant attempt, walked slowly up the steep hillsides in procession behind our landau. Ahead was the craft itself, the body of which the selected pilot had proudly strapped to his body. The light wings - and the new device of a tail fin - had been brought by his pupils Francesco Melzi, Salai Giacamo and his servant Baptista di Villanis. In a wicker sedan was borne his faithful housekeeper, Maturina. The King being absent, those in Leonardo's favour at Court assembled in a place to one side, uncertain as to their intrusion upon the event. The young Dauphin stood proudly to the fore.

The preparation of the machine was simple, so gifted was the design and once the pilot had positioned himself with confidence on a firm spot at the cliff edge, so the assistants bound the wings and fin with ease to the central body. All was ready.

We abated our anxieties and fell silent in the face of this moment and the generous breeze needed to support the maestro's intentions.

There were some present who expected a further tragedy, but the confidence of the pilot was for all to see. He made no special prayer for his safety, nor looked anxiously around. In his mind only was Leonardo.

We waited perhaps for ten minutes, a mass of silent bodies, still in expectation, until the breeze strengthened and pressed against the pilot and the craft's wings, rendering his footing unsteady.

Then with the consent of a white flag in the Dauphin's hand, the pilot suddenly ran forward, slanting the wings as he had been shown in the flight of birds, and at the edge brought his legs sharply up into the footholds of the gearing, and began to pedal rigorously as the whole soared into the emptiness of space.

We truly expected his fall, but the new

weighting fell within his power to carry the machine forward - and more importantly - he managed to exert control from the fin in such a manner that he brought the craft first upwards and then sideways, so as to manoeuvre it to his will - just as Ser Leonardo had predicted.

For some time we could not see how this flight could be sustained, until the pilot proved his control by circling once more in superiority to gliding, and heading out towards the river, then to our clear vision, carried on across the mighty Loire, over the north bank, the houses of the island and the hamlet further, until he was a speck on the horizon, disappearing beyond the tall trees of the forest...'

Another hand has attached a footnote:

Let the record show that the pilot flew five and one third kilometres to the hamlet of Monsartin, and that it was many hours before he would deign to return with us, because of his desire to embrace the feelings of freedom that he had encountered.

LXV

Two last notes pinched together in this package:

> 12 August 1519. Entry in the register of St.
> Florentin at Amboise: 'In the cloister of this
> church was buried M. Leonard de Vincy, noble
> Milanese, first painter, engineer and architect
> of the King, State mechanist, and sometime
> director of painting to the Duke of Milan.'

For three months his body must have lain in the vault of the church before he was interred. It is not known why, but there is one record of the burial service. The King and Queen were elsewhere on State business, yet the Dauphin took steps to be there. At the graveside he made one last gesture, not of patronage, but of the friendship and devotion to the invention that Leonardo had inspired in him too.

As the coffin was lowered into the ground, the young boy brought out a small wooden model of a flying-machine that Leonardo had made for him, and placed it on the top of the casket as it came level with the ground. Then he gathered up loose soil, as is tradition, and scattered it over the model and coffin. He knew that without this genius, the further progress of Flight would be halted. The world would move on, but his maestro had disappeared into the void.

Amboise. April 1519

> Be it known to all persons, present and to
> come, that at the court of our Lord the King
> at Amboise before those present living at the

place known as Le Clos Lucé, who have travelled with me in duty to this haven, that I commend my soul to Him above, duly considering the certainty of death and the comfort it may bring, that they despair not.

For the pattern of life shall continue and man shall learn more as to his welfare and conduct and shall benefit as he may wish from my humble investigations.

But the greatest bond in life is love, and that should receive a fuller understanding and be the basis of righteousness in all dealings between man and woman. That is the great mystery which can provide the logic for our being in this world, and it is more substantial than the creation of machines or weapons.

Dreams are the passionate release of our souls, and in them is the spirit contained by which we should persevere and fulfil our lives, so that in death we will have acquitted our dues and not been envious of others.

In pace, Io Leonardo

POSTSCIPT

Melzi spent years sorting and cataloguing Leonardo's works. In time they passed down his family generations until lack of interest had them sold off and dispersed. Salai returned to Milan, married, but met an early death from a crossbow in 1546, the disposal of his effects unknown.

Cecilia Gallerani was displaced in the affections of 'Il Moro' - Ludivico Sforza, ruler of Milan, first by Lucrezia Crevelli, and then on account of his political marriage to Beatrice D'Este. Being granted estates at Saranno, Cecilia was married off to a Count Bergamini. Leonardo's portrait of her she finally gave to the insistent Isabella D'Este, who long had hoped for a similar portrait by the maestro. Following Cecilia's death in 1536, the picture 'disappeared' in the Milan area, but was bought much later in 1800 by the Polish Prince Czartoryski, which explains its current presence, after many wartime moves, in the museum in Cracow.

This package of Letters has brought issues of its own. Not only did it clearly have a value, some deemed it priceless. Marco, translator, proposed that it be sold directly to a private collector but as it provided payment in kind through the privilege of having it to uncover, hold, translate and read, it was demonstrably wrong for the Letters to disappear into the black hole of private ownership once more. In consideration that we held the translations and thus the meanings of these fragments, I took it upon myself to return the package to its proper ownership, its spiritual home - Vinci.

Typically the chosen day was one that the *Bibliotecca* was closed, but it was possible to approach one of the museums. The Curator was on holiday but the ticket collector met with

304

my request to store the package in the safe. I watched to see it was locked away securely.

At the small terrace shop, with its dedicated mix of gifts for sale - books, trinkets, even caged songbirds and Leonardo memorabilia, I made one more impulsive decision, and bought a canary, and in empathy with that customary action of Leonardo, opened the latch of its cage. It hesitated. Then with a turn of its small head as if to check its luck - and permission to escape - it headed off into the blue tuscan sky. As he would have wanted, its flight was perfect.

When the Curator was rung the following week, he was unaware of any such package being in the safe. The collector entrusted with its keeping had been a temporary vacation worker and had left on the following Monday. At the time of this publication he has still not been traced.